Denise Lawrence

# GO STEAL A BRIDEGROOM

MEZZANOTTE

GO STEAL A BRIDEGROOM

© 2016 Denise Lawrence

Published in Great Britain 2016 by Mezzanotte Ltd, 2 Lyonsdown Road, New Barnet, Hertfordshire EN5 1JB

All rights reserved including the right of reproduction in whole or in part in any form.

Printed by CreateSpace

This is a work of fiction. Names, characters, places, locations and incidents are purely fictional and bear no relationship to any real life individuals, living or dead, or to any actual places, business establishments, locations, events or incidents. Any resemblance is entirely coincidental.
www.mezzanotte-publishing.co.uk

Author's Note: The medieval ship WASA and the WASA MUSEUM actually exist in Stockholm. GREAT KATE, a not-yet-rescued underwater wreck in Portsmouth harbour, similar to the MARY ROSE, is a figment of the author's imagination.

To dear Tracey with many heartfelt thanks for everything.

Love Rosemary.

(Denise Lawrence.)

# CHAPTER ONE

'You must think your little scheme, Miss Claybourne, is about to succeed.' Didrik Nilsson almost spat out the words. 'But you can take it from me, it's doomed to failure. Did you really think no one would realise what you were up to!' The angry Swede turned on his heel and stormed off down the steps of the majestic Church of Ulrica Pia towards his Volvo, parked in the cobbled square below.

'Scheme?' Prue hurried after him. 'What on earth are you talking about?' She reached the bottom step just when he paused to turn and confront her. Disdain and disgust personified, he whipped off his sunglasses and, from his great Nordic height, surveyed her with all the chill of his Arctic forebears.

'The little plan you have so carefully cooked up, my dear,' he told her in his precise English.

'Don't patronise me, please,' she retaliated, her natural spirit beginning to reassert itself. 'Just explain what you mean.'

'Why should I? You'd deny it, naturally, and I have no proof... yet.' His cold smile revealed ice-white even teeth. 'Believe me; you're not nearly as clever as you think you are!' He strode away across the ancient courtyard, leaving Prue stunned and blinking in the late afternoon sunlight.

'What in God's name have I done?' she shouted after him, truly rattled by this time. 'For heaven's sake just tell me!'

Ignoring her pleas he clicked the remote control to open his car and flung wide the passenger door. Then he waited, leaning easily on the bonnet until she reached his side.

'At your service, Madame,' he mocked her, indicating the seat.

With his eyes once more hidden beneath the dark glasses his expression was impossible to read, yet somehow she suspected his anger had turned to brief amusement. Cruel amusement, nonetheless. So setting her chin, she swallowed what was left of her pride and climbed into the car.

'I'm surprised you didn't go to the hospital,' she said, voice unsteady.

'Just get in,' he snarled. 'Hildi is in good hands, she doesn't need me. Although I'm only giving you a lift to please her, it's the last thing I want to do.'

He was holding her gaze - she knew it, even though she couldn't see his eyes behind the impenetrable designer shades. Her own were moist and, to her shame, threatening tears. Mortified, she looked away quickly, uncomfortably aware of his nearness, his powerful physical presence, the overwhelming blondness. She could even detect his shampoo, the toothpaste on his breath and his own smell, masculine and heady. She shivered. What the hell was happening here? She couldn't fathom it but whatever it was, she had to get through it, or be sensible and try to ignore it.

Settling back into the luxurious upholstery, she

closed her eyes and felt Didrik get in beside her. Yet he didn't shut the car door ready to drive off as she expected. Alarmed she opened her eyes, just in time to see him lean across towards her.

He took her chin and pulled her round to face him.

'Oh!' She gave a little choking cry and instinctively tried to jerk away, but the hand holding her jaw was strong and sinewy, his eyes level with her own. A heartbeat later he was pressing his lips against hers.

Gasping for air, she struggled to free herself from the urgency of his kiss, but he had a grip of iron and was in no hurry. She felt his tongue prising her lips apart, probing beyond. As he murmured a few words in Swedish against her mouth she drew a shuddering breath before giving in, just slightly, to the kiss of a man who belonged to another. She relaxed a little, close in the arms of this stranger, a stranger so compelling who, though she could scarce acknowledge it, had suddenly eased some kind of longing in her. A man as immoral as her father, who had abandoned her darling mother for a younger woman. Yes, Didrik Nilsson was just like her father. Yet the kiss was lingering on, deepening, and an instant later almost plundering her heart as if her assailant sensed the weakening of her resistance, and heaven forbid, the wave of pleasure beginning to drift through her. His hand snaked under her blouse and round to hold her slender back, skin on skin. A moment later she touched pure light, felt it, was aware of soft caressing sounds, a blissful stirring...

Then as quickly as it had begun, he pulled away leaving her panting, speechless, embarrassed, overwhelmed with shame, and instantly racked with guilt. She was as bad as he was, wanton, wicked, worthless.

'Now you can boast that at least you got a taste of what you came for!'

Prue gathered her wits. 'You're talking in riddles again!'

She grasped desperately at the door handle, but too late. He'd slammed the door shut on his side, the locks were on, and they were already rapidly backing out of the car park and swinging round into the thick of Gustavkrona's rush-hour traffic.

'Don't forget your seat belt!' he barked as he clicked his own into place.

Prue shook. With trembling fingers she wiped her mouth, dashed away the tears rolling down her cheeks, and smoothed her short dark hair. Then she pulled her best white blouse, now somewhat crumpled, down over her designer jeans. Finally she fastened her seat belt.

'Right!' she said grimly as she strived to regain her composure. 'I assume sexual assault is against the law in Sweden?' It was a statement rather than a question.

'It is, if you can prove it,' was the cool response. 'I doubt you have a mark on you, and don't waste your time trying to pretend you were offended. We both know better, don't we?'

'What? You..!' She glared at his profile, but he just looked ahead.

Her mind was still a ferment when, minutes later, they sped along a winding coast road. The wayside was edged with ripe yellow sunflowers, but Prue was scarcely in a mood to appreciate the beauties of nature. The lovely scenery seemed to pass by in a blur until they left the main highway a short while later. They turned off by a belt of spruce-and-birch which almost immediately gave way to the dappled green of dense forest.

They were already *en route* for the lake, heading directly for the Dahlgrens' isolated summer house. For Norrtorpet.

\*\*\*

This trip to Sweden had been the chance of a lifetime for Prue. She was working as chief illustrator with the project to raise Henry VIII's warship, 'Catherine, Queen of the Waves', affectionately known as Great Kate.

The medieval wreck was lying in shallow waters off the Hampshire coast in the south of England. Only recently located, she was a relic of the same sea battle in which the famous Mary Rose had foundered. But whereas the Mary Rose had already been lifted and returned to some of her former glory, the Great Kate still languished on the bed of the Channel.

Wasa, the beautiful rescued Swedish vessel, was a role model for all such enterprises, and that's why Prue was in Sweden right now. It was one of the perks of working for the Great Kate Trust, a paid-for visit to the famous Wasa in its own museum in Stockholm. As quite a recent recruit into the ranks of the Trust, she had made the trip alone but happily so, as to see the Wasa was such a privilege, a supremely wonderful example of what could be achieved in restoring an old wreck. Her first visit to the museum had turned out to be fascinating as well as informative.

'The Wasa was named after Sweden's royal family. She capsized in Stockholm harbour at her own launching ceremony in 1628.'

Over a pot of coffee Hildi Dahlgren, the museum's elegant public relations officer, was relating the history of the restored Swedish ship. 'King Gustav Wasa himself was watching when she went down in a freak accident - it must have been mind-blowingly horrendous.'

For her part, Prue was well acquainted with the tragic story, but she could see the pretty Swede relished the re-telling of it as well as using her fluent English.

'She vanished beneath the sea on a sunny afternoon,' Hildi went on. 'Can you imagine it? Bands still playing, brand new ship in full sail, gone, in a matter of minutes?'

'It must have been absolutely ghastly,' said Prue. 'The Great Kate went down in the good old-fashioned way - the French got her fair and square with their cannons.'

She smiled warmly at the other girl. The two had

only just met but Prue was getting along famously with the young woman with her Scandinavian blue eyes and rope of mink-blonde hair.

'The Kate's been on the sea bed a long time now,' continued Prue. 'She's only a barren hulk, not complete like your beautiful Wasa.'

The restored Swedish wooden warship, hauled almost intact out of Stockholm harbour, was indeed a fabulous spectacle.

Prue was completely overwhelmed by her first sight of the glorious vessel when, later, they stood together on the viewing platform partly encircling the Wasa.

'She's beautiful,' she breathed. 'Just like a sea-going cathedral.'

Multi-coloured carvings and wooden sculptures decorated the prow and stern - life-size Greek heroes, mermaids, dragons, a raging lion, and more. Feeling the presence of the ghosts of old sea dogs, she shivered a little even though the air in the Great Gallery was warm and smelled of waxy preservative, ancient wood and new pine.

Prue had looked forward to this visit with growing excitement. She seized the moment and made several quick sketches while listening to Hildi's avid explanations about the personal histories, the small and not-so-small difficulties behind the salvaging of the old Swedish ship from the sea. Hildi was such an enthusiast, such an ardent Wasa fan that her stories almost seemed to come to life before their eyes now.

Prue smiled. She was an equally ardent Great Kate

fan and deemed herself incredibly fortunate to be working on the prestigious project back home in England, combining the subjects she loved best - art and history. She was so lucky - just having the opportunity of visiting Sweden as part of her job was a delight. Stockholm alone was breath-taking. She intended to make the most of this wonderful break, to enjoy it to the full. Seeing the famous Wasa with her own eyes was a wish come true, and the warm invitation to Hildi's own imminent wedding a totally unexpected bonus.

It wasn't even as if she knew the Swedish girl that well. Until today, their relationship had been on a purely professional level between PR officer and Illustrator, and conducted solely via telephone and email between England and Sweden. Hildi had arranged Prue's trip with the precision of a choreographer. The two young women had hit it off straight away though, and just hours after meeting for the first time, the invitation had followed - a spontaneous gesture of friendship.

At first, Prue felt she had to decline.

'I'm truly sorry but I haven't come prepared for a long holiday. Apart from that, my boss expects me back at work on Monday, and I've already booked my return flight.'

Hildi immediately brushed aside these objections. 'Oh, please have a word with your boss. Do try to persuade him into letting you stay. I've set my heart on you being there. In any case, tell him that in Sweden it's considered to be really bad luck to turn down a wedding invite.'

In the face of such determination, Prue had happily agreed to give it a go. After all she'd not had a proper holiday for a while. Recently she'd been spending as much time as she could with her mum who'd been left so devastated at the breakdown of her marriage. When her father had left, Prue had been pretty shocked as well, so the two of them had clung together for comfort, never going far from home.

To Prue's joy, the extended holiday in Sweden was soon arranged amicably on the landline phone in the museum's office. Prue was overjoyed. Her mum would be so happy to hear the news.

'Take as much time as you need,' her boss had told her when she rang him. 'Just make sure you tell us all about it when you come back.'

He seemed pleased that she was enjoying her stay in Sweden, bonding so well with the people at the museum. That settled, the two girls delightedly high-fived one another. Then Hildi phoned Arlanda airport to cancel Prue's return flight.

After a couple of nights in Stockholm, they travelled south to Hildi's home town, Gustavskrona, in her Ford Fiesta. The quaint old naval port on the Baltic coast was the location for the midsummer wedding which was still a fortnight away.

'First, we have to go to my wedding rehearsal at the church.' Hildi happily chatted while driving through the beautiful Swedish landscape. 'It's the way we do things here. Then I'll be on leave for a whole month. You'll be my guest at Norrtorpet, our summer house, and I will show you the countryside.'

Prue was bowled over by Hildi's generosity and was ready to enjoy the experience to the full. An extended holiday and, to top it all, Swedish nuptials to look forward to. Bliss! What more could a girl wish for?

Hildi couldn't stop smiling. 'Oh, what a lovely time we'll have. I can't wait to introduce you to my family and to Didrik, my fiancé. You'll meet him at the wedding rehearsal.'

*Didrik, my fiancé.* Not possessing a crystal ball, Prue felt no sense of foreboding at these words. How could she predict that this same Didrik was about to cast his black shadow over her great new adventure?

Having brought only enough clothes for a few days, she thought perhaps she would go shopping for more, but Hildi insisted she shouldn't fret.

'I'll take you to a department store one day if that's what you want, but you can borrow anything you like from my wardrobe - except my wedding dress,' she added with a mischievous smile. 'Most of my clothes will fit you, I'm sure. You are small and dainty while I'm tall, but I have many T-shirts and short skirts that will look fine on you, so don't worry. There'll be plenty of time to sort things out properly when we get there.'

Unfortunately, the journey down from Stockholm took longer than anticipated and they arrived for the rehearsal over half an hour late. Hildi parked the car in front of the church, and nervously glanced at her watch as the two hurried up the steps to the entrance.

Prue was truly enchanted when she saw the wedding venue. The wooden Church of Ulrica Pia, stained burnt sienna, stood proudly at the head of the flight of stone steps. It was austere and dignified, its proportions classic. And if the outside was grand, the inside was a revelation.

'How beautiful! This could be a stage set,' Prue exclaimed as the last notes of a trumpet solo echoed round the exquisitely painted ceiling. 'What a fantastic place for a wedding.'

Her artist's eye took in the ornate turquoise-and-cream mouldings, the ivory cherubs on the cornice, and the many crystal chandeliers reflecting a thousand fragments of colour. She breathed in the combined aromas of incense, lilies and damask roses, and revelled in the utter foreignness of it all.

'Sorry to leave you on your own so soon,' Hildi whispered into her ear. 'I'm sure you'll find somewhere to sit. I have to go now; the others are already waiting for me.'

'Don't worry about me.' Prue patted the shoulder of her friend and watched her retreat to the back of the church to join a group of people. Instantly their voices rose to welcome the bride, and soon they accompanied her into one of the side rooms.

Meanwhile Prue tiptoed past rows of randomly occupied pews. She was well aware of the interested stares of the onlookers. No wonder they were curious. With her petite frame, green eyes and bell of short plum-dark hair she stood out in this company of tall fair Swedes.

Silently she squeezed into a pew near a large pillar. Exhilarated by the majesty of the painted church interior, she took several shots of it on her mobile phone for later reference. Then she searched her bag for her sketch pad and placed it at the ready on her blue-jeans-clad knees.

From being a child, Prue had recorded the high points of her life with pencil and paper in the way others used a camera. This talent to produce swift but accurate drawings had eventually led to her commission with The Great Kate Trust. It had, indeed, eventually brought her to this delightful part of the world.

'Snalla! Du maste!' Hildi suddenly could be heard pleading from the direction of the robing room, followed by the angry reply of a man. Prue's knowledge of Swedish was limited, yet she knew this translated as 'Please! You must!'

Was her friend arguing with her fiancé?

The scattering of people in the church, many doubtless here for later wedding rehearsals, started murmuring and craning their necks, and Prue also risked a curious glance. There was nothing to be seen but even so, she guessed their late arrival was behind the dispute. Hildi was probably feeling tired and edgy after the long drive.

Finally however, tempers seemingly appeased, the bridal party appeared and set off down the aisle. Two little flower girls in T-shirts and shorts led the group with measured steps, followed by the bridal pair and then the minister. With quickening interest Prue leaned forward the better to catch her first glimpse of the prospective groom, Didrik, but from her position half-behind the pillar she was getting only a back view of the procession.

Despite this, while her pencil got to work on a sketch of Hildi in her grey denim and with her knobbly fair plait, she could appreciate that, in a land of tall people, the bridegroom was tall. He was slim and square with shoulders moving easily under his casual cobalt-blue shirt. His hands, surprisingly, were thrust deep in the pockets of his beige trousers. Although he walked beside his prospective bride, he was making absolutely no effort to keep in step with her. From the little Prue could see, here was a person not best pleased with life at this particular moment. In fact, he was making an obvious if silent protest. He was also wearing dark glasses, she realised; designer ones, from the look of them.

'Why keep them on indoors?' Prue wondered. A stupid affectation if ever she saw one. She should have guessed that no man could possibly live up to Hildi's enraptured description of her lover.

'Didrik is the most handsome man you ever set eyes on, but then I would say that, wouldn't I?' She'd given a happy laugh. 'He's so thoughtful and kind, and very clever, too. We shall have wonderful children if they take after him.'

Well, Prue could by now see that at least Didrik's physical appearance hadn't been exaggerated. With the gold of his thick, neatly-cut hair competing with the gilding in the carvings and mouldings in the church he had certainly been blessed in the looks department.

Viking blond, features strong, she listed his assets in her mind while she sketched him with a few confident strokes. Hildi, however, could keep him. Impossibly handsome he may be, but he was clearly also surly and uncooperative. Didrik should count himself truly blessed that such a lovely girl had consented to be his wife.

Prue herself had absolutely no ambition to follow her new friend to the altar any time soon. Early experience of the betrayal by her once-beloved father with a girl her own age had left her with no illusions whatsoever about the opposite sex and its perfidious nature. Yes, marriage could work but only with the right kind of person. She hadn't ruled it out, indeed it would be wonderful to meet her own personal Prince Charming one day, but she would tread warily. Finding a trustworthy, faithful guy would be no easy task, not to mention a little matter called 'falling in love'.

At twenty-two years of age, Prue's one and only abiding love affair was with history in general and a sixteenth century underwater wreck in particular. True love, if it ever arrived, would have to be something extraordinary and special.

The clickety-clack of footsteps on the polished oak floor prompted her to glance up from her drawing. A large fair-haired lady in a bright orange dress-and-jacket was heading towards the lectern and, once there, turned towards the audience. She was just about to read the lesson when a mobile phone started ringing in the body of the church. She frowned but, as soon as the noise had stopped, she began in a loud clear voice.

At the end of the beautiful text from Solomon's 'Song of Songs', Hildi and Didrik turned towards one another and raised their arms to form an arch. Reading from a sheet of paper, held up by the lady in orange, each then said their vows.

'Hildi-Maj, jag vill alska dig…'

'Didrik Rutger, jag vill alska dig…'

A lump rose in Prue's throat. Weddings always did this to her, which was odd as she considered herself a bit of a cynic where love was concerned. Was she a romantic, after all? Probably! Certainly she was moved by the power of the old Swedish ritual - in some ways the same, yet in many ways so different from wedding services back home. No best man and no one to give the bride away, for starters. Instead of waiting in the aisle while the wedding rehearsal took place, the bridesmaids had mounted the wide altar platform to face the congregation. Self-consciously, the two little girls stood together, fidgeting and whispering and giggling. Prue made a separate sketch of each of them; they were so captivating.

In fact everything was charming and fascinating. To Prue all this still felt like a dream - things had happened so fast over the last few days. As if to prove this was definitely no illusion, the organist struck up the first chords of the Wedding March, and the rehearsal group re-formed to process back down the aisle. Finally, the bridesmaids scampered off, the rest of the party dispersed, and the brief practice was at an end. Mr Sour Face Didrik quickly made himself scarce while Hildi returned to the altar rail and was soon deep in conversation with the lady in orange.

After adding a few finishing touches to her drawings, Prue left the pew. Perhaps she should try to find Hildi's parents or even the older brother Hildi had spoken of briefly but with affection. After all, she was to be their guest at Norrtorpet, the family holiday home or 'summer house' which, Prue understood, was nearby.

'Norrtorpet is quite handy for my parents,' Hildi had told her. 'It's only about three miles from their house in Gustavskrona.'

Another wedding rehearsal was now getting under way to the accompaniment of 'Jesu, Joy of Man's Desiring'. Meanwhile Prue meandered through the church, hoping to locate Herr and Fru Dahlgren. She was seduced by the splendour around her, the fat balustrades, and pale turquoise pews. Dark turquoise walls were drawing the gaze up, overhead, to more cherubs and angels painted in vivid reds and blues, and glimmering with gold. Not only the gold-framed religious icons and the cabinets gleaming with gold plate gave the interior of the church a magic sparkle, but that gold in turn caught the glory of the afternoon sun and reflected it through the spacious room.

Full of wonderment, Prue wanted to touch

everything, to bury her face in the pink, mauve and white flower arrangements, and drink in their perfumes. It was all so achingly beautiful and on such a grand scale; ceilings high, windows tall, taking full advantage of the sparkling northern light.

Pausing in a dark archway near the pulpit, she was lightly tracing a finger over the black gothic lettering of a name on a pew, when the smallest flower girl pushed past her, almost knocking her off balance. The child halted in her tracks before looking back uncertainly, then returning.

'Hej, Pru...dence!' Her short flaxen corkscrew curls shook a little; her gaze was solemn and unblinking.

'Well, hello. So you know my name.' Prue was pleased to have made contact with someone at last.

The little girl continued her blatant scrutiny until Prue realised that the child wasn't used to seeing someone with dark hair and sage-green eyes. In a moment of inspiration she leafed through her pad to find the drawing she'd made earlier, only to be interrupted by a male voice coming from behind.

'Anna-Karin!'

Prue whisked round to look up, and up, right into the speaker's face.

Didrik Nilsson towered above her, foursquare in full sunshine as if he belonged there - centre stage. His vibrant hair shimmered and his healthy, clean-shaven skin glowed. Into the bargain he was still sporting the sunspecs. His attention wasn't on Prue though, but on Anna-Karin. He was already addressing the little girl in rapid Swedish. Although plainly admonishing her, his tone was only mock-severe, and Anna-Karin didn't seem too perturbed but answered him in a cheeky fashion when he ruffled her curls placatingly.

As Prue watched the two of them she realised there was something faintly familiar about Didrik. He reminded her of somebody, but she could swear they'd never met, and she hardly dared acknowledge the unwelcome tremor in her heart, refusing to allow herself to be so easily affected by this man.

Swiftly she distracted herself by writing the name 'Anna' beneath her earlier sketch and, tearing it off the block, she presented it to the child. With slowly dawning recognition Anna-Karin studied her own likeness for a few seconds.

'Tack, tack.' The little girl thanked her with a broad smile and scampered off calling, excitedly, 'Mamma! Mamma!'

At that moment the bridegroom looked round, threw one glance at Prue then addressed her in English that was fluent with just a slight Swedish inflection.

'You must be Hildi's new best friend from England.'

He whipped off his sunglasses and started to appraise her, almost insultingly. Taking in every detail of her face his gaze travelled over her eyes, her hair, right down her trim figure, and back to her eyes again.

'Ah, yes,' he continued. 'Now I understand why

she was so keen to invite you to the wedding. But then, with your looks, no doubt you counted on that. I've met your sort before; a gold-digger, hoping to ensnare a rich husband.'

Absolutely taken aback, Prue could hardly believe what she was hearing, could hardly take it in. And truth to tell, she was only half aware of his words because of the impact of two incredible dark blue eyes, defined by thick curved brows. Again she felt that lightning flash of something like recognition, vivid, instantaneous but at once elusive and fleeting. Even as she attempted to hold on to the feeling, it vanished.

'I... I...' she stammered, totally thrown off balance, confused even. 'I'm amazed that your English is so perfect.' Her reply was feeble and utterly stupid she realised immediately. After all, she knew from Hildi that Didrik was an expert in the English language at the university where he worked.

'Maybe it's because I live in England much of the time. I have an apartment in London,' he returned in a flat voice.

Giving herself a mental shake at last, she strived to hang on to the shreds of her pride. 'I must say you've had a darned good look at me,' she snapped. 'That must be the most scrutiny I've ever had to put up with while still being fully dressed.' It was rude and perhaps quite the wrong thing to say but she was still smarting from his insults. This nightmare was not of her doing.

The silence between them vibrated. Prue was

uncomfortably aware that her cheeks were branded by a hot flush; the backs of her legs quivered. At her eye level she saw his chest heave.

'Oh, you've wasted no time in getting onto that subject.' He shook his head. 'Where does Hildi find such low life? However, what's important at the moment is that neither you nor anyone else must spoil this wedding. This is Hildi's special time. So do me a favour and just keep out of my way in future. If our paths do cross, just smile and move on. Now, if you'll excuse me!'

His words, harsh and direct, required no reply. Didrik replaced his shades, spun on his heel and marched up a side aisle and out of the building without a backward glance.

Prue was, at first, speechless then furious. How dare this man treat her in such a cavalier fashion! Who was he anyway? She would not tolerate it, and she was about to catch him up to give him another piece of her mind when Hildi appeared from the other side of the pulpit. This reminded Prue of her recent adversary's identity - he was her friend's fiancé.

For Hildi's sake, she realised reluctantly, she must put the whole unfortunate incident behind her. She swallowed, making a huge effort to bring herself back to normality. It wasn't easy. His reaction had been so unexpected and so disturbing that she was still shaking inside.

Hildi was smiling. 'I want you to meet someone and...' The sentence petered out as she looked round the church. 'It's strange, but I can't see him anywhere. I think we should go and...'

'I'd very much like to meet your mother and father,' Prue interrupted quickly, anxious to forestall any further confrontation with the ill-tempered groom. 'I'd like to thank them in advance for their kindness and hospitality.'

'Oh, my parents aren't here today. Mamma's got an appointment with the captain of the boat. We're planning a sea trip with all our guests - an hour's sailing round our little islands - our arch-i-pel-a-go, I think you call it. That's for after the ceremony but before the reception.'

'A boat trip, what a fabulous idea!' Prue was enchanted.

Hildi giggled. 'Oh, yes, we like to do things in style. There'll be champagne and nibbles on the boat, of course.' Her blue eyes shone. 'As for Dadda, he's gone to see about the birches because, on the day itself, it's his job to put them everywhere - in the church, in the house, on the boat, and in the reception hall. In Sweden the bride's father does this for the good luck. Ah, look who's here.'

Hildi pointed to an approaching group - the two children and the large lady in orange 'Aunt Agnetha has come to say hello.'

After introductions all round, Aunt Agnetha turned out to be Anna-Karin's mother. The dialogue was in Swedish with frequent explanations in English so that Prue didn't feel left out. And all the while Aunt Agnetha kept studying Prue, her head on one side, smiling and smiling, and this Prue found rather disconcerting. Surely even people in Sweden had seen small, dark haired girls before? Even so, she was polite and smiled back. Moments later she followed the rest of the ladies as, still chatting, they made their way outside to linger at the top of the long flight of stone steps leading down into the cobbled courtyard where the cars were parked.

Prue took a moment to cast an eye over the outside of the church - built of vertical planks, its curved blue-tiled roof, crowned with a small cupola, made a popular perch for clamorous white seabirds. Its position was elevated, commanding a breathtaking view of the Baltic but near enough the quay to catch the sounds of the sea slapping against the harbour wall. Even with the faint smell of gutted herring drifting over from the fish dock, the air was intoxicating. A brisk breeze came straight off the water and blew Prue's thick silky fringe about, but it was really warm in the sunshine after the coolness of the church.

Aunt Agnetha had also noticed. She peeled off her orange jacket, saying, 'I feel such hotness.'

In the meantime, evidently bored with grown-up talk, Anna-Karin and her fellow bridesmaid, an older girl, had started a game of 'tag' and were rushing around the slippery granite steps.

The noisy game drew Prue's gaze away from the group momentarily and she laughed at the two girls as they tore up and down. Then, too late, she spotted the groom again. A fresh flush of heat swept along her cheekbones. He'd just entered the courtyard below with a tall, stately girl, his sunglasses still firmly in place. The two walked slowly, their heads turned towards one another. On reaching a large cream Volvo he folded his arms and, still talking, leaned against it.

In spite of the distance, Prue could feel his disturbing influence strongly. A twinge of something approaching pain touched her deep inside, making her instantly cross with herself. The man was deplorably unpleasant and totally unimportant to her. She just couldn't understand why his mere presence affected her so much. In future she'd avoid him completely, however difficult this might prove.

Of course, Hildi would be eager to show him off, but Prue decided to keep her distance. She only hoped her friend wouldn't notice him and drag him up here to introduce them. She wasn't keen to experience a further encounter with the fiancé from hell. Thankfully Hildi was still totally engrossed in the conversation with her aunt.

Hildi's voice broke into her thoughts. 'I'm just telling Aunt Agnetha about your work; that you make a drawing of every item the divers find in the Great Kate.' Her friend turned back to her aunt, who'd just reprimanded the little girls for repeatedly bumping into her during their running game. 'Prudence is Chief Illustrator for The Great Kate Trust in Portsmouth, in England. It's a great honour for someone so young to hold such a position.'

Prue felt herself blushing again. She was earning a

living doing the thing she loved. Few people were so fortunate. 'I got the job because I was in the right place at the right time, that's all. My supervisor at university put in a good word for me.'

Aunt Agnetha looked suitably impressed. 'It was through The Trust you first met Hildi, yes?'

Prue nodded and stepped quickly out of the way of one of the children who, immersed in their play, were getting really excited. 'It was my turn to visit the Wasa museum and Hildi did all the arranging. It's a lovely bonus for all of us connected with the Great Kate.'

'Bo-nus?' Aunt Agnetha was puzzled. 'Excuse me, my English not good.'

'Oh, I'm sorry - bonus. It means that we all get a free trip to see the Wasa. I'm afraid we come to Sweden to pick your brains, to learn how to preserve an old ship that's been on the sea bed for centuries. You are the experts, you see.'

'Oops!' Aunt Agnetha said as again one of the children bumped into her. Yet unperturbed, she continued speaking. 'History is good. I am nurse for little children but I visit Wasa Museum many times. My niece fix everything for me, too.'

'Hildi is wonderfully efficient,' Prue agreed. 'She booked me into a gorgeous hotel in the Old Town in Stockholm and made all her official appointments as well. She even pointed out the best bargains in the museum shop. I bought a lovely embroidery of the Wasa.' With a chuckle she put a friendly arm around her friend to give her a quick hug.

Hildi blushed with pleasure.

'She's made me feel so much at home,' Prue added with feeling. 'I've never met anyone so friendly.'

This was the utter truth. Prue was absolutely amazed by her new friend's helpfulness. She couldn't believe that none of her colleagues at The Great Kate Trust had ever experienced the same immediate rapport with Hildi as she had; it had been friendship at first sight. Not that she was complaining. To stay in a Swedish summer house and attend a Swedish wedding was an unexpected development to be grasped with both hands even if it had thrown up a black spot, namely the strange and unpleasant altercation with the bridegroom.

The children's game continued around them, becoming more and more boisterous. By this time Anna-Karin had bumped heavily into the chatting women several times. What the little girls were doing was quite dangerous as the flagstones and steps were shiny in places, polished by centuries of countless feet.

Prue was quite relieved when, eventually, Agnetha turned around.

'Var forsiktiga, barn! Ni kan ramla!' she called to the little girls, clearly asking them to be careful, but to no avail.

Unfortunately, Hildi used this moment to glance down into the courtyard. She smiled when she spotted her fiancé, who was still leaning against the Volvo and conversing with the tall girl. In fact, the blonde had a hand on his arm while whispering in his ear and Didrik laughed in response. The two seemed very familiar with one another. Prue couldn't help wondering who this beautiful girl was, and what Hildi made of their apparent closeness.

Hildi didn't seem bothered. 'Hej!' She shouted and waved, beckoning Didrik to come up. She turned to Prue. 'At last, I can introduce you to the best person in the world. I've been looking for him everywhere, and there he is, talking to Ulrica.'

With fast-beating heart, Prue was just steeling herself to deal with the approaching situation when little Anna-Karin let out a squeal of excitement and dashed right into the middle of their little group.

Prue had the presence of mind to jump aside, but her companion wasn't so quick. Anna-Karin barged smack into Hildi who missed her footing on the top step. Plait flying, she tumbled heavily, at the same time letting out a yelp of surprise and pain.

'Oh, no!' In a flash Prue ran down several steps to kneel at Hildi's side. She put an arm about her friend's shoulders to support her. 'Oh, Hildi, what a thing to happen! No, dear, try to keep still.'

Hildi's stricken face was frighteningly pale, almost chalk white.

'Where does it hurt?' Prue asked thickly, choking back tears of sympathy.

Hildi was too shocked to answer in English. She winced then, nursing her left arm, panted out something in Swedish. People gathered around them, the air was filled with cries of alarm and concern, and

Hildi's husband-to-be came bounding up the steps two-at-a-time. Aunt Agnetha bustled up to take charge in her motherly way, wrapping her own orange jacket round Hildi who'd begun to shiver violently with shock.

Recalling Aunt Agnetha being a nursery nurse and as such no doubt trained in First Aid, Prue reluctantly moved aside.

Suddenly she felt useless and in the way. Not for long, though. There was soon something practical for her to do when poor little Anna-Karin burst into a torrent of tears. Instinctively, Prue hurried over to console the little girl, guessing she was feeling guilty as well as upset.

'There, darling,' she soothed the child. 'Don't cry, everything will be all right, you'll see.'

She found a tissue in her pocket and wiped Anna-Karin's eyes, hugging her gently. The language barrier didn't seem to matter at all.

'Hej! Hej! Hej!' A masterful voice now overrode the general commotion.

The crowd parted and a minute later Hildi was being carried down the steps to the Volvo in her fiancé's arms, accompanied by a fretful Aunt Agnetha and several of the by-standers. When they all arrived at the car a discussion broke out and Prue, who was still at the top of the stairs comforting the child, could hear Hildi's voice, faint but insistent, protesting, 'Nej! Nej! Ulrica…Fiesta!'

Soon the argument seemed to be resolved. Aunt Agnetha and the tall blonde detached themselves from the small gathering and climbed into Hildi's Fiesta. Ulrica took the steering wheel. Hildi was then helped, carefully, into the front passenger seat while, to Prue's relief, an elderly lady came to claim the still-weeping Anna-Karin.

After giving the distraught child a parting kiss, Prue looked at the crowd below. She felt so helpless and wished she could comfort Hildi and be at her side during her ordeal, but even as she watched the little knot of worried friends, the Fiesta reversed over the cobbles and drove away.

Disconsolate, Prue turned her back on the scene and went to find a seat in the church porch. Reaction had set in and she felt suddenly shaky, but she was stopped in her tracks by the commanding tones she knew only too well.

'You, Miss Claybourne, are nothing but a nuisance!'

His tone was low and tight, edged with animosity. Today had Prue heard that voice for the first time, yet now she would know it anywhere. Pivoting on her heel, she found herself facing the one person she'd vowed never to speak to again.

She looked up prepared to meet the strong, rigid chin, the unpleasant manner of the now-familiar brute in the sunglasses. His expression was strained, his manner as brusque as ever.

'Hildi asked me, or rather ordered me, to give you a lift to the summer house, to Norrtorpet. To see you settled in as there is no one else there at the moment to show you the ropes,' he barked at her. 'Agnetha and Ulrica have taken her to the hospital.'

Prue knew she should make allowances for him; he was naturally pretty upset over Hildi's accident. Nonetheless, she felt as though she'd been dealt a physical blow by his rudeness, and there was nothing she could do about it. He had her at a complete disadvantage. Yet why should she care? As Hildi's intended, the guy was her friend's problem. As if that poor girl didn't have enough to contend with...

She lifted her chin defiantly.

'The last thing I want is to be a trouble to you or anyone else, especially after what's happened. I'm not an idiot. You could come to the summer house after you've been to the hospital, just to show me the ropes. Hildi told me that Norrtorpet is about three miles from here. So if you write the address down, and point me in the right direction, I can easily walk it.'

Denim jeans, socks and sandals - at least she was dressed okay for a hike.

'Walk? To Norrtorpet?' A dimple appeared; his laugh was brief and grim. 'Well, I suppose it's a possibility. Mind you, every Swedish mile is worth about six English miles so you'd better get cracking if you want to get there before bedtime.' His tone became jagged again, his features set. 'No, Hildi made me promise to look after you and I'm not going to add to her misery by reneging on that promise. I've already explained, somebody has to show you where everything is, including the door key which is hidden in a tree.'

So Prue was cornered; the situation beyond her control. She would just have to go with the flow. She had to call a truce with the dreaded Didrik, or Hildi would wonder what was going on. Much as she hated to acknowledge it, he was right. There must be no more upsets for her injured friend. She could see that from now on she would have to pretend to like Didrik, simply for Hildi's sake.

'I see what you mean. In that case we'll be driving together to Norrtorpet, you and I, and...'

'You must think your little scheme, Miss Claybourne, is about to succeed!' Didrik interrupted her. 'But you can take it from me, it's doomed to failure. Did you really think no one would realise what you were up to?'

And with that the angry Swede turned on his heel and stormed off down the steps of the church towards his Volvo, parked in the cobbled square below.

The journey to Norrtorpet got under way, with Prue shocked into silence by Didrik's unsolicited and mocking kiss. The world had tilted, her thoughts were in chaos. It was outrageous! There was no sense to her friend's fiancé behaving in such an appalling manner. Why was he so obviously hostile towards her? Naturally, he wasn't about to give her any answers. She was caught fast in a nightmare.

The kiss, mocking though it was supposed to be, still lingered in her mind. Why had he done that? He belonged to Hildi. That trusting girl was in for a shock when she'd married him. He was a babe-magnet, and he knew it.

Prue's emotions were a complete mess. She felt the pull of him, even now. Worse, she couldn't get that kiss out of her head. What a traitor she was to live in hopes of it being repeated, to feel his lips on hers again. She was no better than others she affected to despise, including her own father.

Trying to ignore her troubled thoughts, she glanced out of the window. They'd left the town behind with its pretty postcard harbour and scores of gently bobbing yachts and dinghies, their slender masts breaking the smooth pastel blue sky, and now drove along a coastal road. Fields of sunflowers flashed past before they veered off by a belt of fir-and-birch forest. Pop music streamed from the CD player in the dashboard, lively and tuneful. Usually Prue loved this kind of music but right now she wished it would stop. The day's events had given her a headache. She maintained her silence however, and the music continued unchallenged.

She found herself looking out for a sign to Lunneby - the name of the nearest village to the Dahlgren's summer residence. When eventually they passed it, Prue was much relieved - that was until she remembered something. Her luggage!

'Oh no! My suitcase, my clothes, my lap-top... They're all in the boot of Hildi's car!'

Her shout of dismay was spontaneous and unheeding because the realisation was nothing short of disastrous. All she had with her was a little airline bag.

Didrik's gaze never left the road, but he did have the grace to turn the music off.

Biting her lower lip in vexation, Prue sucked in a long, thin breath. 'What shall I do?'

'I'm sure you'll think of something.' His words were heavily laced with sarcasm. 'Believe it or not, worse things can happen and frequently do.'

Prue, her fingers kneading and working together in agitation, was in no position to argue with that. Compared to Hildi's present plight, her own mislaid luggage was nothing but an inconvenience. All the same, dejection swept over her as they motored on. The pretty woodland gave way to plum and pear trees, apple and cherry. Finally the car turned down a long drive, and came to a halt in a natural clearing before a large rambling house.

'This is it,' announced Didrik tersely.

Prue gave an involuntary gasp - the house was breathtaking, a vision. Constructed of stout timber logs, it was painted in that rosy brown colour the Swedes call red ochre. The gables and windows were outlined in white. Bushes bursting with fresh green leaves crowded up against the front porch of hand-made Swedish glass glinting in the sunlight. Soft winds stirred through random red currant bushes and brambles. A swing hung lazily from a low apple bough while somewhere a bird was singing.

She gazed around. The whole scene was straight out of a bedtime story book, an old-time nursery illustration. She half expected a flock of white geese to wander into view tended by a little goose girl in a floppy sun bonnet. It was all so quietly glorious.

Ever alive to beauty, she put aside her troubles for a second and allowed the rustic peace of it all to flood over her. This was the Dahlgrens' summer residence, Norrtorpet, a place of timeless serenity, a home at the heart of an age-old orchard. They had arrived.

## CHAPTER TWO

'You'll find a key hanging on a nail in the second tree past the swing,' Didrik barked at Prue, bringing her down to earth. The Volvo's engine was still ticking over. 'Please return it to the same spot when you...'

The sentence died on his lips and he cocked his head in a listening attitude. Prue caught the sound, too - a telephone was ringing inside the house.

Switching off the ignition, in one bound he was out of the car to retrieve the key from its hiding place, unlock the front door and disappear inside. Prue was only a minute or so behind him. Setting foot in the lovely glassed-in porch she removed her sandals, as was customary. In spite of the fraught situation, she was entranced by the tiny bells nailed up round the inside of the door. The slightest movement caused them all to jingle musically - no intruder would dare to break in by this entrance.

The smell of polish and old seasoned wood met her as, in her pale blue socks, she wandered through a lobby stacked high with walking sticks and boots, and a child's yellow-painted sledge. By-passing the study where Didrik was on the phone, she entered a large kitchen with a small scullery off to the side. Her artistic eye immediately imagined the room as a water colour - sun-yellow cupboards stencilled with blue flower shapes, a mirror-backed mahogany chiffonier, and the whole dominated by a white, floor-to-ceiling tiled stove. Split logs and twigs for kindling lay tumbled in and around a log basket.

A click indicated that Didrik had terminated the phone call; a moment later he stood in the doorway. He'd removed the sunglasses at last, and Prue found herself trembling again as she re-lived that insulting kiss. As best as she could she suppressed the disturbing emotions raging inside her and met his gaze with all the boldness she could muster. He stared back with narrowed eyes.

'I'm leaving now, the family needs me. That was a call from the hospital. Hildi has had an X-ray and, amongst other things, she's broken a bone in her hand.'

'Oh no, it's so not fair!' exclaimed Prue. 'Close to the wedding date, too.'

Almost defensively, he folded his arms across his chest.

'Hildi needs nursing care. Naturally she'll be staying at the house in Gustavskrona while she recovers.' His dark-blue eyes glittered with antagonism. 'There's a message for you: Hildi hopes you'll make yourself at home here. Not quite what you were expecting though, is it? Being stuck in an old wooden house with no luxuries, no modern facilities, and right in the middle of nowhere.'

Again a bitter jibe; unexplained and inexplicable. Yet before Prue could reply in kind, he'd gone, the outer door slamming behind him. The little doorbells were still ringing furiously as his car set off with an unnecessary roar.

His accusing words lingered on in the kitchen, though.

*Not quite what you were expecting, is it?*

What was she to make of them? Unnerved, she felt she was taking a leading role in a drama for which she'd had no chance to consult the script. Feeling defeated and deflated, she sank into the deep green-cushioned basket chair by the stove and found herself perilously close to tears. The fact that her belongings were sitting in the boot of Hildi's car just added to her misery.

'Enough of this!' Rubbing her damp eyes with her fists like a child, she firmly banished her self-pity and glanced around. Hildi wished her to make herself at home, and that was just what she would do.

The house was old and full of character, with ancient beams and walls painted in white and pastel colours. The kitchen with its floor-to-ceiling tiled stove was invitingly cosy. She had to tell her mother about it, and about everything else that was happening; she would give Mum a ring very shortly.

Pale gold daylight filtered into the room through creamy curtains of stubbly hand-made lace. The faint winey scent of apples came from a door bearing the legend, Appelforrad - Apple Store, next to the pantry. This scent mingled with the tangy fragrances from bunches of drying herbs, rosemary, sage and bay, strung up on wall brackets. Small terracotta pots of growing parsley and basil and a jug of wild cornflowers decorated the window sill, and Prue realised she'd already fallen helplessly in love with this beautiful timber dwelling. Its atmosphere was stealthily folding itself around her, and she couldn't wait to explore. Just one thing prevented her - a ravenous hunger.

Jumping up to investigate the cupboards she was relieved to discover a good stock of tinned food and a packet of wheat biscuits. In the fridge was a carton of fresh milk, a vacuum pack of smoked reindeer meat and soft Swedish cheese. By a cafetière, in a jar labelled 'Kaffe', she found ground coffee - just what she needed, but first she wanted to speak to her mother. Prue tried her mobile but there was no signal, so she went to the study to use the landline.

It was a quaint, old-fashioned phone, in keeping with the old-fashioned house. With urgent fingers she dialled the number, longing for the solace of a familiar voice - and a familiar one was what she got: her own.

'We're not available just now, but please leave your name and number...' droned the answerphone.

Pulling a wry face, she left a message. 'Hello, Mum, it's me. I'm just letting you know I'm... er... everything's fine.'

She held back from revealing too much, because she didn't want to cause her mother any distress.

'I'm having a wonderful time,' she concluded the call, adding the house phone number, in case her mother wanted to call back. 'Put 0046 first, that's the code for Sweden. Also if you see Claire, tell her I'll be in touch. Lots of love, I miss you. Bye.'

Claire was Prue's old school friend and best pal. She had even come to the airport to see her off with friendly kisses and hugs when Prue had left for Stockholm.

She dialled again, this time to speak to her boss. The office number was engaged so once more she had to leave a message.

'This is Prue Claybourne phoning from Sweden. Could someone please tell James Bickford that I'm having a great time? I'm also dying to know all the latest news...'

Prue returned to the kitchen, a little disappointed she'd not managed to speak to anyone. A coffee would cheer her up again, but there was no electric kettle. After spending several minutes searching for one, she gave up and filled the saucepan with water to put on the hotplate.

As she sat sipping coffee and snacking off cheese and biscuits, she remembered all the exciting experiences she'd had so far here in Sweden, the many interesting things she'd seen and done in Stockholm. Too bad Mum had been out this afternoon. She was usually home this time of day on a Saturday, even allowing for the hour's difference between Sweden and England.

Actually, it was good that her mother went out more these days. She was finally getting over the deep hurt she'd suffered when the tight loving triangle that was the three of them, Mum, Dad and Prue, had been so cruelly shattered about eighteen months ago.

Her mother had clung to her for a while and had needed a lot of tender loving care, but the bitterness was passing and she had started to go out with friends and enjoy herself again. Yes, Mum's life was definitely getting back to normal.

Prue bit a hard biscuit in two and popped a piece of cream cheese into her mouth. As much as she'd looked forward to a chat, perhaps it was fortunate Mum wasn't in. She was feeling so strange at the moment, confused by Didrik's hostility and by the kiss that she wouldn't forget in a hurry. She felt her cheeks redden at the memory of it now, and she might have been tempted to spill everything out over the phone. It would have sounded absolutely crazy.

*'The bridegroom insulted me and then kissed me like he really meant it...'*

No, no one should ever know what had happened between them. Not ever.

In an attempt to get Didrik off her mind, she cleared up the remains of her scratch meal and set off to explore the house. Clearly much loved and lived-in by the family, it would provide accommodation for the wedding guests shortly to converge from all corners of Sweden. Some would be staying here, some at the Dahlgren's house in Gustavskrona, and some at local hotels.

Prue gently fingered the old paintings and books, and admired the exquisite embroideries and needlepoint. The many quaint holiday souvenirs, which included tiny bits of Limoges porcelain and a tiny castle and windmill made of Swedish crystal, were especially enchanting. Among the many framed photographs on display she came across one of Didrik. It showed him seated at a piano, smiling his marvellous smile, the single dimple etched deep in his lean cheek. He certainly must have been in a better mood that day.

The bedrooms, up winding stairs, were all a delight, especially one on the first landing. It was a room with child-size furniture and an old white-painted dolls' house with a family of colourful rag dolls propped up, rather drunkenly, against it. Fascinating as this room was, Prue finally decided she would sleep in a back room overlooking a birch wood, simply because it contained the only bed made up with duvet cover, sheet and pillow case.

She also took to it because it was so feminine, all white frothy curtains and pink furnishings. The single bed with its padded headboard smelled faintly spicy, of sandalwood, perhaps. Something else drew her to this particular room, though - a wall tapestry depicting a chapel, the walls probably wooden. Its green dome was surmounted by a small and simple model of an old sailing ship.

It was entitled 'Wasakappellet' and signed 'Hildi-Maj Norberg Dahlgren', all in beautiful petit-point. A Wasa chapel - how intriguing! An earlier comment from Hildi came back to her.

'I've been a Wasa fan ever since I can remember. There's a strong connection between the old ship and our family. When we go to Norrtorpet I'll show you something that will interest you.'

'Tell me about it now,' Prue had pressed her, bursting with curiosity.

'It will be a surprise,' was all Hildi would say.

She was plainly a girl who revelled in secrets, and here was Prue discovering at least a part of this secret for herself.

Where was this Wasa Chapel?

She was eager to know more but it would have to wait until she saw Hildi again.

Her friend's middle name of Norberg had also caught Prue's attention. She guessed this was a family name from the distaff side. Norberg - Norrtorpet, it seemed to fit.

She wandered over to the sash window and raised it. Through the slim trunks of the trees she glimpsed a shimmer of water; enticing, inviting inspection – but not yet, she was too tired, she realised suddenly.

It was only around six o'clock but it had been a long day. On impulse, she flopped down on the bed, closed her eyes and, lulled by the drowsy murmur of insects in the garden in no time at all she was asleep. Yet running through her dreams was the mysterious, disturbing accusation, 'Your little scheme, Miss Claybourne, is doomed to failure!'

When she awoke, confused for a second by her strange surroundings, it was still daylight and still Saturday by her digital watch. She'd slept for nearly two hours. A change of clothes was out of the question but a refreshing shower would be welcome and she set off in search of one. Ten minutes later she had to face the fact that such a thing didn't exist -

the nearest approach to bathroom facilities seemed to be the scullery off the kitchen. Judging by the inadequate curtain that served in place of a door, plus mirror and range of tooth and shaving brushes on a shelf over the shallow stone sink, this was it - the only bathroom! Not only did it lack privacy but also hot water, Prue quickly discovered.

With a resigned sigh and in the absence of a kettle, she prepared a largish pan of cold water and put it ready to heat up later. A strip wash would have to suffice but first she decided she would like to explore the beautiful garden around the house.

She slipped her feet into one of the many pairs of wood-and-leather clogs arranged in a neat row at the back door. Clattering down the stone steps into the extensive, half-wild garden, she pushed through a tangle of currant bushes and past a picnic table and bench. After crossing a field of elderflower bushes she clambered over a pile of birch logs, their axe-blunting bark stripped off and ready for chopping, to make her way down towards the water glimmering through the trees.

In the wood, small birds twittered and sang; a robin fluttered from branch to branch. Heavenly green fragrances invaded her senses. She could almost taste them as her feet rustled along the part sunny, part shadowy path meandering through purple foxgloves, mauve bell flowers, pale stitchwort and red campion, all buzzing with white butterflies, lacewings, and the occasional fat bee.

'Our part of Sweden is famous for its wild

flowers; we've got every kind you can think of,' Hildi had told her.

Her friend obviously adored the unspoilt, fairy tale countryside with its divine scents - and so she should.

The lake, when she reached it, seemed to be waiting just for her - a jewelled mirror, a looking-glass set in a leafy frame. Nearby, under the alders, a dinghy swayed slightly at its mooring by a floating pontoon. Across the lake, through the thick forest canopy, a little dome was visible, the brilliant green of corroded copper that Sweden was famous for.

Prue caught her breath in a little rush of excitement. Was this the chapel she'd seen fashioned in needlepoint and displayed on the wall of her room in the house? There was certainly something fixed to the pinnacle of the dome. Although it was not easy to be certain at this distance, it could be a small model of a sailing ship, perhaps fashioned in wrought iron to withstand the elements. The more she looked at it, the more she was certain. Yes, this must be the chapel depicted in the tapestry. The Wasa Chapel - Wasakappellet.

Prue glanced around. This place was pure magic. Life had its ups and downs, to be sure, but here was a moment to cherish. Her fingers itched for paints to do justice to the colourful reflection of trees, sun and sky in the lake. Her body felt a primal urge to be immersed in the water and restored to full vitality.

Stepping out of the clumsy clogs, she pulled off her socks and tested the water with her toes. Almost child-like, she rolled up the legs of her jeans and began to splash about in the shallows. It was incredible; compared with the chilly tidal waters of the English Channel where she often took a dip, this lake was so warm.

Should she go in for a swim? Standing still, she gazed around to check that, apart from a couple of two-tone, black-and-grey crows, the shore was deserted. Still she hesitated – dare she go for a skinny dip? Why not? There was no-one about and it would be miles better than a strip wash. Without delay she began to pull off clothes and underwear until she was suddenly struck by a thought. No towel! But there was one in the scullery, she recalled. Sorted! Quickly she tugged on her jeans and blouse. She rubbed her still-wet feet with her socks and picked up her underwear.

By this time used to the loose-fitting clogs, she rushed up to the house where she threw her socks, bra and panties over the back of a chair. She would rinse them through later and they would all dry quickly, she hoped. She grabbed the kitchen towel and some minutes later arrived back at the lake shore, glowing from her exertions.

Wasting no more time, she stripped off her clothes again and stepped into the water. Oh, it felt so refreshing! She began to wade further into the clear inviting lake. This was paradise. The sky was a cloudless blue and the birds sang a lyrical tune.

As she moved, shoals of small fry turned tail and swam away. Now large gentle fish came to investigate her legs, making her squeal with delight. Innocently she took one more step - and gave a shriek! The sandy, gravelly lake bed had taken a steep downward slope and the water had instantly changed to freezing cold, just when she least expected it.

Lapping round the tops of her legs now, the icy water caused her to gasp and gulp until she was forced to acknowledge what a prize idiot she was. The scarcely moving shallows had been heated all day long by the sun but here, further out in the deeper part of the lake, the chill was penetrating right through to her bones. Her thighs were already turning a sort of mottled blue and red. She'd better take the plunge quickly and get it over with, or maybe not. It was so icy and her legs already stiff and awkward.

'I've heard about you Brits - that you're a foolhardy lot, but surely even the intrepid Miss Claybourne will have to draw the line at swimming in meltwater.' The mocking voice was calling out from the shore behind her. 'Less than a month ago this lake was packed solid with mini icebergs. We've just had the worst spring in living memory!'

'Who on earth…?' In a swish of water Prue whirled round to face the land, yet she already knew.

Who else but Hildi's infuriating fiancé who seemed set on haunting the whole of her stay in Sweden? He still wore the fancy blue shirt, but had dispensed with the sunglasses for a change. Legs slightly apart, he stood at the lakeside some ten or twelve yards away, thumbs casually hooked into the pockets of his beige designer trousers. His trademark wicked smile was playing round his mouth.

It could hardly get more embarrassing than that, and almost instinctively she plunged deep into the lake on the spot, to hide her naked body. Returning to the surface she struggled for breath; her mind, her reason, snatched away for a moment by the Arctic chill.

'Go away! Please, go away!' she managed to splutter out, wildly thrashing about and treading water.

'Not likely. That's not what you really want anyway, is it?' His resonant voice carried easily to her. 'I've got to hand it to you; nothing puts you off, does it? Only a truly dedicated schemer would risk bathing in a lake which, this year in particular, is a notorious death trap.'

A flock of white birds flew across the water, wheeling and crying.

'Listen to that!' he went on. 'Even the gulls are laughing at you!'

But he couldn't catch her with that one. She knew these birds were the ones the Swedes called, laughing gulls. Hildi had pointed out a similar flock over one of the many lakes they'd passed on the drive down from Stockholm.

'That's a very feeble joke - is it the best you can do?' she deflected his attack but didn't really care anymore.

She had to get out of the water, and quick. She was already freezing cold! Modesty forgotten, her feet sought and found the gritty lake bottom and, with a defiant lift of her head, she began her unsteady return to the beach. Dignity was her sole protection from his exploiting gaze as she emerged from her ordeal, wondering if her legs would carry her back to land. Her wet hair dripped dismally, and her teeth chattered uncontrollably.

Given the right circumstances she was no prude but nor was she an exhibitionist. So, when she gained the sandy beach and he made no attempt to avert his devouring gaze, she lost her self-control.

'Watching a girl freeze to death; is that how you get your kicks?' She snapped out the accusation through teeth clenched in an effort to stop them from chattering. Shivering violently, she reached down for the towel which looked woefully thin and small. 'You've obviously picked up a lot in England, but one thing you haven't learned is how to behave like a gentleman. You... you unspeakable...'

Words failed her as she tried to rub some life back into her arms and legs. It was scarcely believable that this male relishing her dilemma was Hildi's intended.

Although she'd relinquished eye contact, she knew he was highly amused, gloating at her predicament as she struggled into her jeans and blouse.

'You may as well leave now,' she sniped at him, ashamed of the sob of humiliation in her voice. 'Sorry to disappoint you but the show is definitely over.'

'I'm only doing precisely what you planned I should do,' he replied. 'I am a man after all. You clearly gambled on that.'

Planned? Gambled? Riddles again, she could stand no more of them.

'You've got to be clean out of your skull,' she flared, pausing to pull the clogs on before attempting to negotiate the woodland path. 'I can't think why, but you believe I've somehow deliberately engineered this...this scenario.'

'Since you mention it, I do. Oh, don't bother to deny it again. Women have used stranger tactics to worm their way into my life.'

'Worm my way into your life! Me? You've got to be joking! It just goes to show you're the most insufferably conceited man that ever walked the face of God's earth, ever!' Snorting her derision she stalked past him and turned up the rise into the sweet-smelling wood. 'How do you imagine I arranged it all then? Come on, you must have worked that one out!'

'It was pretty obvious.' He caught her up, counting out his assumptions on his fingers. 'One: you heard my car arrive. Two: you hurried to wait by the lake and hoped I'd come looking for you - as I did, especially as you'd left your sexy lace underwear draped around the kitchen. I couldn't miss it, and I took that as a 'come on'. Three: the house was empty, I checked. That told me you hadn't gone far, as you knew it would.' Points emphatically made, he pushed his hands into his pockets. 'I had no choice but to investigate, you arranged it all quite neatly - and don't forget I found you naked!'

'That all sounds pretty damn complicated to me.

Waiting by the lake!' Prue was utterly annoyed by his assumptions. At the same time, she could see how bad the whole scenario looked for her. 'I couldn't find a bathroom to have a shower, so I decided to go for a swim instead. Initially I was going to heat up some water to wash myself but I changed my mind. It's as simple as that.'

He'd gone on ahead, his blue shirted figure striding through the glades of wild flowers. She followed him, not sure whether he'd heard, yet he made it clear that he had been listening.

'I must say it's a good story. Some people might even believe it but don't expect me to.' He shot the words over his shoulder as he left the shade of the trees and entered the grounds of the house. 'The only thing I don't get is, why are you back-pedalling now?'

He shook his head, clearly puzzled that she appeared to have no intention of following what he saw as her plan, to its inevitable conclusion.

Devastated by the way things had turned out, Prue plodded behind him. Some demon inside her wouldn't let it rest there. 'And how was I supposed to know you'd come back here? Perhaps you think I'm clairvoyant or something?'

'I didn't say you were expecting me,' was his comeback. 'I only said that people like you are opportunists - you heard my car. After that I give you credit for a bit of fast thinking.'

'Oh, go to hell!' responded Prue, who rarely swore. Awkwardly she clambered over the log pile after him. 'Apart from anything else, you've forgotten one crucial fact. Hildi is my friend!' Surely that would touch a chord in his vile nature!

'So what's new?' was his sneering rejoinder. 'Many of the girls I've met, who had seduction in mind, and more, have been so-called friends of Hildi. Scores of females make a point of cultivating her acquaintance so they can get an introduction to me.' His laugh was unpleasant, cynical. 'Lots of them, like you, aren't even subtle about it. However, you might be interested to know that, apart from the immediate fascination of a nude female body - any female body - pushy girls are a big turn-off for me. I find them revolting.'

Pushy! Prue couldn't believe her ears. He had his camp followers then, at his university, no doubt just because of his male-model appearance. Yet the arrogance of the man was staggering.

'Surely you're not suggesting I'm a sort of... groupie! I can assure you nothing could be further from the truth. If you knew my history you'd never even think it. Oh, I'll admit I'm quite normal, whatever normal is. At least, I once believed in romance, in true love, that sort of thing. Something happened, though, something I can hardly bear to talk about.'

Perhaps it was the break in her voice that caused him to look around. He regarded her curiously.

Prue gave a little cough, reluctant to reveal her private anguish but, apparently all ears now, he'd slowed down, had indeed now halted and was looking at her expectantly amid the lush wild garlic mustard that grew among the birch trees.

'Go on,' he prompted.

'My Mum and Dad used to be the ideal couple,' she began. 'We were a threesome - I was surrounded by love, but about a year-and-a-half ago, absolutely out of the blue, my father left. He walked out to set up home with a butcher's daughter; a girl I knew from school.' She paused, choking on the memory.

'That kind of thing's happening all the time. I can't believe it upset you that much, a tough cookie like you!'

'You know nothing about me! I was so devastated I cut off my hair - with nail scissors to make a complete mess of it. My hair has always been long and Dad loved it - he'd never even let me have it trimmed. Since his betrayal I've always kept it like this, simply because Dad doesn't care for short hair.' She flicked a hand through the dark, dense mass of it and her voice shook with emotion at the memory. 'I'll always hate him for what he did to Mum - to us both. For this reason alone chasing men figures very low on my list of priorities. So you see you're quite safe from me.'

'Safe? That's what they all say.' He dismissed her story with a flick of his hand and moved off to trample heedlessly through the pungent wild garlic. He crossed the lawn and climbed the back steps. 'Quite the little drama queen aren't you? Your pitiful tale cuts no ice with me, so if you're expecting a round of applause, prepare for disappointment.'

There was no answer to that. Prue's small hands

were clenching and unclenching, she could almost have hit him.

She followed him into the kitchen, not caring whether she'd ever get through to him. Why couldn't he see that as Hildi's almost-husband he was off limits to any decent girl? Anyway, he was nothing. Nobody. Invisible to her from this moment on. In any case, her own needs were suddenly paramount. She was cold and clammy and really could do with a hot drink to get her circulation moving.

While the water was heating up, she collected mugs from the drying rack in the scullery. She didn't even have to check in the mirror to know what a complete fright she looked - face streaked with mascara, eyes bleak and colourless. Her hair, she knew, was plastered to her head, giving her the appearance of a painted peg doll. She was, without question, very far from her best. The knowledge disheartened her further.

On returning to the kitchen she was astounded to find Didrik making himself useful. He was kneeling on the red-and-yellow rag rug before the open doors of the stove, striking a match. Soon the screws of newspaper and kindling caught fire and he began to feed the crackling flames with sticks from the log basket. In spite of herself, Prue felt a surge of gratitude. Quietly she set about making the hot drink, enough for both of them.

'There's coffee if you want some. Help yourself.'

She was half-a-mind to take her own mug to another room but decided to show some bulldog spirit and stay. Truth to tell, she was drawn to the life-giving fire. So she sat in the basket chair and, while her hands warmed round the hot beaker, slowly her blood started to thaw. Her jeans, damp because she hadn't dried herself properly, began to steam gently.

Although the last thing she wanted was to open up another conversation, she just had to know. 'How is Hildi?'

'Resting at home,' he replied. 'As well as the broken bone and some bad bruising, she twisted her ankle. All the same, she hasn't forgotten your luggage and persuaded me to drive over with it.'

Hearing of her friend's additional injuries, Prue felt a heavy pang, yet she couldn't help offering up a silent prayer of thanks for the arrival of her own possessions. It was the first positive thing that had happened all day and she let out an audible sigh of relief.

'I suppose Hildi's original plan was to keep you company here for a few days?' He glanced up at Prue and she nodded. 'That's my Hildi, always considerate.'

Too considerate over some things, Prue agreed silently. 'A sprained ankle - that can be so painful but I suppose it could have been worse.'

The warmth creeping through her veins released the throbbing tension in her muscles.

She began to relax as she watched him lodge an awkward branch in the flames. In peace, she studied the back of his neck and noted how sexy it was; she could well imagine the difficulty he might have fighting off some of his female students. Hildi had told her all about his posh job at the University of Gustavskrona.

'Didrik's really into British culture. He's an expert in your language and customs, and earlier this year he was made Head of Department.'

This would account for his excellent command of English, his fluency and familiarity with it. It also explained why he had a flat in London. Prue couldn't help wondering how Hildi felt about this.

'By the way, I made a long distance phone call earlier, to my mother,' she said. 'I'd like to pay for it. How much…?'

'Forget it.' He dismissed her offer with an airy wave of one hand while the other plied the fire with chippings of juniper and cherry wood, which spat resin and whiffs of fragrant smoke into the room.

'Oh, but I must settle my debts.'

'There's no more to be said. You're Hildi's guest. In any event, the decision is mine. I took on all the expenses of Norrtorpet some time ago. As I'm sure you're well aware, I'm quite a rich man.'

'Of course I didn't know, it's of no interest to me,' she stammered, acutely embarrassed, but even as she spoke she thought what a wonderful gesture that was. Didrik wasn't even a member of the family yet. Hildi, and perhaps more to the point, Hildi's parents were probably very grateful for his financial help.

He had left the hearth to pour himself a coffee. Then he returned to sit near Prue on a polished wooden settle by the wall. In the flickering light from the fire the two of them acquired an air of companionship, albeit a false one. At the very least he'd stopped kicking off for the present, and Prue was grateful for small mercies.

'So how do you manage to work and live abroad at the same time?' she asked, her curiosity getting the better of her earlier resolve to cold-shoulder him.

'No problem. I can work as easily there as here, and I come home frequently.'

'I should hope so, for Hildi's sake.' It sounded like a strange set-up to Prue, but there was no accounting for foreign ways of doing things.

The logs were now flaming as orange as the sun that could be seen through the window. The heat caressed Prue and soothed the frazzled edges of her nerves. She put a hand to her cheeks as they tingled, not with vexation this time, but with the glow of warmth and well-being. It occurred to her that they had been chatting like ordinary acquaintances, and perhaps he too, had noticed their dialogue had been borrowing instants of normality.

Didrik stood up, having finished his drink, and the spell was broken. He took his mug to the scullery, rinsed it out and up ended it on the dish drainer.

'Incidentally, this - what would you call it? - "kitchen annexe," serves as a bathroom.' He dragged the skimpy curtain across its entrance to demonstrate exactly how private it could be - not. 'It's just your bad luck if you happen to be prudish. We Swedes have no hang-ups about our bodies. Or anyone else's body, come to that.'

Was he smiling? At the very least, he was striving not to, Prue guessed as he launched into further details.

'The house is very old and there's no modern plumbing. We're lucky to have running water this far out of town. It was only this spring that we got electricity laid on, and we're still waiting for a hot water heater. Sorry, but there it is.'

He didn't look too sorry, though, as he walked out through the door into the light evening. A second later he came back, but stopped in the doorway. There was the suspicion of a smile in the corner of his mouth as he spoke again.

'This is Norrtorpet, and "torp" means "little place out in the sticks".' She could clearly see a twinkle in his eyes now. 'The veneer of Swedish civilisation is very thin. At heart we're really primitive, close to the earth. It comes from the centuries our ancestors spent living in the forests. That's why there are no hot showers, no cold showers even, no *ensuites*, no three-course dinners and no waiter service. Welcome to Hotel Dahlgren!'

He withdrew swiftly, but not too swiftly for Prue to miss the wide grin on his face. He obviously thought it was funny. She did herself, in a way, and conceded that she still had a lot to learn about Sweden and Swedish ways. At least, Didrik had tried to lighten the atmosphere between them. Why, the guy might even possess a sense of humour. If she was completely honest, she could forgive an awful lot for that.

A few minutes later he returned carrying her white jacket and suitcase, and immediately went off to fetch a plastic cool box and several supermarket bags containing the groceries Prue and Hildi had shopped for on their journey down from Stockholm.

'I got you some frozen dinners from the supermarket while I was out,' he informed her, removing foil containers from the cool box and stowing them in the scullery freezer. He nodded in the direction of the cooking area. 'There's a microwave oven over there. The instruction book is somewhere about, in a drawer, I expect. Don't worry, it's written in several languages.'

He behaved as if his former flash of good humour had never existed; as if outside he'd given himself a good talking-to. His features were once again stern, severe even. 'I've eaten already so I'll leave you to it; I have to work.'

When he'd gone, Prue put the groceries away - bread, milk, cornflakes, lingonberry cordial. Taking account of Didrik's disappearance to work, he had presumably made the generously glowing fire for her sole benefit. After all it was still light outside, the weather mild. It had certainly been a considerate gesture and he hadn't even stayed to share the benefit of it. It had been more than polite; it made him look genuinely concerned for her welfare. The food he'd brought too, when he had so much on his mind, was more than welcome and Prue was truly grateful.

She took a quick peep into the freezer, at the

food. How thoughtful. Perhaps she shouldn't think too badly of him after all. He was an odd mixture of good and not-so-good, which described most people, come to think, and she'd given up trying to fathom him out in any case.

Somewhere along the line, there must have been a misunderstanding. He'd mistaken her for someone else, maybe. That was the only possible solution, the only explanation she could come up with. Perhaps it would all be explained when Hildi was better. Yes, that was it, and she decided to cling to the hope that, in the end, it would all come out in the wash as her grannie used to say. Even so and bearing his sustained animosity in mind, Prue couldn't entirely rid herself of the idea that he harboured more than a little interest in her welfare, something more than mere politeness. After all, he'd made a fire for her, brought groceries and food, not to mention that kiss...

She took a deep breath; she was on dangerous ground again. Nonetheless, she found the idea provocative and, heaven help her, more than a little exhilarating.

# CHAPTER THREE

Once she'd put away the coffee and washed and dried the mugs and spoons, Prue lifted her suitcase onto the settle and opened the lid. Just the sight of her own clothes, sponge bag, lap-top computer and field set of water colours warmed her heart. She glanced out of the window. Didrik's car was in the drive, so he was still around somewhere, but as he was working she should take advantage of his absence to complete her toilet.

The scullery was cosy from the heat of the stove, so she brushed her teeth. Wary of interruptions, she turned the key in the outside door and wedged a chair against the inside one. Only then dared she shed her clothes and get ready to shampoo her hair after the inevitable wait for hot water. Later she donned a nightie consisting of lace-edged shorts and matching negligee. The apricot-pink material was delicate, but not transparent. All in cream and peach, she stood before the mirror and combed her hair. It had grown a little too long of late. It reached already below her ears; never mind, she liked the effect.

She didn't consider she was bad-looking and she liked to look glam for special occasions, but sometimes what she saw in the mirror quite surprised her. This was one of those times. Bathing in an icy cold lake plainly suited her.

It was as if she had willed herself to be really

attractive. Suddenly she wanted it, oh, how she wanted it. She ran her fingers lightly over her face, the contours of her rather full mouth, straight nose and finely fleshed cheeks. She turned her head a little and with a slight shock saw how much she resembled her father. She went on to check different aspects of her face, slanting her chin upwards, turning slightly to observe the effects sideways. The flow of her hair moved with her, the thickness of it falling attractively. Yes, the likeness to her father was less obvious from this angle. It was the hair that did it and she might let it grow again, long as it once had been. She wondered if Didrik would like it better. Didrik! Now where had that thought come from? In an instant she recognised the yearning for what it was, to look pleasing for the partner of another, to covet the lover of a kind friend. She was being selfish again, wicked, evil.

With her mouth set in a firm line of self-disapproval, she removed the chair guarding the door, then took out a foil container marked 'fiskpaj' and heated it up. The food was delicious - white-fish pie with a potato and cheese topping and a hint of nutmeg. She ate it while sitting in the basket chair that had already become her favourite. After helping herself to a rather wizened red apple from a rack in the apple store for dessert, she added more logs to the fire. Fizzing and crackling, the flames cast spurts of blue smoke and danced shadows about the room. To the soothing sound of the breeze rustling in the thick foliage outside the window and notwithstanding her earlier nap, Prue dozed off.

Her hazy dreams of walking down a lane to a hospital to visit Hildi accompanied by her own father, of all people, were enhanced by soft music. The melody seemed to come from far away, the sounds reverberating distantly like the echoing bells fastened to the porch door.

At around three in the morning, she awoke to complete silence. The fire had burned out and the foliage outside the window had stopped rustling. Sleepily and rather stiffly she rose and made her way out of the kitchen and up the stairs to bed.

The middle of the night it may have been yet outside the summer night sky was not quite dark. She opened the door of her bedroom and located a light switch just inside the door. A tiny pink-shaded lamp on the dressing table lit up. Her face and figure were immediately thrown into soft illumination, reflected in the dressing table triple-mirror. She paused, taking a minute to appraise herself critically again.

Shrugging out of the negligee she let it fall to the floor, and the short nightdress clung to the gentle curve of her breasts which really needed no support. She adjusted the mirror a little so that it showed how the cream lace border on the flimsy material formed a flattering pelmet, setting off slim fair thighs and slender legs. Yes, her figure was fairly okay, but she could do with a few extra inches in height.

'One of your frequent pastimes, is it - admiring yourself? I was always taught to despise vanity.'

The sudden, throaty voice in the confines of the low-ceilinged room threw Prue into a panic. She flung herself back, defensively, catching her arm on the edge of the dressing table, crying out. In the dim moonlight that flooded through the room she recognised Didrik on the single bed, bare-chested and raising himself on his elbow.

'It's you!' How could this be happening? She was jinxed!

'Who else did you expect?'

'No one, I...'

Totally embarrassed she trawled around the floor, frantic to find her dressing gown. Obviously she was destined to keep making a dreadful idiot of herself in the presence of this man.

'I... er... This is entirely accidental...'

'Accidental-on-purpose, I'm sure.'

Her heart thumped painfully as he watched her retrieve the pale apricot gown and, all in a fluster, pull it on - inside out. She rubbed her arm which was sore where she'd just knocked it.

'It's the middle of the night and I need my beauty sleep,' he said. 'So, what the hell are you doing here? And don't even think of giving me any of your long-winded excuses.'

She felt his heavy lidded gaze on her body, rather wolfishly, and she clutched the negligee closer around her.

'I ... I'm sorry.' There was nothing else she could say, her mind had gone blank. 'I thought...'

'I know what you thought - that you'd sneak into my bed,' he interrupted. 'If you don't mind my saying so, you should wait until you're invited!'

Prue groaned inwardly. Oh no! It was too late at night to have to listen all over again while Didrik allowed his wild imagination run away with him.

'I just made a mistake, that's all. I had a nap in this room this afternoon.' She made for the door. 'Go back to sleep. I've got no designs on you - whatever you may think.'

Unfortunately, he wasn't about to let her go so easily.

'Come, come. Why so coy all of a sudden - lost your nerve?'

The accusation cleared her brain in a flash. All fired up, Prue stalked back to the centre of the room.

'When you've quite finished, I've had just about enough of your insults!' She stood, hands on hips, the better to do battle if that's what he wanted. 'I don't expect you to believe me, and frankly, I'm not bothered, but I slept for at least two hours in this very bed this afternoon. How was I to know that the room was yours? First of all, I didn't know you were still in the house. Second of all, this is a girl's bedroom, for pity's sake, all pink and frilly.'

There was nothing girlish about the smell of the room now, though. A faint tang of body cologne hung in the air; sandalwood, probably, underscored by a warm seductive perfume she couldn't name; musk perhaps, and certainly male.

'Third of all, the bed's far too small for you!'

'I was in my studio all evening,' he countered, raking the fingers of one hand through his hair. 'My travelling bag has been on the top of this wardrobe since I arrived from England two days ago. A blind person couldn't miss it. What's more, the drawers in the chest are full of my clothes.'

'For all I knew the travelling bag was a permanent fixture,' she retaliated. 'That's what the top of a wardrobe is for! As for your clothes, I'm afraid I didn't examine the drawers.'

A tremor of weariness ran through her, reminding her it was the middle of the night. 'Oh, think what you like! Why should I care?'

Yet the trouble was she did care. She was uncomfortable with the whole situation, even more so since he'd mentioned the fact that he supported the summer house financially. It meant she was his guest as well as Hildi's, and that put her in a very difficult position.

However before she could retreat towards the door his long athletic body, clad only in bleached white boxer shorts, moved swiftly, lunging across the space between them. A second later, her forearms were imprisoned in a grasp of iron.

She gave a yelp of alarm while the aromatic smell of his body was overwhelming her now, engulfing her senses.

'Leave me alone! How dare you?' Frantic, she struggled with him for several seconds, but it was hopeless. His grip was steel and he was not about to slacken it. 'What is it you want, then? Make up your mind!'

His eyes were black pools of midnight in the diffused glow of the lamp. 'You deserve ten-out-often for sheer bloody guts, and such persistence merits a reward. It's probably time I taught you a lesson.' His voice became ragged as he pulled her in to his chest, breathing harshly.

A moment later, with one swift movement he had her fast, locked to him with one strong arm. Prue felt the fierce tension of his body; a matching urgency flicked like a whiplash through her sinews and blood. When his mouth found hers, she closed her eyes, aware of the heat of his lips, the hard pressure of his kiss. Her own lips, her mouth, were forced open as he demanded more, a deeper kiss. The wild sweetness billowing in her loins was near unbearable. She didn't intend to submit to his will yet she found herself returning his kiss, starting to lose herself in the primitive joy of lovers from time immemorial.

Yet before she knew it, the brief squall was over. Without warning he let her go, leaving her feeling shocked, abandoned, quite bereft even.

'Perhaps that'll make you think twice before you play with fire in the future,' he growled. 'Better be careful; next time you might not get off so lightly.'

Suddenly not supported by the strong embrace of his arms anymore, she staggered foolishly for a couple of seconds.

'You know, you've got quite a plausible tongue.' He shook his head sadly. 'You almost had me fooled. In fact, I was on the point of giving you the benefit of the doubt. I have to admit it - you look so… virginal.'

'That's because I am a virgin,' she burst out.

'What's more, I'm not ashamed of it — not that it's any of your business!'

'Untouched and untouchable? I don't think so. As I said, I'd nearly persuaded myself to believe it, but after this...' He spread his hands eloquently. 'For goodness' sake, go away, or I shall refuse to be responsible for my actions.'

An instant later he was back in bed and had turned his back on her.

Glad to escape, Prue ran out, still tense and agitated. She located the room with the child-size furniture and, overcome with humiliation, she switched on the light briefly. Since she'd been in here earlier, the bed had been made up with a fresh rose-patterned duvet cover and matching pillow slips. The only person who could have done that was Didrik. The man was such a puzzle, full of suspicion, yet caring. Prue sighed, lay down under the duvet and closed her eyes.

Many good-looking men demanded adulation. It was what her mother had given her father for eighteen years, and look what had happened to her. Yes, lots of men were spoiled, first by their mothers, then by the female population at large. From now on, Prue was determined not to add herself to the list of women who worshipped at the shrine of Herr Didrik's handsome looks. Even if it meant causing offence, she'd keep out of his way and, promising herself she'd do just that, against all the odds, she fell fast asleep.

Prue awoke blushing at the memories of the

previous day's disasters and to the distant sounds of a piano being played. Was there even a piano in the house, with Didrik being the pianist, or was he playing a CD?

She took the ewer from the pine wash-stand by the bed and fetched water from downstairs, first checking that the landing was clear. She was pleased to see her suitcase standing by her bedroom door. Didrik must have carried it up for her. He could be kind when he wanted to be then.

After unpacking, she decided on fine wool navy trousers and a jade silk, short-sleeved shirt which brought out the intense green of her eyes. For the first time this holiday she put on a little make-up - she felt she could do with the moral support. Her brows and lashes needed no emphasis, but she brushed her face with a translucent powder and finished off with a natural pink lip gloss.

When she went down the stairs, Prue noticed a piece of paper on one of the treads. She bent to retrieve it.

*In case you are wondering where to sleep, the bed in the children's room is ready for you.*

She took a quick, surprised breath. So that confirmed it: Didrik had made up the bed especially for her and had even left a note to let her know. She hadn't noticed it the night before, and that's how she'd come to end up in the wrong room.

Heavens, what an idiot she was. She blushed at the memory. In retrospect, how could she blame him for suspecting her motive for invading his sleeping space?

The music was louder here on the ground floor, and she traced its source to the long corridor off the hall. This, she'd already noticed, was a separate wing of the house, a single storey with one small window reaching out into the shadowy green of the orchard; a recent extension from the un-weathered look of the wood, built for the man about to marry into the family. At a guess it was a music studio. From behind the door came the practised, sure notes of a born musician. As the chart-topping tune was repeated over and over, first in one style, then another, Prue was forced to conclude she was listening to a live performance. Surely the performer could be only one person, and that person, beyond all shadow of doubt, had a rare gift in his fingers. Against all her inclinations, she was totally impressed. Didrik obviously took his hobby seriously. To Prue's ears, here could be a professional musician at work.

Dear heaven, who was this Didrik, this enigma with his handsome looks, his hostile attitude tempered with small kindnesses, and now demonstrating his musical prowess? He was, seemingly, a person of many parts and immense talents, exciting and intriguing. Although she was reluctant to acknowledge it, Prue realised only a special kind of woman would make a fitting partner for such a man – someone like Hildi.

Wondering why Hildi had never mentioned her beloved's flair for piano-playing, she went into the kitchen and dropped Didrik's note into the bin. When she and Hildi had driven down from Stockholm, they'd even spoken about music and romance in their lives, but her friend hadn't said a word about her fiancé's musical talent.

The car radio had been switched on to Abba singing their old hit, 'Dancing Queen', Prue remembered.

'I'm a glam-rock fan myself,' Hildi had remarked, conversationally. 'You know, that seventies' stuff. I also like middle-of-the-road pop. What about you?'

'Oh, I enjoy most kinds of music really, jazz and anything classical from Chopin to Bach. I like indie rock, and I'm mad about disco music because I just love dancing.'

Hildi had turned and smiled at her. 'I'm glad because you're like me. I love my job, but you know what they say about all work and no play.'

Prue had happily agreed and talked a little about her job at The Trust. Hildi was interested in the way things worked in England. Prue had taken a minute or two to elaborate on the Channel currents, high water and low water. With there being little or no currents in the Baltic, having to dive when the tides were right was a new concept for her.

'It can take ages to draw everything the divers bring up - they find so many beautiful items down there in the wreck.'

'You don't have much time to do any painting for your own pleasure, then?'

'It's all a pleasure to me, but I know what you

mean. In my spare moments I do water colours of local scenes for The Trust shop. I enjoy that, and it earns a bit extra for The Kate funds.'

'So, do you have time for a little love then, a little romance?'

'There's no-one special at the moment.' Prue had given a small laugh. 'We're not all as lucky as you, you know. Since I was a little girl, I've been waiting for my knight in shining armour to come riding by on a white horse. He hasn't turned up yet!'

'Perhaps you read too many romantic stories.'

And so they'd moved away from the subject...

So, until this morning, Hildi's close association with music had remained an innocent secret. Prue's own secret was different, and her forehead felt clamped in an iron band of worry and guilt. She'd been so disloyal to her injured friend and was totally ashamed of her forbidden feelings, the way she'd been drawn into returning Didrik's mocking kisses – it had all been absolutely and totally out of order.

She would make up for it with an extra special wedding gift, one of her own paintings. A set of water colours of Norrtorpet, the wild garden with its many flowers and the lovely lake, would be perfect.

Prue looked round the kitchen. Various packets of cereal as well as a clean bowl and spoon stood ready on the table. That was also obviously Didrik's doing as there was no one else in the house, yet she didn't feel in the least bit hungry. So she decided she would make an immediate start on the artwork. Minutes later, she was wandering about the sunny grounds, taking a few photos with her mobile, casting her eye over the house. It was utterly important to assess every aspect of her surroundings before she began the first sketch.

All at once a sound broke the peace of the garden, the rhythmic clip-clopping of a horse's hooves. A minute or two later a pony-and-trap emerged from the orchard, and Prue was charmed to see Aunt Agnetha holding the reins.

'Whoa!' The capable lady brought the pony to a halt and, followed by Anna-Karin, climbed down from the driving seat. She was full of happy hand-waving; the little girl, however, was pale and subdued. Mother and daughter were soon engaged in lifting various bags down from the cart, and also a wire pet basket. The occasional 'Miaow' announced the occupant to be a cat.

Prue regarded the little scene with rapt attention. In spite of the drawbacks she'd encountered, Sweden was one enchantment after another.

'God morgon, Prudence. What sunny day, and you look so nice in lovely green,' Aunt Agnetha called cheerily.

She, herself, was wearing grey leggings and a blouse in her favourite orange. 'Hildi sends love. She is much better in the good care of her mamma.'

'Hi!' returned Prue, smiling broadly, and prepared to give them both a welcoming hug. She was thrilled to see them. Now perhaps life would return to normal.

'Hildi will come soon, but her mamma wish she

rest today. I come to make a meal,' said Agnetha. 'You like Janssons frestelse?'

'Jansson's Temptation? Yes, I do,' Prue confirmed as she helped them into the house with their parcels. 'I had it for dinner in the hotel and loved it.'

'This is Kattis,' Aunt Agnetha introduced her to the cat with its multi-coloured fur - white, black and various shades of brown. She opened the basket, produced a fleece-lined harness with an extended lead, and fastened it on the little animal. 'I bring him because Anna-Karin has distress for Hildi. My little child is much crying and crying, so I think you do some good thing for her. Draw cat, please, for Anna-Karin.'

'What an excellent idea!' Prue was only too happy to oblige with helping to console the child. 'I'll do a picture of the pony, too, if you like.'

'Ah, the horse. He does working for us on our farm, but today is... er... special for Anna-Karin because she is sad. The horse is very good boy in all the many traffics.'

Amused by Aunt Agnetha's quaint turns of phrase, Prue sprinted to the house to sort out her painting materials and prepare coffee. While she put water on and waited for it to heat up, she watched through the window as the little girl tied her pet's lead to a drainpipe. The drainpipe was metal and somewhat rusty.

Some fifteen minutes later they were drinking coffee, or milk in Anna-Karin's case, and eating the home-made almond cakes Aunt Agnetha had brought with her.

Afterwards, Prue cleared their coffee cups away, and Aunt Agnetha took a colander from the kitchen dresser, saying, 'Now I wish apples for the cooking.'

While her mother adjourned to the apple store, Anna-Karin found cushions and an old brown check picnic blanket and ran outside to spread them under a tree. Prue followed her into the sunshiny garden, eager to make a sketch of the pony before he was taken out of the shafts of the cart and left to graze at will. There was little he could spoil. The grounds of the house were informal, with areas of out-cropping blue-grey granite, grass and wild flowers as well as trees and bushes.

Using the tree as a back rest, Prue settled down on the blanket with her painting materials. She snapped a strong rubber band over the pages of her pad to hold them down in the balmy, but occasionally blustery wind and started on the drawings, the pony first, then the cat. Anna-Karin sat close, her pretty face absorbed, as under Prue's skilful fingers likenesses of the animals emerged.

Kattis, the cat, was a lively creature and never still for a moment, but Prue enjoyed the challenge of capturing him in varying positions. Normally she didn't care for an audience while she worked, but this was different - she was delighted to have Anna-Karin there. The two of them quickly evolved a language of pats and nods and giggles, and under Prue's tutelage Anna-Karin added splodges of gingery-brown and black paint to the picture of her pet.

'You get on well with children, at least.'

The all-too-familiar voice initiated a knot of tension at the back of Prue's neck. Her paint brush trembled ever-so-slightly, but she didn't allow it to pause in its stroking in of the cat's ringed tail. Without looking up, she offered him a 'Good morning.' Courtesy cost nothing.

'Did you want me for something?' she added.

'Phone call for you, from England. Your mother.'

'Oh!' Prue instantly dropped the brush into the water container, scrambled to her feet and shot into the house and to the study.

'Hello, Mum,' she said breathlessly into the phone.

'Darling, how are you? I'm just making sure you're all right and having a nice time.'

'Oh, Mum, you got my message then. It's good to hear your voice. I've got so much to tell you.'

'Yes, and I've made a note of the phone number in my address book. It's a lovely weather here at the moment, by the way. It's getting really hot in the conservatory. What about you, is the sun shining in Sweden?'

Prue laughed. 'Mum, our weather's gorgeous. It's not as changeable as in England.'

'Well, I must admit we did have a shower this morning, but never mind that. I want to hear all about your new friend, the bride-to-be, and the wedding, and don't miss anything out!'

'Oh, Mum. Hildi had an accident; it was all too awful...'

She went on to tell her mother much of the news, the ups and downs of her trip to Sweden but she was careful not to say anything about Didrik and her difficulties with him.

'By the way, I'm listening for the doorbell. James will be here soon.'

'James? Do you mean…?'

'Yes, love. Your boss. He's coming for lunch.'

The news gave Prue quite a jolt. As far as she was aware her mum hardly knew the man. The two had met maybe twice before, and always at official functions.

'I'll tell him that your fine, enjoying yourself. And he'll want to know what you thought of the Wasa.'

'Tell him…,' said Prue, still taken aback by her mum's casual reference to James. 'Tell him I was completely knocked out by it. Marvellous, no, more than that, mesmerising and quite unearthly in that massive chamber.' She hesitated before embarking on the big question. 'But how did you come to invite James for lunch?'

'Don't sound so surprised, darling. He got in touch to ask if I'd heard from you, and we sort of got talking. You know how I love those medieval whodunits? Well, it came up in conversation and James said he'd read several himself and would I like to borrow them? He brought them round a couple of days ago. Er… he took me out for a meal as a matter of fact.'

Feeling rather stunned by this revelation Prue replied, 'I see. Well, will you thank him again for letting me stay on here?'

'Of course, darling. In fact, he's here now. I can hear his car. By the way, before you go, I saw Claire in the library. I told her you were staying on in Sweden for a while and about the wedding and so on. She sends love and hugs.'

When finally Prue went back into the garden after the call, her thoughts were occupied by the question of James's apparent involvement with her mother. This was quite a turn up. Her mum was an attractive woman, but romance with Prue's boss? That would be a surprise. Although come to think, James was single and fancy-free; his divorce had come through in the spring. Also he was a considerate boss, a pleasant man.

Like Prue herself, her mother was perhaps beginning to realise that the end of her marriage didn't mean that every man was bad news. It seemed she was ready to move on. Prue certainly hoped so. It would be wonderful to see her beloved mother happy again! In truth, she found the whole idea of her mum and her boss being an item more than a little exciting. Maybe it was better to check her thoughts which were running away with her - she might already be assuming too much. It was likely that they were just two lonely people, making friends. Still, the two had quickly discovered they had tastes in common, like those historical crime novels. So with a bit of luck, they each may have found a soulmate!

There was now no one in the garden apart from

the animals – the cat was still tied to the old iron drain pipe near the kitchen door. The pony was now roaming free. Prue could hear Anna-Karin's bright chatter in the kitchen, so she decided to get on with the painting.

She was aware that Didrik came to the window of the music studio every now and again, glancing in her direction across the lawn. Maybe he was curious about what she was doing, although Hildi would surely have mentioned that her new English friend was an artist.

Progress on the painting however was somewhat slow as the cat was still restless, rushing about, pouncing on imaginary mice then rolling on his back. Prue lost count of the number of times she was obliged to stop painting, get up and disentangle his lead from the red currant bushes. After a while she turned her attention to the grazing pony which she'd drawn earlier. She now needed to paint his shiny chestnut coat. Absorbed in the task of completing the picture she didn't look up for a while. Finally, it was nearly finished and she was quite pleased with her efforts.

Rinsing out the brush in the water pot she casually glanced round and, my goodness, the pony was ambling across the wide, rough lawn towards her. Not being used to dealing with such a large animal, she realised she needed to move, and there wasn't much time. She emptied the water pot onto the grass, then hurriedly gathered paints and artwork together and set them aside behind the tree before taking hold of the blanket to drag it out of harm's way. All the while Prue kept her eye on the pony. No doubt he was a gentle, friendly creature, but she was getting quite nervous.

Just when she was about to shout for Aunt Agnetha, the pony changed tack, veering towards the house and the restrained Kattis. Now it was the poor cat's turn to panic. On seeing the approach of the pony he shot off and ran as far as his lead would allow, which wasn't very far. Prue watched in horror as it was immediately obvious that the rusty old drainpipe was going to have to give – it made a clattering noise as the frightened creature pulled frantically on his leash. A moment later, accompanied by several 'miaows' and cat-shrieks, a section of the drainpipe tumbled down with a loud clanking noise. With a final pull Kattis broke free. In an instant he was away, streaking across the garden and through the orchard, trailing his long lead.

Prue stood aghast, bewildered by the speed of the events happening before her eyes. Then she pulled herself together. There was no time to lose. She dropped the blanket and set off after the terrified cat as fast as she could. Over and over again she kept shouting his name, hoping, trusting someone in the house would hear her.

'Kattis! Kattis!'

She daren't stop to raise the alarm because the little creature, revelling in his new-found freedom, was already out of sight, maybe even lost in unfamiliar territory.

Prue hurried along as best as she could, much hampered by the wooden clogs she'd pushed her feet into earlier. Frantic with worry for Anna-Karin's sake as well as the cat's, she went after him, still constantly calling his name. She only hoped that Kattis wouldn't get trapped or injured by his long trailing lead.

Leaving the orchard she crossed a field, an outcrop of blue granite, and then entered the wood. Unfortunately, there was no sign of the cat. Even worse, the paths were tortuous, obviously unfrequented, and many of them overgrown with yellow broom, or spattered with mushrooms. Clumps of tiny red spotted toadstools were thriving where there was a whiff of decay. Breathing hard now, Prue pressed on. Once she thought she saw a flash of the cat's coat, the white harness, yet when she rushed forward she found nothing but a plastic supermarket bag in the undergrowth.

The forest canopy thickened, darkened, and soon there was only the occasional rustling of a wild animal, or the odd chirping of a bird to disturb the quiet. Constantly scratched by brambles and baby firs, her bare arms began to bleed. The quest seemed hopeless, but guilt and compassion compelled her to keep going. Finally, though, a stitch in her side brought her to a halt. Her rasping breaths were loud in the eerie, enclosed space, and she had to face the fact that she was lost. There was no certainty that anyone had seen her run into the woodland. In the vast forests of Sweden, she'd heard, one could walk in circles and never be found.

She was staring round helplessly when something caught her eye shimmering through the endless grey and silver-green tree trunks. Different colours, solid brown, a glimpse of emerald — were those stained wooden walls and a green copper roof? The Wasa Chapel!

In front of her, a small animal suddenly darted swiftly along the ground.

'Kattis!'

Clumsy in the clogs and with resurging hope, Prue rushed through the trees but the animal bounded up a tree trunk just as she stumbled and fell. Slightly dazed, she lay there for a moment, tears of shock and disappointment filling her eyes.

'Can't you tell the difference between a red squirrel and a cat?'

The sudden sound in the comparative hush of the forest scared the wits out her - she'd heard no one approach. Still, her heart did its usual shaming somersault because she'd immediately recognised her rescuer's voice. Before she could even attempt to stand, a pair of strong hands had gripped her arms and hauled her to her feet.

'Are you hurt?'

She shook her head.

'I thought the English were such animal lovers, but you can't even keep an eye on a cat.' Yet in spite of the accusation in his words, there was no harshness in his tone.

She felt him watching her as she brushed moss, pine needles, and a few stray ants from her clothes.

There were even more scratches on her arms now.

'What about Kattis? Did you catch him?'

'He's okay, he didn't go far. Anna-Karin saw what happened in the garden. She fetched me, and we soon found the cat down by the lake. As you were nowhere to be seen it dawned on me that you must have gone in the other direction, so I came to look for you.' He paused and his expression told her that he was quite relieved. 'Now I've found you, safe and well.'

'If the cat's all right, nothing else matters.'

'You're right, so stick close to me and don't get lost again. I've got lots to do, and that includes mending a drainpipe.'

'Well, I hope you're not blaming me for everything - and that somebody has put the pony in a place where he can't do any more damage.'

He made no reply but turned round and started to walk away.

She couldn't resist one last dig. 'I wasn't really lost, you know. That building over there is the Wasa Chapel, isn't it?'

Her comment seemed to grab his attention; at least he stopped in his tracks.

'Actually, since I'm here, I'm sure you won't object if I stay to look inside it,' she went on.

'No!' His negative response was no real surprise, but the vehemence of it was. He half turned. 'I've already told you how busy I am. I can't spare the time.'

'I shan't need a guide,' she replied. 'You go on

ahead, don't worry about me. I already know that the chapel is near the edge of the lake. I saw it yesterday before I went for my famous swim.'

'I said no and I mean no.'

Prue wasn't put off. 'It's easy to work out - all I have to do to get back to Norrtorpet is to find the lake-shore. It can't be far away.'

'It's dark in the chape,l and it's locked up. The key's up at the house…'

'I'll get the key and I'll borrow a torch.'

'You wouldn't see a thing, even with a torch. ' Visibly annoyed, he spun round to face her. 'There is no proper lighting in there, so you wouldn't be able to…' His sentence trailed off. His mouth was bunched tight, his resistance to her request almost a physical thing. 'You are being very awkward!'

'Please, I'd love to see inside,' she pleaded. 'You must understand, the Wasa was the reason I came to Sweden in the first place. I want to find out all I can about it. The idea of a chapel in its memory intrigues me so much; it's driving me to distraction.'

'Enough! I expect Hildi will be happy to give you a tour when she's better. In fact, she likes showing it off. She was the one who introduced my late wife to the chapel…' He left the sentence unfinished, his features contorted with emotion.

Completely baffled, Prue's eyes widened in surprise. This was the first inkling she'd had that Didrik had been married before; that Hildi would, in fact, be his second wife. It was also interesting to hear his first wife and Hildi had been friends. Still, even this new mystery didn't distract her from her determination to view the chapel. 'It wouldn't take you long to get the key. I know the way here now, I could come back.'

'Goddammit!' he exploded. 'The best thing you can do right now is get yourself some first-aid. You need some antiseptic on your arms. You've made a real mess of them.'

'Don't exaggerate. I'm not going to die from a couple of tiny scratches, so if...'

'No! From now on, Miss Claybourne, the subject is closed!' He emphasized the last four words as he strode off through the trees. Obviously his patience was at an end.

Giving the chapel one last lingering look, Prue resigned herself to following him. She had no choice, yet she wasn't fooled. Oh, no. He thought he'd fobbed her off with his promise of Hildi and a guided tour which, when it came to the crunch, he would never allow. For reasons of his own, he seemed passionate about keeping the Wasa Chapel off limits.

In any case, walking down the aisle would be more than enough for her injured friend to manage in the near future. There'd be no stumbling over boulders and through thickets of bramble and broom for Hildi yet awhile.

Never mind, she would return on her own, and soon. She'd made up her mind on that score. Prue definitely intended to see inside the strange little building before she was very much older. Her laptop was in her suitcase, so in the meantime she would try Google with the name of the chapel. She would have to ask for permission to get online at the summer house so she intended to keep on the right side of Didrik until that was accomplished, at least.

Today's events had only served to arouse her curiosity even further; now it burned at fever pitch inside her. The Wasa Chapel was a place with a secret, one which Didrik Nilsson was clearly determined to keep.

## CHAPTER FOUR

When they arrived back at the house, Prue discarded the clumsy clogs at the door. She had rescued her painting materials from behind the tree and left them on the kitchen window sill together with the water colours for Anna-Karin; one of the cat and one of the pony.

Although the sun hadn't set yet on this bright summer evening Aunt Agnetha endearingly displayed a typically Swedish love of lighted candles. The table in the dining room that evening was adorned with them, deep fuchsia pink with matching damask napkins on a plain white cloth.

While Prue was getting changed beforehand, the mouth- watering aroma of cooking filtered through the house, onions and anchovies blending with the sweet smell of cinnamon and cloves in the apple crumble. She'd cleaned up the abrasions on her arms and discarded her dusty clothes in favour of white jeans and a matching Great Kate T-shirt. The shirt portrayed the ship fully rigged and holed by cannon in a battle with the French fleet as it had been on the day it had sunk in the English Channel. The black-and-white drawing had been done by Prue herself, and identical T-shirts were on sale in the Trust Shop. She'd dressed up the plain outfit with her lapis lazulis; these were polished, graduated beads of a deep ultramarine blue. Semi-precious, they'd been handed down in the family for generations, and Prue was very attached to them. Actually they needed restringing, this time properly, with a little knot between each bead just in case the string ever snapped. Somehow Prue had never got round to having it done, but she promised herself this would be at the top of her 'to do' list as soon as she got home.

At Aunt Agnetha's request she drew up a chair to the table, relieved to note that with the cut-glass candelabra and its flickering candle glow between them, it was easy to avoid eye contact with the man seated opposite. For his part Didrik confined his remarks to Aunt Agnetha and Anna-Karin, albeit frequently in English, and often provoking them to a titter, or even a real outburst of laughter. Prue, however, wasn't about to act the wilting violet and tucked into her Jansson's Temptation.

'It just melts in the mouth,' she complimented the cook. 'What I had in the hotel was nice, but yours is different somehow - I can't quite decide what it is, but it's really scrumptious.'

It was - a full, mellow flavour with a tangy bite to it.

'Spice,' Aunt Agnetha supplied, rosy with pride.

'Agnetha, don't you mean allspice?' Didrik corrected her gently and looked over the top of the candles at Prue to explain. 'It's her secret ingredient.'

'Ah, yes, allspice.' Prue gave a nod. 'I recognise it now. Mum uses it sometimes.'

Why was he so pleasant, all of a sudden? Seeing

him in this affable mood just confused her. She wanted to continue to dislike him, but how? In spite of her outward bravado, she couldn't even control the butterflies in her stomach, so powerfully did she feel his nearness just across the table. Even her hands were shaking slightly, ready to betray her, so when she wasn't actually eating she kept them in her lap, out of sight.

The evening was balmy, the company was perfect. Sitting here so companionably with perhaps the most beautiful man in the world - a man who, at present, was displaying a warm, likeable side to his personality - was magic. Her imagination could so easily run away with her if she allowed it to. In many respects he was all she'd ever wanted, or dreamed of in a man. Strong, sexy, intelligent... she could go on and on. Yet she must never allow herself to forget that he belonged to someone else. Not just 'someone' but a wonderful, sweet and generous friend.

Prue brought her mind back to the conversation at the table and the excellent meal. As well as the crumble there was home-made blueberry ice cream and elderflower cordial to drink, to please Anna-Karin.

Afterwards Aunt Agnetha declared it time to re-harness the pony to the trap in readiness for their departure. Prue helped with the clearing up and promised to wash the dishes later; it was the least she could do in return for such hospitality.

She sat down at the kitchen table to quickly write 'With Love to Anna-Karin from Prue' on the backs of the studies of the animals. Below, after asking Aunt Agnetha the name of the pony, she added 'Kaspar' and 'Kattis,' ready for the little girl to take away with her.

'Anna-Karin!' Aunt Agnetha could be heard calling shortly after. 'Come here, please. Do not forgetting your lovely pictures, then we go home!'

Still looking for her daughter, she came in to untie Kattis from the table leg where he'd been fastened up for safety because of his earlier flight.

'Tomorrow Hildi must go and try on dress for marriage day, but she will see you in little while,' she said, settling the cat comfortably in his basket. 'Please be happy till we come again for "midsommar".'

'Midsummer?' Prue had heard that in this part of the world, midsummer was celebrated in some style. 'When is it?'

'Fredag...er...'

While Aunt Agnetha fumbled for the word in English, the translation was supplied by Didrik.

'Friday is Midsummer's Eve - a national holiday.' Again, he spoke politely as he strolled in from the garden where he'd been helping Aunt Agnetha deal with the pony.

Prue's glance was drawn upward; she felt she would never get used to his height. Already a concentration of heat was spreading out from the small of her back and when it flared under her collar bone, she looked away abruptly. This was school girlish idiocy to tingle every time she heard the sound of his voice. She pursed her lips as if it would stem her growing feelings. Didrik had been behaving in a perfectly civil manner for a while now. He was constantly blowing hot and cold; she couldn't keep up with his changes of mood. Into the bargain she knew herself to be reprehensible for the daydreams which sometimes, no, frequently, rampaged through her head since she'd first met him. The physical attraction he exuded had a power she'd never come across before. Yet there seemed to be something more underneath, something indefinable binding them together.

The next instant she cast aside the notion for the foolishness it was. To cover her confusion, she left the kitchen for the sitting room where, with the pictures, she cajoled Anna-Karin away from an Australian television soap about a dingo.

'Ah! Bra!' The child placed a smacking kiss on Prue's cheek. She was visibly excited and proud to have had a hand in the creation of the pictures and raced outside to show her mother. Prue followed to see them off.

'Heydor! Goodbye!'

A few minutes later the two of them waved as they lurched off along the uneven track through the avenue of trees. Sad to see them go, Prue blew kisses until they disappeared from sight then she returned to the house.

Didrik was stacking the dishes in the sink. There was a saucepan of water already heating up.

'I'll dry and put away if that's all right with you,' he said. 'I know where the dishes belong in the cupboards.'

Again surprised at his civility, she half smiled. 'Okay, that makes sense.'

When the water had boiled they started to wash the pots together like an old married couple. She almost started a conversation about a pop group that had recently formed in Portsmouth. The girls called themselves 'The Mary Roses' and, since appearing on a television talent show, they were making a great success of themselves. However she thought better of it.

Noticing the efficient way he handled the crockery, she couldn't help smiling.

'You've done this before.'

'I have indeed.' He closed the cutlery drawer. 'Is that everything?'

When she nodded, he lowered the clothes airer that hung over the draining board, draped the tea towel over it to dry, and pulled it up to the ceiling again. Then he left the scullery and she heard the door in the kitchen closing firmly.

Prue felt suddenly lonely after the excitements of the day. She helped herself to a glass of the elderflower cordial left over from dinner. Sipping it slowly she wandered through the ample-sized kitchen, just looking at the china knick-knacks and the little holiday souvenirs displayed on the shelves. She stopped at the chiffonier to gaze at the large studio portrait of Didrik. He was sitting at a baby-grand piano and, in the distortions of light pouring in through the window she could almost see him move.

As if by magic, music from perhaps that very same piano began to percolate softly through the house, like a murmuring wind. It was eerie how the music seemed to bring the photograph to life. The atmospheric, heart-wringing melody, half familar, had a curious effect on her.

Her paints, brushes and pencils were still where she'd left them on the window sill. She set them up on the kitchen table then, lost in contemplation, she sat down. Almost absently, she started to draw, then paint a portrait of him; from memory, from the picture of him inside her head. His hair, white-gold; eyes, level with a remarkable lustre which she tried to capture in purple madder touched with Prussian blue; dark-gold lashes and brows; straight nose with proud nostrils; mouth, sensually smiling, showing the strong white-as-white teeth and, lastly, she did not overlook the dimple. She placed it carefully, almost lovingly.

As an afterthought she added a sketch of herself at the side of his portrait; her own reflection in the chiffonier mirror. Glossy bright-dark hair; brows as fine as her own sable paint brush; eyes a lustrous grey-green, flecked with yellow; straight nose, too short for true beauty; full lips, almost pouting over white, even teeth. Lost in her self-appointed task, it was a second or two before she realised she wasn't alone. Didrik had entered the kitchen.

Prue was startled - she hadn't noticed the cessation of the music. Unsettled by his arrival, her gaze followed him to the fridge where he helped himself to a can of lager.

He came to stand behind her.

'Drink?' he offered, snapping off the ring-pull and taking a long draught straight from the can.

Prue declined with a shake of her head, again disarmed by his friendly demeanour. Too bad she hadn't had the time to cover up her work of the past couple of hours. Now he took it upon himself to comment on it.

'Hmmm... Is that how you see me? You've made me really handsome and have given me a very fetching dimple.'

'I...er...I've done it for Hildi.' She fiddled with her pencil. 'That's why I've made it so flattering, to please her.'

She felt the inevitable flush creeping over her face and was cross with herself for giving such a feeble performance.

'But what a shame, look!' He jabbed a finger at the other painting. 'The one you've done of yourself is unrealistic in a different way. You've made your eyes too small for example, and they're a very wishy-washy colour.'

Before she could object, he'd turned her face with his free hand, bringing it round to the light from the window. 'Yesterday these same eyes were like birch leaves. Tonight they're as green as the green in your paint box.'

'Very poetic.' Prue jerked her head out of his grasp. She was annoyed with herself at being caught out so revealingly, at exposing the inner recesses of her mind so unwittingly. Flicking the still-wet paper up and off the sketching pad she tore it across, twice.

Didrik gave a soft snort of laughter at this petty display of temper. He was clearly enjoying himself. 'Why so touchy? Are you in love?'

'In love? What do you mean?'

'Oh, don't look so offended. I just wondered; that's all. Predatory women can become infatuated just as easily as anyone else. Makes their self-appointed tasks easier, I imagine.'

Again he was mocking her. Prue started to fume inside.

'Are you suggesting I may be infatuated with you? If so, your conceit is appalling!' Now she was getting truly worked up, livid. 'I object to the fact that you think you can scoff at my work. I've never claimed to be Picasso, but I am a professional.'

'Calm down, miss! Surely there's no need to get so agitated.'

She ignored his remark, picked up her drawing pencil and waved it at him. 'To me, this is a tool with which I earn my bread and butter.'

His well-defined brows shot up, almost in apology. 'I wasn't criticising your expertise, merely pointing out that in the case of your own portrait you've been less than kind. You didn't do yourself justice.'

'Well, please keep your comments to yourself in future. I wouldn't dream of setting myself up as a critic of your musical talent.'

Prue was now uncomfortably aware she was being unreasonable. She'd over-reacted to his remarks and realised it was because, in her painting, he'd seen more than a glimpse of her inmost feelings. She took a long sip of the cordial. Then, in an effort to bring the conversation to an end, she pushed herself energetically out of the chair and gathered her painting materials together.

Regarding her closely, he took a quick swig of his beer. 'So you think I've got talent, eh?'

His tone hovered half-way between teasing and irony. She could make no sense of it at all.

'Stop fishing for compliments,' she flung at him. 'You're a fantastic pianist and don't need me to tell you that. If you'd wanted, I'm sure you could've made your living in the world of music. You're obviously a natural.'

'Really?' He gazed at her, perplexed. 'A natural, am I?'

'You are, definitely. I'm not so small minded that I can't acknowledge a true gift for music when I hear one.'

'Hmmm...' He rubbed thoughtfully at his chin which was glinting ever-so-slightly golden with stubble, and she caught him staring again, his eyes focused intently on hers.

Disconcerted by his look which she'd seen before but couldn't fathom, she took her paint box to the sink to rinse it along with the brushes. He followed and leaned on the wall - at the entrance to the scullery where there should have been a door, but was only a curtain.

Knitting his brows, Didrik drained his beer in two

gulps. He seemed to be considering her last remarks as if he'd been testing her.

'It's strange but, against my better judgement, even now I'm tempted to believe you're naïve; a total innocent,' he remarked eventually. 'On reflection, though, I've said it before and I'll say it again - you ought to have been an actress. Your timing and credibility, your sense of drama - flawless. You've got the looks for it, too, though no-one would ever guess from the self-portrait you've just ripped up.'

Riddles again, never to be resolved. Prue was driven to further exasperation as she could hardly complain to Hildi.

'Your fiancé is convinced I'm chasing him, and that I won't rest until I've seduced him.'

How would that sound? No, she'd have to work through the situation as best she could by herself, and do her utmost to keep out of his way.

She groaned inwardly, fed up with his barbed tongue - it was really getting to her. Hildi had proudly told her that Didrik was 'an important person' at the university. His professional know-how obviously gave him an extremely high profile, not to speak of his piano playing. With his magnetic combination of looks and talent, he must be the focus of much female attention.

'Putting on an act of any sort is beyond me - I should be so clever. I'm not the… the camp follower you take me for.' She spoke wearily for this was becoming repetitive. 'I'm sure you've got your following of groupies, girls of a certain type, but I'm thankful to be able to say that I'm not now, nor ever shall be, one of them.'

Prue snapped down the lid of her artist's box. She was utterly tired of the cut-and-thrust of any dialogue with him. It was time to end it, once and for all.

'Perhaps we could come to some arrangement, you and I. In future, I'll ignore you if you'll ignore me. Deal?'

Without waiting for a reply she made to leave the scullery, but he was blocking the exit.

'Hold on a sec.' He took her arm, almost gently. 'Come and sit down.'

He indicated the basket chair in the kitchen and she was so taken aback she sat in it without comment. As before, he chose the settle for himself.

'I wanted to ask you...' He hesitated before going on. 'The man who phoned you yesterday, is he... a close friend?'

'Er... you could say that.' Astonished by his question, Prue neglected to parry it with a sharp response.

'Well, he is quite persistent.'

He had all Prue's attention in an instant. 'I don't understand.'

'He telephoned again, twice, while you were playing hide-and-seek with the cat. Agnetha told me. I promised to pass the message on, but forgot. He did say he'd ring back, though.'

'I wonder...'

'He stressed that his call wasn't urgent. He was just anxious to check that you're all right.'

Prue couldn't resist another dig. 'I hope Agnetha told him I'm being persecuted unmercifully.'

'She did say he sounded concerned. Boyfriend, is he?'

'What? My boyfriend? That's a laugh. My mother's boyfriend, more like! Since I've been in Sweden he seems to have been hooking up with my mum. While the cat's away, the mice will play!'

'Come on, now. They are adults. Is your mother single?'

'Yes, she's divorced from my dad.'

'There you are then.' He spread his hands expressively. 'They don't need permission.'

'But I think we do,' said Prue, seizing the opportunity to mention something that needed to be said. Still, it was an awkward subject and she started to finger the beads at her neck nervously. 'You and I... here together... It doesn't look good.'

He, who was about to be married, living alone in the house with a single girl. Why did she need to point this out?

'I... have you got... I mean, is there somewhere else you could stay?' The question had been on her mind for some time.

It was now his turn to look confused. Prue guessed that her remarks had totally shattered the image he had of her as some kind of groupie, out to ensnare him.

'At present I'm in residence here.' His voice sounded quite resolute. 'It's peaceful, one of my favourite places. Only this spring the garden room was extended and converted into a music studio, soundproofed, triple-glazed. Surely I mentioned that. It was all done when the electricity was laid on. I'm in the process of testing all the equipment; keyboards, amplifiers and so forth. There is much work to do and I have to get on with it when I can.'

He spoke with pride and Prue supposed that as a self-confessed rich man, he could afford to indulge in such expensive whims. She gulped a little at his words. Surely her reasons for speaking up were obvious yet he plainly wasn't bothered.

'Are you implying that we need a chaperone - at our age? You're perhaps twenty, and on my next birthday I shall be thirty.'

There was a gleam of amusement in his eyes and the laughter lines around them deepened; something was tickling him. 'On second thoughts, though, you might be right - maybe I do need someone here to protect me from you.'

He was deliberately misunderstanding her!

Prue didn't dignify his remark with any acknowledgement; his wit was wasted on her. She'd merely been worried what the world in general, and Hildi in particular, might think. Her mouth tight, she got up to leave the room, shooting him a glance of aggravation as she did so. It was then that she detected something else in his eyes, something beyond the flippancy of his answer; a question that was perhaps troubling him. He carried himself like a conqueror yet, at times, he seemed so vulnerable. She had to admit she was baffled by him, his curiosity about James, for instance. In anyone else this might have been construed as jealousy. Then something else crossed her mind, something amusing.

'Did you say the music room was soundproofed?' She gave a little laugh. 'I don't think they made a very good job of it.'

'Sometimes I leave the door open,' he replied with a smile. 'And the windows.'

'Okay.' So that was explained then.

She was ready to retire to the sitting room when she remembered that she needed to get online sometime soon. So, instead of leaving the kitchen, she had to eat humble pie and ask Didrik politely if he would mind giving her his internet password. He obligingly wrote it down on a piece of paper while she explained that, amongst other things, she wanted to send emails to her mother and The Trust.

Prue thanked him, then went into the sitting room and made herself comfortable. It was a family room rather than a showplace, light and airy with filmy white curtains at the windows and well-worn easy chairs in dark green. Beside a pinky-red Ikea couch stood a sagging settee in a different, clashing red. The atmosphere was laden with the sweet smell of apples from the nearby apple store.

For the little that was left of the evening she kept herself to herself. She thought of fetching her laptop from upstairs to read over the notes she'd made about her impressions of The Wasa. Or, out of curiosity, she might look for the website of the university where Didrik was such an important person. In the end, though, she simply watched a television programme about Strindberg and his plays. The programme was, conveniently enough, in English with Swedish sub-titles.

At bedtime Prue noticed that the dolls in her room had been moved about and rearranged. She smiled to herself, imagining the fun Anna-Karin must have had earlier in the day. Last thing before going to sleep, she took out her laptop and wrote an email to her mother.

*'...so apparently the Wasa Chapel is gloomy inside and it's too dark to see anything,'* she rounded it off. *'I'm determined to see inside it before long, all the same - it's such a mysterious place. I'm now keeping a sharp look-out for a torch to borrow.*

*I've been told that Hildi will give me a conducted tour of the chapel when she comes but I shan't rely on that. She's got a sprained ankle as well as other injuries, so walking that far will be out of the question for her.*

*Weather still fine, beautiful and warm in fact, although I'm told it does rain sometimes!*

*Bye for the time being. Love and Hugs and Kisses.*

*Yours,*

*Prue*

*P.S. Didrik, Hildi's husband-to-be, has been married before, and I gather his first wife was very keen on the chapel.'*

Next morning Prue dressed in a pretty blue cotton skirt with a clean matching sleeveless top - hopefully she would soon get an opportunity to do a bit of laundry.

The house appeared to be empty apart from herself, so she sat down at the kitchen table with her laptop and checked her emails. There was a message from James to all the staff to which she sent a brief reply. Afterwards she looked out of the window into the garden – it was full of sunshine. Only an hour ago morning mist had covered the ground. Amazing! So she grabbed her painting materials and went outside.

With a feeling of regret that she hadn't brought her best paint box with her, and vellum - more difficult to paint on than paper, but so much more rewarding as regards bringing out the colours of the paints - she looked round for the best spot. There was a hardwood bench and table on the front lawn, so she dragged these to a secluded place which gave her an unrestricted long shot of the house. It looked fabulous, truly inspiring to a painter, its timbered walls a lighter, rosier shade in the white morning light. There was one small irritation, though. Someone had placed a wooden ramp over the front steps. When she sketched in the porch she would have to imagine the ramp wasn't there.

Sitting among the veils of rising mist, the rich scents of ripening fruit, and with a background of birds twittering and singing, she set about measuring up the building. With half-closed eyes she squinted at it in the time-honoured fashion, sizing it all up with her pencil. Soon enough she was absorbed in the activity of trying to capture the magic of Norrtorpet on paper.

She'd just loaded her brush with paint ready to put on a pale umber wash, when the Volvo drove up and stopped exactly between herself and her subject. Feeling rather frustrated she put the brush down and watched Didrik alight with a tall man carrying a guitar case.

Didrik looked more gorgeous than ever, dressed all in black and wearing the inevitable sunglasses. As soon as he came into sight, her heartbeat increased. The other man, all casual in jeans and red T-shirt, wore his sunshades pushed up into his chestnut-brown hair. A new house guest, Prue hoped. This would ease the tension and her guilty feelings.

As soon as he spotted Prue, the visitor left his guitar case leaning against the porch and walked purposefully towards her. He had piercing light eyes, a wide smile and big friendly teeth. His expression suggested that he'd been searching for a pot of gold and Prue was it.

'Goddag, trevligt att traffas!'

She guessed at his greeting and echoed it. 'I'm pleased to meet you, too, but I'm sure you don't take me for a Swede. Do you speak English?" She smiled pleasantly, instantly warming to him.

'Ah, Englesk - ja, little bit.'

As he spoke Prue noticed his single earring, a shining gold stud with a red stone that toned in nicely with the colour of his T-shirt.

'Hej!' Didrik called to his companion.

'Ah, see, Maestro - he speak.' The newcomer gave a Nordic shrug. 'His voice, it is angry, in rage. He think I am stealing you away. He is keeping you a secret to himself. He did not tell about you, about beautiful girl at "sommarstuga".'

'You're quite wrong about your Maestro, you know.' Prue paused, amused by the apt nickname. 'He doesn't even like me.'

She raised her eyebrows and shook her head to emphasize the point - she didn't want any false tales getting back to Hildi.

'Not like you?' He snorted, disbelieving. 'Then he is brain-dead man.'

The subject of their exchange still stood by the house like a god, waiting for his companion, his stern features rapidly turning to a scowl.

Now she'd made the man's acquaintance, Prue wasn't about to relinquish this useful source of information so easily, no matter what The Maestro ordered. 'Are you a wedding guest, like me?'

'Ja, and I come also for making midsummer music. We practise. My name is Rolf.' He clicked his heels together smartly, took her hand and kissed it.

'I'm Prudence - Prue.'

'Ah, Prudence - nice.' He leaned forward to give her arm a friendly shake, the typical Swedish greeting. In doing so, he knocked the table clumsily. The little pot tipped over and some of the dark-coloured water splashed over Prue's blue skirt and top.

'Oh, no...,' she couldn't help groaning. The painting had suffered, too; she would have to start again. Never mind, she had plenty of time.

'It's all right, don't worry, it'll wash out. I've got

every intention of doing some laundry today,' she reassured Rolf as he sprang back, apologising profusely in Swedish. She dabbed at the stain with the piece of tissue she was using as a paint rag, making things worse. 'Come and sit down. Your Maestro has gone inside now.'

Didrik had indeed vanished through the front door, so Rolf joined her on the bench. 'You paint house?'

'I was going to until you turned up - now the Volvo's in the way,' she pointed out, replenishing the empty container from her bottle of clean water. 'It's spoiled my view of it.'

'Then for Prudence-the-Painter, Volvo shall move - for price of one kiss.' Boldness was plainly Rolf's middle name.

'Please, I want to get on; the sun's moving round, the shadows are changing. Water colourists have to work very quickly.' She couldn't take this benevolent flirt seriously, but before she could prevent it, he'd put his jolly face up close to hers. His huge hand went round the back of her slender neck and, holding her head firmly, he placed a kiss squarely on her lips. It happened before Prue could stop it. Cringing from his undesired attentions, she pushed him off, strongly and just so he made no mistake about how she felt about the liberty he'd taken. The silly bloke; she just wanted a friend, nothing more. Almost shuddering, she wiped away his kiss with the tissue. One stranger's kiss should be much like another's, but this was not so. The first unsolicited one, in the Volvo outside the church, had stayed with her. Although she'd fought it at the time, it kept surfacing in her dreams, the memory of it moving her beyond all measure. This latest effort was simply almost vomit-inducing. Rolf was a likeable person, but he was also annoying. She would keep him at a distance in future.

An impatient summons again rang out across the garden. Didrik, The Maestro, was back.

'Rolf! Kom hit!' The voice was laced with more than a liberal helping of edginess; nevertheless, at this juncture Prue was relieved to hear it.

Rolf's brows lifted in mock exasperation, he rolled his eyes. 'I go. Maestro, he is jealous, sure thing.' Giving her an extra squeeze he got up and ambled off over the grass, collecting up his guitar on his way to the house.

'I don't think so. He just likes to give people the run around,' Prue called after him, her voice intentionally loud so Didrik would hear.

Unfortunately Rolf must have instantly forgotten to tell Didrik about the Volvo or, if the car was going to be moved, Didrik was taking his time about it. After a five minute wait Prue went across to the house. She needed some clean tissue from the kitchen anyway.

The music she could now hear told her a rehearsal was already in progress. Should she dare disturb the musicians? Prue pulled a face and decided against it. She'd crossed swords too many times with The Maestro to relish that idea. Instead, she went up to her room and changed out of the stained clothes and into a pretty primrose slip dress that she accessorised with the heavy blue beads. She collected up her laundry and her new white sandals and carried them all downstairs. Leaving her sandals at the door she dealt with her laundry. Someone had thoughtfully left liquid detergent and fabric softener on the top of the washing machine in the scullery. So far, so good. Luckily all her laundry was colour fast, the diagrams on the containers were easy to understand and soon her soiled clothes were spinning round merrily.

She'd made up her mind to walk into the village to see if she could find a cash machine. Then perhaps a dress shop, she was getting rather short of clothes! Mindful of the fact that it might rain she found a plastic tablecloth in a drawer. Then she slipped her feet into the sandals and went outside where she covered up her paints and water colour pad with the cloth which would also keep the insects away.

The walk to Lunneby was further than she'd anticipated and, although the day was warm, the sky was clouding over. After about thirty minutes she reached the village. It was a reasonable size with attractive wooden buildings, a church, and a row of quaint little shops. In the wall beside a supermarket she spotted a cash machine.

Opposite was a boutique with pretty summer outfits on display in the window. With the help of a young assistant she decided on a green-blue flowered dress and another dress in a romantic apricot-and-white patterned material. She added three silky bra-and-panty sets and a plain pink top for good measure.

Inside another store she discovered some simple birchwood picture frames on sale, in exactly the right size for her planned paintings of Norrtorpet. She bought four and was delighted to find that they even came with ivory card mounts. Pleased with her purchases so far, she had a quick browse round a nearby souvenir shop where she bought a piece of amber for her mother.

Meanwhile the clouds had increased and a soft, persistent drizzle had started to fall. Luckily her new clothes and the picture frames were in a large plastic bag and therefore protected from the rain. When she eventually arrived back at Norrtorpet, her hair was plastered to her head and her yellow dress was clinging to her figure. She would make a good candidate for a wet T-shirt competition, she thought ruefully, except she wasn't wearing one.

During her absence, the Volvo had been moved further along the drive, nearer the entrance gate. The daylight had altered and the wet garden had that wonderful smell of summer rain and fresh vanilla. It meant, though, that there would be no more painting outdoors today. Disappointed, she rescued paints and sketching boards and went towards the house just as Didrik and Rolf came through the front door into the porch. They were obviously about to go out.

Anxious to get out of the rain which was getting heavier now, Prue entered the porch and flashed the two men a quick smile before depositing paints and shopping bag on a convenient chair. Leaving her sandals under the chair she went into the house and through to the kitchen. Clearly impressed by the sight of her, perhaps because she presented an arresting picture with her ringing wet dress clinging to every curve, Rolf followed. A little alarmed Prue turned to face him just as he slipped a practised arm around her and noisily planted a kiss on her cheek.

'The car - it is moved. The kiss, it is promised me.'

'You are nothing but a menace!' Prue said in her best 'cross' voice, affronted by Rolf's liberty-taking. Yet she had to admit his kiss had only been a friendly one on her cheek and in any case she couldn't be at odds with him for long. 'You've been paid twice, then; that's the second kiss you've stolen. In any case, you were too late. Look, it's raining.'

'We go eat - very good home-cooked Swedish food at restaurant. You come?'

'Thank you, but I'm not hungry,' Prue declined.

Although Rolf seemed set on refusing to take no for an answer, she remained adamant.

'Look, your Maestro is expecting you,' she said when, through the window, she saw Didrik already waiting for Rolf in his car.

Her words were accompanied by a continuous honking of the car horn. The Maestro was plainly getting impatient! So reluctantly Rolf departed.

Prue watched them go, then set about drying herself. Once again she changed, this time into a clean navy cotton skirt and a crisp blue check blouse. Still feeling chilly, she added a navy waistcoat and went downstairs to empty the washing machine and put her laundry on the airer in the scullery. Afterwards she made herself a substantial cheese and tomato sandwich. She really was starving.

When the men returned several hours later, Prue was reading. In the book case she'd found a number of volumes in English, including a paperback of 'Jane Eyre' which she'd enjoyed as a teenager. Soon she was engrossed once again in the doings of gentle Jane at Lowood School and had lost all track of time.

Rolf was the first to enter the sitting room and, sitting heavily on the sofa beside Prue, he took the book from her and examined its cover. This was rather luridly illustrated and showed the two lovers, Jane and Rochester, in a passionate embrace with Thornfield in the background.

Rolf started to talk in Swedish, then, belatedly recalling whom he was addressing, translated his words in slurred English.

'Romance. You like love?' He encircled Prue with two bear-like arms. 'Rolf give you good romance, better than stupid book.'

Already overpowered by the fumes of alcohol on his breath, Prue was struggling with him frantically when the command came from the doorway.

'Rolf!'

This was accompanied by a battery of acerbic Swedish.

Prue listened anxiously as an argument developed between the two men. Clearly enraged by something Didrik had said, Rolf pulled himself to his feet with difficulty and began to wave his fists menacingly. The temperature in the room seemed to soar and the shouting match escalated into a fight as Rolf swung out wildly at his opponent. He missed by inches and the next instant, carried forward by his own momentum, went weaving towards the far wall. Crashing into a small bamboo table, he groaned, slumped awkwardly to the floor and then into a prone position. The next second he was breathing deeply and heavily, lost to the world in an alcoholic stupor.

'Fortunately he won't remember any of this in the morning. I didn't think he'd taken that much drink this evening, but I was obviously wrong.' Didrik bent over the unconscious Rolf the better to search the man's pockets. 'The answer must be here somewhere...'

He removed a wallet; comb; mobile phone. Then, with a loud, 'Ah!' he extracted a practically empty whisky bottle from an inside compartment in Rolf's coat.

'Why does he do this to himself? It's a crazy way to carry on. He's his own worst enemy as you like to say in the UK.' Didrik threw up his hands in despair. 'The drink gets him into trouble every time. He's been banned from driving, so I'm landed with the job of acting as his chauffeur. The guy's the best classical guitar-player I've ever heard - but where drink is concerned, he's weak.'

'Yes, I can see he's a man with problems. Such a shame.' Prue glanced down at the sleeping guitarist as he emitted a drunken snore. 'I do think we should try to get him to bed, though, don't you?'

'He doesn't deserve it but, okay, you're right. Let me see…' He tapped his temples. 'His bedroom's in the top attic, but there's a day bed in the studio. He'll be out of the way there till morning.'

The two of them slowly half carried and half dragged the grunting sleeper to the long corridor where there was a brief pause in the proceedings while Didrik opened the door of the music studio.

Prue was supporting Rolf's head. She couldn't help feeling sorry for him, a man in the prime of life with such a weakness for alcohol.

Inside the studio, it was dim but not dark, and once Rolf was settled on the day bed in the corner, Prue looked around. She got the impression of a grand piano, a set of drums, amplifiers, computer station, desk with fax machine plus photographs pinned all along one wall. The whole was overlaid by the strong, pleasantly pungent smell of recently-sawn wood.

'Thanks for your help,' said Didrik. 'He'll be all right when he's slept it off.'

They were standing close, arms almost touching, and she could feel the heat from him, drawing her towards him. The effect he had on her was tearing her apart. He was Hildi's man, for goodness' sake, and absolutely forbidden. As she strived to suppress the desire to touch him, she was convinced he must be able to hear the beating of her heart; it was so loud in her ears. Prue swallowed hard. Her feelings were running away with her and for the sake of her pride, she had to hide them.

'Goodnight, then... Maestro.' This last was added on impulse - it was a well-deserved nickname and she couldn't resist teasing him with it.

'Maestro?' He strode across the road quickly to plant himself between Prue and the open door, barring her way like a deep-rooted tree. 'No one is allowed to call me that except my fellow musicians!' His voice was gruff.

'Oh, come on, it was only a joke. You're not seriously upset, surely?'

He made no reply. His gaze in the semi-dark was a rapier ready to lance her heart, a sword thrust holding her motionless. Prue gave an involuntary shiver. She was aware of small things suddenly - the rain sliding noiselessly down the window panes, the massing green of foliage outside, a pricking of the skin at the nape of her neck and the harsh, rushing sound of his breathing.

The atmosphere was in an instant electric. With great strength of mind Prue decided to disregard it.

'I'm afraid I can't get through the door. You must know you're standing in my way.'

He remained silent.

'This is getting out of hand,' she went on, trying to be stern but feeling more than a little apprehensive. She was conscious of his size, the way he towered above her, his pulsating nearness. 'In the name of heaven, what's going on?'

In an effort to call his bluff she adopted a no-nonsense stance and made to push past him. He caught her effortlessly, trapping her in the vice of his arm. She tried to shrug him off, but her fruitless attempts only engendered a low chuckle.

'You can carry on struggling, but you won't get anywhere,' he said.

Silently she had to agree. One of the first things she'd noticed about him was how rugged, muscular and fit he was. He probably worked out a lot.

Now she was clamped in place against the iron hardness of his body. The sharp, clean smell of his aftershave, the potent maleness of him, made her senses swim. She felt his trousers against her legs, her bead necklace tapped faintly against one of his buttons.

Through the crisp cotton of his shirt she felt his heart hammering, vibrating strongly, and her own responded in kind, the pulse throbbing in her throat threatening to choke her. Instincts aroused, she felt the urge to take flight, or cling.

'God knows what you think you're doing,' she managed to blurt out, at last. 'Aren't you forgetting yourself?'

'A kiss.' His tone was ragged, raw. She felt the waiting hunger in him. 'My punishment for calling me "Maestro". A kiss releases you.'

The dimness lent an intimacy to the room, gave it a closed-in, soothing, other-worldly atmosphere. Yet the situation was beyond belief and it crossed Prue's mind that maybe he, too, might have had too much to drink.

'In case you were wondering, I haven't been

drinking.' He anticipated her suspicion before she could voice it. 'In Sweden we don't drink-and-drive unless we want to go to prison. Our friend, Rolf, has been there for precisely that. It's quite a hobby of his. I give you my word, I'm stone cold sober.'

He spoke without loosening his hold. Every muscle was steadfast.

'Then why... why... this farce?' she wanted to know, short of breath now with longing.

'Don't struggle, please, and I'll tell you. You've been giving your favours out very freely, so I thought it was about my turn. No, don't try to run away.' He pinned her arms to her sides as she made a rather feeble effort to twist out of his grasp. She was fighting with her conscience but not very hard. He wasn't hers to kiss, and yet... and yet...

'I haven't been handing out favours to anyone,' she said, breathless. 'But I do respond to friendliness. I can be quite human at times, you'd be surprised.'

'Friendship is not what Rolf has in mind. All through dinner he's been quizzing me to find out whether I've got an interest in you, a romantic one. I told him you were here merely as an early wedding guest.' He readjusted his grip on her but did not loosen it. 'Incidentally, the enquiry was quite sensitive coming from Rolf - he's not usually so considerate. He makes passes at women wherever he finds them, never mind that they might be committed to other men. Anyway, from then on I had to listen to a whole catalogue of things he'd like to do to you and with you, all in glorious technicolour.'

Revolted, Prue gave a shudder, then sensing a relaxing of his attention as he spoke, she broke away. They were not meant to be together, yet there was no escape. He filled the exit, legs stolidly apart, the mask of his face thrown into bright relief by his black shirt. His scorching gaze rested on her like a laser. It penetrated the depths of her very being and ignited her carefully concealed longings until they burned, treacherous, like the fire he'd made for her on her first night here. His lips relaxed, parting to reveal the pointed tip of his tongue.

Heaven help her, she wasn't strong enough. How was she going to resist? She felt like drowning in her own feelings, almost overcome by them, but thankfully reason suddenly came between them and Prue knew she couldn't do it. She did not belong here, in the arms of this mesmerising man. Abruptly, thankfully, she came to her senses.

Prue's head was beginning to clear. Didrik was playing with her, like a cat with a mouse. The realisation pulled her up short. Perhaps he was out for a bit of fun in his last moments of freedom before his wedding. He plainly thought it was quite acceptable to have a little fling on the side as long as nobody knew about it.

Ignoring the betrayal of her body and her blood still pulsating with hormones, she smoothed down her skirt and gathered her wits.

'On the whole I must say men just make me sick. Now, I'm tired. Let me go, please.'

His answer was to lean forward and pluck up her

hand. His eyes were large and dark, as black as his shirt.

'Just one kiss?' He wasn't pleading but requesting nicely, coaxing her. 'Please don't say no. I'm only flesh and blood, and it's not much to ask, is it?'

'You're despicable.' Prue snatched her hand away. 'Only yesterday you called me predatory. When we first met you stole that kiss you're now asking for so nicely. I've had to put up with the vilest of insults from you, and now you're acting in this perverse and outrageous way. It's... unspeakable behaviour.'

'You may be right. I just can't quite make up my mind about you. My head tells me one thing, my heart another.'

'Oh, that's a good excuse. It seems to me you just believe what suits you at the time.' Her voice faltered with emotion, tears gathered in her eyes, but the logic of her argument lent her the courage to continue. 'According to your reckoning, this is the moment I've been waiting for, scheming for, all along. Yet the fact that I'm not taking advantage of it must tell you something.'

She was well aware that her lengthy protest came out in a strangled fashion. Her heart was in her throat, choking her, her body shook with the force of her feelings, and her eyes were filled with un-shed tears of anger. It was so unfair, the way she was having to battle with the instinct screaming inside her, 'Yes! Yes! I want to kiss you! I will! I will!'

With no little effort she now relapsed into silence.

'Resistance is part of the thrill of the game, too,

isn't it?' He stepped forward as he spoke and took her face in his hands, masterfully. His heavy hair fell across his forehead as he bent to her, gently kissing the teardrops from her eyes.

A swift intake of breath was her sole protest, a weak one, she knew. So be it, her emotions were spent. She was almost lost; her backbone seemed to be in a state of imminent melt-down.

His own breath, sweet like pineapple, was on her face as he whispered two words, three - the most powerful words in her vocabulary.

'Please, Prudence... Prue...'

It was the manner in which he said her name, the catch in his voice; the deep, warm timbre of it muted, so soft, so caressing. Prudence... Prue... It was her final undoing.

A fury of heat fanned out from the pressure of his hands on her cheeks, spreading downwards through her body with a warm flowing softness, invading her secret recesses like molten gold. Where there should have been fear, revulsion, she felt only waves of primeval longing somewhere in the depths of her being. He placed a hand on the small of her back and propelled her steadily towards him, towards his broad chest, the pearl buttons.

The room was full of shadows, encouraging, encompassing the two of them. His hot breath was intoxicating as she made one last desperate appeal.

'You don't even like me!'

Her words were suppressed, smothered, as he took her mouth with his, not hard as she would have expected but with a velvet touch, his lips trembling with passion. She felt him working her mouth open with a searching gentleness. His hands moved to the space between her shoulders and he drew her even closer, cupping the curve of her head in his firm fingers. Her lips moulded to his and moved under them. She was beyond controlling the wantonness within her as his other hand travelled down her spine, slowly. Hands that caressed magic from the keys of a piano were now teasing notes of pure joy from the instrument of her body. With each small pressure messages flew from his fingers straight to some inner, secret fastness.

Acute dizziness invaded her head and the recesses of her heart while waves of previously unsuspected sweetness shimmered through her small quaking frame.

'So little, so fragile. I'm glad she brought you here. She did the right thing, after all, my Hildi,' he murmured.

*Hildi!*

The mist cleared from Prue's brain. Not for the first time her friend's face, her name, forced itself between them, instantly writing itself in Prue's mind in capital letters. HILDI.

Coming rather belatedly back to the reality of what she was doing, Prue put up her hands and pushed at him. His arms tightened about her, lifting her clear of the ground for a second. What were they doing? This was insane. Deeply troubled and battling with her conscience, she struggled to get away from him.

'Nej, nej, Prudence... relax... It's good between us, so good,' he whispered, his Swedish accent more pronounced now.

The magic of her name on his tongue weakened her resolve once more. He claimed her mouth again and she was lost, helpless, in his thrall. Her arms lifted of their own accord and her hands met to entwine at the back of his neck.

There was a heavy thud! The interruption was mega-loud in the shadowy room. The sound was followed by a curse, then a burst of song, the words a burbling mixture of Swedish and English.

*'Alskling, you're a candle, shining bright,*
*In the darkness of my night.*
*Du mast...'*

Rolf had rolled off the couch onto the floor. His drunken rendering of a well-known pop song ricocheted off the ceiling and shot them both back to reality.

On the instant, Prue recoiled from her partner in crime. The horror of her betrayal of her friend now reeled through her brain. She was about an evil business. It must be in the genes - like father, like daughter. Drenching shame lending a strong motive to her actions, she pulled violently from the arms enfolding her still.

Didrik reached out to prevent her flight. Unfortunately, he caught her precious beads. The string snapped and they now fell, bouncing and scattering all over the studio floor with tiny pattering noises.

'Oh, no!' With a sob, she darted away through the open door before he could stop her.

The next morning was radiant after the rain, the garden a watercolour of bright clean washes. During the night Prue had tossed and turned in bed over the way she and Didrik had carried on. Who knows how far things might have gone but for silly old Rolf rolling off the couch. Hildi would doubtless soon be here. Prue was mortified at the thought that she had to face her lovely friend and to act as if nothing was wrong while her conscience was screaming, 'Traitor!'

She was worried about her blue beads, naturally, but she would just have to look for them. The breaking of the string was somehow symbolic of her cheap behaviour. Disgusted with herself, she hadn't even stopped. She'd just given that little cry of dismay and bolted out of the studio and up to bed.

The musical outpourings of passionate hands had kept her awake as well. The piano keyboard in the music room had become a battleground. The sounds had not been subdued as before, but overpoweringly loud, the beat of the music echoing round the house. One tune was repeated often, a beautifully haunting melody which Prue had not heard before. Clearly Didrik had left the studio door wide open, and she doubted whether even the inebriated Rolf had managed to sleep through the expression of so much naked emotion.

The tumult inside her head had been in concert

with the reverberations from below, but it hadn't taken her long to come to a decision about her sojourn in Sweden. She must end it, make her excuses and return to England as soon as it was feasible. If it was true that her breathless longings, her wickedly responsive body, could be attributed to a perverse trick of nature, then she knew she stood no chance of controlling or taming them. The attraction between herself and this charismatic guy was on a physical level, it was true. Yet there was more to it, she actually felt herself hovering on the brink of a deep and genuine love. She had to be honest with herself, she was falling for him. It was time to admit it. He could be gentle; she'd found that in his kiss which had been passionate but not rough - and yet, there was an aura of excitement around him too.

All this was shocking to Prue's sensibilities. Even though the fresh new day invited her to change her mind about leaving, she knew what had to be done. The fact that Didrik was Hildi's fiancé overshadowed everything else.

Recoiling from the bracing effect of cold water, she washed quickly, making a guess that it was well past breakfast time. A few minutes later she was pulling on a crocheted lilac top that clung to her firm curves, matching it with slender lilac trousers, when downstairs the little bells rang out lustily. Someone had obviously opened the main door.

Out of curiosity Prue pushed up the sash window to look down onto the drive where a large crimson car was being parked neatly. She could also see Rolf who had just left the house to greet the new arrival, but before he did so, he spotted Prue first.

'Prue, baby! Prudence!' he called up to her. With a disarming grin, he fell to his knees in mock supplication. 'Come, slap me, Prudence. Yesterday night I am naughty boy.'

With an expansive, theatrical gesture of his arms he proceeded to give his own wrists several sharp smacks.

At this Prue couldn't help but burst into laughter. She found it hard to be miserable with the man for long, he was such a clown.

'I forgive you, but don't let it happen again,' she called back with mock severity.

Rolf got to his feet. 'Pardon,' he said and bowed low to Prue before turning in the direction of the new visitor.

The driver, a young guy, had got out of his car by this time and was searching for something in the boot. As far as Prue could tell he was neat-featured, fair-haired and a little bit overweight, a complete stranger to her. He and Rolf were soon engaged in conversation. She surmised that he was another early wedding guest.

The wedding. It was dreadfully disappointing to think she was going to miss it after all. With her spirits swinging back to zero, Prue closed the window, got out her laptop and proceeded to check the flights to Heathrow from Arlanda Airport. There was one at seven fifty that night. She'd have to cadge a lift, get a taxi, or even a train to Stockholm in order to catch it. She needed to think about that, perhaps enlist Rolf's help. In addition she'd also have to invent some dire emergency to excuse her leaving in such a hurry.

In the meantime the aroma of fresh coffee was wafting up the stairs, so tempting, she was ready for a cup. But first things first, she needed to speak with Rolf.

She shut down her laptop and looked through the window. Outside Rolf and the fair-haired man were walking across the lawn, carrying between them a tall cruciform pole which sported two large rings, one each end of the cross beam. This, Prue realised, was a maypole, and it had been brought out for the midsummer celebrations. She would miss those, too.

She hurried downstairs and out through the porch where she found Rolf at the front door, leaning on the door frame and about to take off his outdoor shoes. He was alone. The visitor had returned to his vehicle where he was now cleaning the windscreen.

'Rolf, is there a train station near here? I need to get to Stockholm today. It's urgent.'

Rolf straightened up. 'Train, today? You are going back to England now? You not stay for wedding?'

'No, but it's a secret, Rolf. Don't say anything yet. Something has happened. I have to leave as soon as possible.'

Prue held a finger to her lips. She was just about to launch into her invented and lurid excuse that her mother was ill and had been rushed to hospital, when a phone rang out in the nearby study.

Rolf glanced down at the heavy shoes he was still wearing. 'Please, Prudence. Telephone rings. You answer.'

She hurried into the study and picked up the receiver. 'I'm sorry, I don't speak Swedish,' she said politely to the caller. 'Will you hold on for a second, please?'

'I would like to talk with Rolf.' The female Swedish voice switched easily to English. 'Please tell him this is Ulrica.'

Grateful for the diversion Prue left the phone to Rolf who had followed her, shoeless now, into the study. She could consult him later about taxis and trains. Making her way to the kitchen she wondered casually, who the caller was. Ulrica was a name that rang a bell, the tall blonde girl she'd seen talking to Didrik at the wedding rehearsal, maybe. Now, she would have a quick coffee first and then try to locate her missing beads. There was no time to be lost if she was to catch that plane.

When she entered the kitchen all thoughts about Rolf, her impending trip home, and even her beads were driven right out of her head. Pale but smiling with mischief and clearly enjoying the effect of her big surprise, Hildi stood at the kitchen table, buttering rolls for breakfast.

'Hildi!'

'Prudence!'

With a gasp of pleasure and a flush of shame all mixed up together, feeling absolutely overwhelmed,

Prue ran to her friend and the two girls hugged affectionately. For a minute or two no other words were necessary. In the end, Prue held Hildi away from her. She looked nice and casual in loose navy shirt and pants. There was a small plaster cast on her hand but the sling which should have been supporting it, hung loosely around her neck.

'I can't believe it! How are you? You look a bit on the frail side but very well, considering.'

'As good as new, almost,' said Hildi cheerfully. 'What about you? Have you been all right in our summer house?'

'I love it here,' Prue answered truthfully. 'It's fantastic!'

At this point the two men entered the kitchen; Rolf and, behind him, the driver of the crimson saloon. Maybe this plump, pleasant-faced chap in the smart beige linen jacket was Hildi's brother, Torsten.

Hildi hadn't spoken too much to Prue about Torsten during their early acquaintance, but it had come over loud and clear that she was devoted to him. She must have arrived with him in the crimson car, entering the house before he had parked it properly.

It was plain that Hildi and Rolf were old friends. They fell upon one another with glad cries until finally Hildi pushed him aside, gently but firmly, and went over to the new arrival. She kissed his cheek before taking his hand and turning to Prue.

'I am so glad, at long last, to introduce you two,' she said in the manner of one making a grand announcement. 'Prue - this is Didrik. Didrik - meet my English friend, Prudence.'

# CHAPTER FIVE

*This is Didrik.*

Prue was thunderstruck. Had Hildi really said that? Had she? It was impossible, surely! The Maestro was Didrik, wasn't he?

She gasped and then put the back of her hand to her mouth to conceal her shock. Horror of horrors! Could it be that she had gone and got it wrong all along? Alarm and confusion was sweeping over her. She fought physical weakness as she struggled to take it all in, completely overcome by the enormity of her apparent mistake. The moment was mind-numbingly hideous. Feeling an urgent need for some support, she gripped the edge of the kitchen table.

As her brain started firing questions, the fair, plump man came forward, smiling, to take her hand in greeting. 'This is Didrik' seemed to be etched like a neon sign in the air above his head.

Remembering her manners just in time, Prue let go of the table and shook hands with the newcomer.

'How do you do, Didrik? It's so good to meet you,' she managed to say, but her mind was still reeling.

How had she come to make such a terrible error? If this man really was Didrik, who was The Maestro? She gulped and forced herself to simmer down. There had to be a simple explanation. Didrik's response to her greeting was lost to Prue as her mind blanked him off before going into immediate overdrive.

Didrik was the name of Hildi's husband-to-be, true. Then again, Didrik was a name common enough in Sweden. Perhaps the man before her was another Didrik, a close friend, a relative. Yes, that was it. That had to be the logical explanation.

All the same Prue could feel her face burning, her toes curling in the socks she was wearing as slippers. She chewed at the fullness of her lower lip and tried to sort out her spinning thoughts just as she realised that Didrik was still speaking.

'Hildi has told me so much about you. Welcome to Sweden!'

'Er... Thank you for having me,' she returned.

'You would like coffee?'

When she nodded he went to the kitchen counter and poured out three mugs of coffee from the large cafetière; one for Prue, one for Rolf and one for himself. Prue thanked him, added milk and sipped it gratefully.

'Help yourself to rolls and cheese,' Hildi urged, passing her a plate. 'I must tell you that my parents have invited us to a meal later - Didrik, you and me.'

'How kind, I'm looking forward to meeting them.'

Prue had trouble acting normally. She hardly knew how to begin, but she simply had to clear up the mystery. The two men had taken their coffees through to the sitting room, which was a great help. It would be less embarrassing.

'Didrik, the... er... man in the other room with

Rolf...' she addressed Hildi, making an effort to keep her voice steady but not succeeding very well. 'He's not your fiancé, is he?'

Prue's hands were shaking as she put a roll on her plate.

Looking perplexed, Hildi paused in the act of tipping the rest of the buttered rolls onto a serving dish. 'He is my bridegroom, yes. Who did you think he was?'

'Sorry, don't take any notice of me. I just got a bit mixed up.' Prue brushed a hand across her brow. You could say that again! 'Didrik's... er... he seems really nice, you're so lucky.'

Hildi took a seat at the table, still with a puzzled look on her face. 'Please, eat breakfast and you will feel better. Your face... it is a little bit white.'

'I'm all right, really. Surprised to see you but so pleased you're recovering well. Here, I'm an idle so-and-so, let me help. I'll get some knives, shall I?'

Prue took a few small knives from the dresser drawer and put them on the table. Then with legs that suddenly threatened to buckle, she lowered herself hurriedly onto the nearest kitchen chair and gave herself a moment to gather her scattered wits.

'Are you sure you are O.K.?' Hildi regarded Prue with concern. 'Please, have some cheese or a sweet roll. Mamma made them.'

Prue pulled her chair up to the table and took the offered sugary pastry out of politeness, but her appetite had deserted her. Steeling herself, she drank some more of her coffee then cleared her throat, her next question inevitable. 'Who... who was the man who brought me here, Hildi? The man who acted as your bridegroom at the wedding rehearsal?' Her voice was thin with strain.

'Torsten. My brother, Torsten,' answered Hildi simply, puzzlement accentuating her Swedish accent. 'You really did not know this? You have not learnt also that he is...?'

Hildi clammed up at that point and Prue scarcely registered the evasion as she shook her head slowly, her mind still occupied in trying to make sense of this bombshell. 'But why did he...?'

'Why did he take Didrik's place at the rehearsal?'

Prue nodded.

'He came to church with the message that Didrik was with the police - something urgent to do with a break-in at the university. So I asked Torsten to step in.' Hildi gave her a helpless look. 'I couldn't walk to the altar alone, not even at the rehearsal. This would bring me really bad luck! I was going to explain everything to you, but look what happened! I fell over, didn't I?'

Prue reached out and touched her friend's arm sympathetically just when the two men came back into the room and joined them at the table. Apparently the morning news they'd been watching on the television was finished. Chatting amiably in Swedish, they started on the rolls and cheese.

The quivering around Prue's heart persisted. Biting on her knuckles one at a time, thinking, ruminating, she tried to take it all on board. The wedding rehearsal re-ran through her mind like a film. The whole scenario was finally falling into place. Now she understood why Torsten, the substitute groom had looked unprepared for his role, not truculent, but rather indifferent.

Meanwhile, Hildi was conversing in Swedish with the real Didrik, her bridegroom. As she spoke, a smile spread slowly across his face until he finally burst out laughing.

Didrik, then turned to Prue and it was clear that Hildi had just informed him and Rolf about the way Prue had got her wires crossed. Rolf too kept glancing at her and grinning, also highly amused.

'So you were a little confused at the wedding rehearsal?' Didrik addressed her. 'Sorry about that. There'd been a break-in at the university where I teach, in my department - a nasty affair, lots of stuff smashed up. I had to wait for the police.'

Hildi nodded. 'He tried to phone me, but we must have been in a spot with no mobile reception when we were driving up from Stockholm.'

'Next I tried Aunt Agnetha, but her phone was switched off because she was already in church.' Didrik gave a sigh. 'In the end I managed to contact Torsten. He offered to go to the rehearsal and break the news to Hildi. There was simply no other means of letting her know.'

No, there wouldn't have been, Prue acknowledged. Hildi and herself had been on the road non-stop, and on arriving in Gustavskrona had driven straight to the rehearsal.

'The burglary involved my own department so I couldn't refuse to co-operate,' Didrik continued. 'I was counting on the minister to delay the procedure until I could get there. However, his programme was too full to alter the arrangements. In any case, dealing with the burglary took longer than I thought it would.'

Feeling stunned, not to say somewhat stupid, Prue thought that at last she'd got her head round some of the complications of the silly mistake.

'I suppose... er... Torsten didn't tell me he was Hildi's brother because he simply assumed I already knew,' she said to nobody in particular.

Hildi's accident had put a brake on all those questions Prue had wanted to ask at the time. Now, with some of the misunderstandings cleared up, she could start again, maybe. Yet she still had no explanation for brother Torsten's ambivalent attitude towards her; the perverse way he blew so hot, then so cold. Never mind, at least she could discard the guilt she'd been carrying around. What she'd just heard was good news, after all. She wouldn't now have to miss the wedding for one thing, or the midsummer celebrations. She summoned up a bright expression, finally determined to make light of the whole matter.

'Where's Torsten now?' asked Didrik, spreading wild strawberry jam on a little fairy cake and popping it into his mouth whole.

'He is sleeping,' Rolf supplied. 'He has been practice, practice piano, all night long. Many times I wake up with music noise.'

Prue couldn't help smiling at this and the memories of the previous night.

'How did you get on with my brother, Prue?' Hildi asked. 'I hope you and he have become good friends.'

'Well, I'm afraid we... er... that is... your brother and I... we rather got off on the wrong foot. I'm sorry...'

'Forbanat!' Hildi's blue eyes glittered. She thinned her lips but said nothing more.

Prue easily recognised the expression as strong language, quite unusual for her friend, and filled the ensuing silence by complimenting Didrik on his English; perfect because it was, of course, his subject.

So if he was the university man, the lecturer, what was The Maestro - Torsten? Music teacher? Professional pianist? The latter seemed more likely, he didn't have the patience for the former.

Prue helped herself to more coffee and sat with it, staring into the mug, lost for a while in a world of her own. Inevitably, as Hildi's brother, she now saw him in a different light. Was he available, as in 'not romantically attached', for instance?

She clamped down on the word 'available' even as it sneaked into her mind. Torsten Dahlgren might be devastatingly attractive, but he was unspeakably big-headed, and that didn't sit easily with her.

Just the same, nameless sensations had been triggered off somewhere inside her, and her heart felt like a trapped bird, tripping and fluttering under her rib cage until she thought it must take flight. She had no time to speculate further on the kind of musician Torsten might be, because another car came screeching to a halt outside.

'Ah, Gunnar!' announced Didrik.

Hildi went out to welcome the new arrival, whoever he might be, and Prue noticed that she walked with a pronounced limp. There was obviously a thick bandage round her lower leg, under her trousers. Yet however painful and incapacitating Hildi's problems were, they were only temporary. The disability of the new guest was permanent. Prue watched as he manoeuvred himself slowly and awkwardly into the room. That's why the ramp had been installed at the front door - Gunnar was sitting in a wheelchair!

'Hej!' Gunnar shouted the usual greeting cheerily, balancing a concertina across his knees, while Hildi hastened to get some breakfast for him.

Heaven Almighty! Young, brown haired, with a thin clever face that she would know anywhere! Shock on shock, like high voltage electricity, arced through Prue's small frame. The jolt had nothing whatsoever to do with Gunnar's handicap - that only invoked her profound compassion. Instead, she was having a moment of enlightenment that threatened to engulf her. Coming hard on the heels of the new knowledge that The Maestro was Torsten, Hildi's brother, this latest revelation was mind-blowing, a lightning bolt!

Speechless and stupefied, Prue took refuge in her hot coffee, swallowed it down too quickly, and choked on it. Unavoidably, this resulted in an embarrassing fit of coughing. Even so, when she was largely over it, she got up, hurried over to Gunnar and, stifling the urge to splutter, warmly gave him the accepted forearm grasp of greeting. His reaction to her was not incurious. He turned a solemn but hard gaze on her before smiling in return. She, for her part, fished around futilely in her pocket for a hanky, then begged to be excused.

Out in the garden she almost fell onto the sawn logs stacked against the back of the house and gradually, the acute discomfort in her lungs subsided. Her hands, though, were shaking, so she crossed her arms and balled her fists, pushing them into her armpits in an effort to still their trembling. In her crocheted cotton top she shivered as the strong breeze found her, blowing her hair over her eyes and rattling the blinds of the open windows on the first floor, above her head. While she sat recovering, Rolf appeared, shambling down the back steps and out of Prue's sight round the corner. A car door was opened, slammed to, and he reappeared with a music case.

Instead of returning to the kitchen he came to join Prue on the logs.

'You are O.K., yes?' His tone was conciliatory; his one earring gleamed in the sun.

'No! I'm not!' She flew at him, eyes glaring. He didn't deserve this treatment but she had to take her feelings out on somebody, and Rolf was handy. 'That man in there – Gunnar…'

'Gunnar - ja. He is the most best of men.'

'He is also the most well-known of men. He is Gunnar Holm! I'm not a pop music expert, but, heavens above, I've not spent the last five years under a stone either! I am fully aware there's a Swedish trio with a drummer who is confined to a wheelchair.'

'Ja,' interposed Rolf. 'Poor Gunnar!'

'I know, tragic, and this same drummer also plays the concertina.' Prue's voice, her whole body, shook with the knowledge. 'It can mean only one thing - you are Rolf Kalmar.' The statement was an accusation. 'You and Gunnar and Torsten – The Maestro - are *Scandinavia*, the famous pop group. No, let me amend that - the world-famous pop group! Hildi should have warned me!'

The sentences had come tumbling out almost incoherently, now she was seething and breathless. There appeared to have been one massive conspiracy against her!

Rolf looked as crestfallen as a little child who'd been reprimanded. 'It was not secret,' he said, reproachfully.

'From me it was! I knew you and your... colleague... looked familiar, but the beards have gone - you both used to have beards.'

Rolf nodded, rubbing his chin. 'We cut off beards a few weeks ago.' He started chuckling with glee. 'But the girls, all the lovely girls, they still like us.'

Prue hardly listened. She kept talking, more to herself than to him, voicing the questions that were rapidly beginning to surface.

'The sunglasses, that's why he, this Maestro of yours, always wears them in public - they're a disguise. That's why he assumes I'm after him.' She paused to think. 'Who's to blame him? Every single girl he meets is probably after him. He's the world's most well-known heart-throb! I remember something about his wife, too. Something happened to her, what was it?'

'Sad thing, very sad thing,' said Rolf. 'Jill was girl from London… and she killed in accident, in Spain.'

'That's right, it's coming back to me. Jill was her name and she had a boating accident in Spain last year. She was there with a girlfriend. It was headlined in all the newspapers just after I got my appointment with The Trust.'

*Scandinavia*! The group was globally renowned!

'There's something else, Rolf. Your Maestro, he is Sten Norberg, singer, song-writer, universal dreamboat!'

'Sten' she knew, meant 'stone' in Swedish. She liked it! She'd also heard him referred to as 'Sweden's hero-composer'.

'Yet you all call him Torsten,' she continued.

'Sten Norberg is name for stage. Family, friends, we call him Torsten. Sometimes we call him Sten - or Maestro.' He placed his hand on her arm. 'But Prudence, talk to me about airplane. You still go home today, to England?'

'Oh, no. I… er… changed my mind. I'm staying for the wedding. There's something else. Do you know the Wasa Chapel in the woods?'

She would be able to fit in a visit to the mysterious chapel now that she didn't need to go running home!

'Wasakappellet. Ja,'

'Is there...do you have to have a key to get inside?'

'Key? Ja, there is key. Big key. In kitchen key cupboard.'

'Thank you, Rolf, that's all I need to know.' She had noticed the key cupboard on the wall and would investigate it very soon.

'Not much people go Wasakappellet,' Rolf added with a frown.

'No, I guessed,' Prue answered absently. In truth, she was still striving to come to terms with the recent revelations, to convince herself this wasn't all a dream. Her fingers went to her neck, out of habit, to fidget nervously with her beads - but the pretty lapis lazulis weren't there which brought home to her that she still had to go to the studio and find them all. The excitements of the morning had driven them completely out of her mind. 'Rolf, I'm so sorry, you must excuse me. I have something urgent to do.'

Quite hastily she got up and left the log pile.

The music studio wasn't locked - with all the musicians assembled at Norrtorpet this was no surprise. What did puzzle her, though, was that it took no more than one glance for her to see that the beads were no longer there, she didn't even have to search. She did look round on the cabinets to see if they'd been put in a little pile somewhere. But no, someone had obviously collected them up and taken them away, perhaps because they were a bit of a hazard on the floor to the unwary. There wasn't time for making enquiries now, though. She had to smarten herself up ready for the trip to the Dahlgren's house.

Prue left the studio and went upstairs where she freshened up and changed into one of the dresses she'd bought from the shop in Lunneby, the greeny-blue flowered one. It was simple but flattering and in her luggage she had a white knitted jacket she would wear with it. She brushed her hair and put on a little make up. She wanted to look her best when she met the parents of Hildi and Torsten.

She was ready now and as she had a few minutes to spare, she picked up her lap top. A minute or two later she had googled, 'Sten Norberg.' She longed to find out more about him, his girlfriends, anything she could.

When Hildi called to say they were ready to go, Prue had viewed several photos of him, with and without the other two musicians. Oddly enough there were no pictures of Jill, but she'd found some of him cosying up to the tall girl, the one she'd seen before at the church. Ulrica! The blonde seemed to have been an item with The Maestro since his wife's death. So, tall and blonde was his preferred type.

With a disappointed sigh Prue read the information below one of the pictures. Apparently, Ulrica was *Scandinavia*'s agent and road manager, or 'roadie.' An important person in more than one respect then.

Hildi called again and this time, Prue replied, 'Coming!

As she hurried downstairs, Prue could hear discordant notes; obviously the three musicians had started to tune up for their practice session. She felt herself grow hot again as she recalled the many blunders she'd made just because she'd mistaken Torsten's identity. She was also apprehensive about bumping into him, perhaps at his parents' house later. He must have been thinking she was an absolute idiot, mistaking him for the bridegroom.

Hildi was waiting in the front porch where, full of apologies, Prue put on her best black stiletto-heeled shoes.

'How pretty you look!' Hildi glanced at her approvingly as she led the way to the car where Didrik was already waiting behind the wheel.

The first thing Prue noticed was a small branch from a birch tree tied to the car bonnet. The second thing was a large black rubber torch on the back shelf, and she made a mental note of this. When she went to explore the Wasa Chapel, she might need to borrow it. That was for future reference though. For now, as she settled herself into the back seat she asked about the birch branch.

'It's what we do in Sweden to welcome midsummer,' Hildi explained. 'You will see many more cars decorated like this in town.'

'How quaint,' Prue nearly said but thought better of it. It would perhaps sound patronising, so she settled for, 'Cute!'

They left the house, driving round Gunnar's Mercedes, which he was allowed to leave near the front door. Conversing amiably on general topics, they motored along the forest-lined road until they reached the town. Here, at Prue's request, Didrik stopped the car at a street market so she could buy flowers for Hildi's mother.

The market was bustling and distractingly colourful. Still, in spite of all the noise, a name, his name, was never at any time displaced from the forefront of her consciousness. Torsten.

Her arms full of fragrant yellow jasmine and blue love-in-a-mist, Prue climbed back into the car and they drove off once more. A little later, in as light a tone as she could muster, she brought up the question looming large in her mind.

'Hildi, when Gunnar arrived this morning, it suddenly dawned on me that Torsten is a member of *Scandinavia*, the pop group. Actually, I believe he *is* the group - I understand he formed the band, and writes and arranges all the music.' She'd learnt that much from their website.

Hildi nodded. 'Ja. He is the lead singer, too.'

Prue considered for a moment before delivering her next sentence. She mustn't sound belligerent - maybe Hildi had an excellent reason for keeping quiet about the brother who was a household name. Perhaps being boastful wasn't in her nature. Indeed, Prue had heard that Sweden was a society of true equals where a dustman was as important as a brain surgeon, and that Swedes rather despised fame. This didn't alter the fact that a celebrity of his stature was likely to be mobbed when he was out-and-about. It explained why he wore his sunglasses so often; he was easily recognised in public.

'I really wish you'd told me earlier, prepared me, sort of,' Prue said in the end, rather lamely.

Hildi cleared her throat and appeared to be having trouble with her seat belt. 'Well, yes, but I wished the two of you to be friends. I didn't want you to be put off by all the lies that get into the newspapers. Torsten is a very private person and won't give interviews, so journalists invent their own stories. I wanted you to meet him first, and then make up your own mind about him.'

'Torsten gets a very bad press, terrible.' Didrik changed gears to take a sharp bend which took them into a road of yellow-and-white-painted wooden houses. 'The media makes him out to be a womaniser which he certainly is not. He likes women, but accounts of group orgies are complete fabrications. He has girlfriends, naturally, one at a time, but he's never been in love since he lost Jill, his wife.'

'How do you know that?' Prue's voice was almost a whisper.

'He's written no songs of any note since Jill's death, because he's pining for her,' replied Didrik. 'Torsten produces his best music when he's in love. All the family have noticed this, and all of us worry about him.'

His voice faltered and faded out, but from her

position in the back seat Prue hadn't failed to notice the jab he'd received from Hildi's elbow.

Even so, Prue had heard enough.

A man, bereft of his beloved woman, still in mourning for her - Prue could understand and empathise with that. It indicated a capacity for deep abiding faithfulness. As for the rest, the supposed orgies, she'd read about those but took it all with a pinch of salt. Sensation was what sold newspapers, she knew that from her own experience with The Great Kate Trust and their dealings with the tabloid press. Some newspapers had to sensationalise everything.

She leaned back, relaxed, and reflected on this latest information. So Torsten was fancy free and not about to marry Hildi. Yet, paradoxically, he was still hardly available to the likes of herself simply because of his talent, his looks and his fame. She was way out of his league. He could have any girl he wanted. Any girl!

Another thing took him even further out of reach. He was still in love with his wife, with Jill, even though she was lost to him. That was the kind of love Prue wanted for herself, a forever relationship, lasting beyond death itself. Indeed, it proved that true love did exist. If she could only have that with Torsten, with the great Sten Norberg, but she was forced to be realistic. She was dreaming... just dreaming... because apart from anything else, he might fancy her physically but, as a real person, he didn't even like her! And he was probably having a relationship with the blonde Ulrica anyway!

The Saab slowed down to motor round a pretty bluff of rocks and silvery trees, then turned along by the harbour wall. Most of the other vehicles, and that included the scores of cycles, were sporting sprigs of birch on their bonnets or handlebars. Prue was tickled pink, what a charming tradition! What an old fashioned, lovely place Sweden was!

Celebration was in the air. She caught the excitement with a feeling of lightness, headiness, and joyous anticipation. In the serenely smiling land of Sweden, in spite of everything that had happened here - the misunderstandings, the accident, the frustrations - she felt alive, reinvigorated. Yes, she loved her job at The Trust, but there was more to life than work. There was fun and that had been severely lacking in her own home life for some time now. She missed her dad for one thing, although she'd made the choice not to keep in touch with him because of his disloyalty.

Even her beloved mum seemed ready to move on these days. Oh, what a blessing that was, and her boss was such a nice man. If this new liaison turned out not to be permanent, at least there was a little light and frivolity in her mum's life at last. It also meant that Prue was now let off the hook, because for a while she'd stayed home a great deal, to keep her mum company, as she didn't like to see her lonely and sad. So hoorah for James!

'We're nearly there,' Hildi broke into the happy haze of Prue's daydreams as Didrik steered onto the quay-side. He drove along for about a hundred yards before taking a left turn by a life-size bronze of a traditional 'fish maiden' with her gutting knife and box of bronze herrings.

'See that restaurant across the road?' Hildi pointed towards a quaint looking house with a red door in the middle of the row of shops. 'The food's really lovely and there's a wonderful view of the harbour. Torsten should take you there before you leave.'

Simultaneously, a strange fact registered with Prue. The back of Hildi's neck, previously white, was now stained by a scarlet flush that was most noticeable, contrasting as it did with the fair hair scooped up into an elastic band. Then, with a flash of insight, a possible answer surfaced. Hildi, the dear, scheming little minx, was guilty of an age-old pastime – she was trying her hand at match-making!

Prudence and Torsten - the idea must have appealed to Hildi, for some unfathomable reason. Prue frowned. Didrik's earlier remark could supply at least part of an explanation.

'Torsten produces his best music when he's in love,' he'd said. 'We've all noticed it.'

Quite clearly, the joy of her own impending marriage had not blinded Hildi to her brother's unhappiness. She wanted him to fall as deeply in love with someone as he had with Jill. Prue was certain that Torsten had no difficulty in attracting women. Indeed, by all accounts, he had to fend them off all the time. With a huge choice of tall Swedish blondes, why did Hildi think Torsten might be tempted by a petite brunette from England? Could it be because, like Jill, she was English also? Prue wasn't convinced by her own reasoning. Somehow it seemed a feeble solution to the puzzle.

For the time being the mystery would have to be put on hold. At least the burden of her dangerous infatuation with Hildi's 'bridegroom' had been removed. Whatever unfinished business existed between her and Torsten would hurt no one but themselves - and for that Prue was extremely grateful.

The car pulled up outside a three-storey cream-washed stucco town house, and they all clambered out of the crimson Saab. Even before Hildi could knock at the door, it was opened by an older, slimmer version of Aunt Agnetha. It was obvious that the two must be sisters.

With an all-enveloping smile Fru Dahlgren kissed Hildi and Didrik, and gave Prue the usual Swedish arm grasp.

'Valkommen, welcome,' she said warmly. After profusely admiring the fragrant bouquet, she seemed much taken with Prue herself. 'Hildi has told me about your lovely English face,' she commented, briefly cradling it between her hands.

She hurried off to find a vase for the flowers, leaving Prue feeling a mite uncomfortable, yet pleased to have made a favourable impression.

Hildi was already leading the way through to a conservatory. Here, they sat in the sunshine in cane chairs among tall plotted plants, framed family photographs, plus hand-painted porcelain knick-knacks, which Prue guessed were from Sweden's famed Rorstrand factory. A few minutes later, Fru Dahlgren served them lingonberry cordial and Swedish pastries.

'It's so peaceful here, yet we're right in the centre of town.'

Prue marvelled at the lack of noise. There was so little traffic compared with back home in England. She stood up and wandered round the conservatory, admiring the many proudly displayed photographs of the Dahlgren's celebrity son. Here he was shaking hands with the Crown Princess of Sweden; the American President; receiving Platinum Disc Awards... The pictures made Prue appreciate even more fully Torsten's defensive rudeness, caution, and suspicion. His was fame with a capital F, and this made him vulnerable to all kinds of scams.

There was a little niggle, though. Next to the photos of Hildi and her mother, of Aunt Agnetha and Anna-Karin, there was an imposing one of the musicians. All three smiled into the camera, with Ulrica standing next to Torsten, their arms entwined. The two looked very happy and cosy together. There was another little niggle, too. There were no photographs of Jill.

Prue turned to Hildi. 'I recognise you in the photos, and your mother, but I haven't seen one of Jill. I'm just curious, that's all, as to why.'

'Mamma took down all her pictures - at Torsten's own request.'

'Oh, I see.'

To be truthful, she didn't see at first but when she thought about it, of course, it was obvious - photos of Jill everywhere would force Torsten to keep confronting the anguish of his loss. This fresh insight caused a little knot of worry to form between Prue's shoulders. He was, at heart, a decent man. She had to review her opinion of him and give him credit for that. Would he ever accept that she was no fortune hunter, that she'd never known his true identity? Could she convince him of the truth, that the name mentioned to her - Torsten Dahlgren - had triggered off no recognition? Without the trade-mark beard, his much published likeness had been only vaguely familiar to her.

In the afternoon, the two young women walked over to a nearby arcade of shops. Encouraged by Hildi, Prue bought souvenirs; a couple of carved wooden Dalarna horses, a blue and a red one, and a decorated glass jug by Boda.

'My mum will love the jug. Crystal is her passion.'

After their little outing together they returned home just in time for dinner. Herr Dahlgren was home from his job in the Tourist Office near the harbour. He bore a close resemblance to his famous son; similar build, his hair dulled a little with age but still thick and vigorous; compelling lustred blue eyes, all of which made Prue wish that Torsten was here.

'So this is Great Kate,' was Herr Dahlgren's initial teasing comment to Prue. Then glancing at her petite figure, he added. 'Not very aptly named if I may say so.'

So he had Prue laughing right from the start.

Soon after, dinner was served. Hildi's mother had roasted a joint of elk meat. It had an unusual and distinctive flavour which Prue, always keen on new experiences, thoroughly enjoyed. In addition, in fluent English, Herr Dahlgren talked and joked with her throughout the meal, making her feel relaxed and very much at home.

After dinner, Prue persuaded Hildi to rest while she helped Fru Dahlgren with the clearing up. Later, in the soft light of the Swedish midsummer evening, Didrik drove them back to Norrtorpet.

The house was silent, its occupants in bed. Gunnar was sleeping in the study and there was an improvised 'Keep Out' sign hanging from the door knob. A badly drawn skull-and-crossbones with his name underneath gave it a humorous touch.

Hildi had elected to stay overnight at the summer house and so had Didrik. He chose a little bedroom separate from Hildi; he was plainly an old-fashioned guy. Pleading tiredness, he excused himself and disappeared into his room. Hildi, too, looked exhausted.

'Are you feeling all right?' Prue asked her, concerned.

'Yes, thank you, but I must get some sleep soon.'

Hildi yawned, yet before she went off to her own bedroom she indicated a chest of drawers under the stairs, full of tops, T-shirts and shorts.

'You're more than welcome to wear any of those clothes if you like. By the way, have you got a pretty frock for tomorrow?'

Tomorrow was the first day of the midsummer celebrations, but Prue had already given thought to this and put some of her clothes through the washing machine.

'I bought a couple of new dresses and a top in the village yesterday.' She indicated the dress she was wearing. 'This is one of them. My primrose dress might be okay, but it needs ironing. There's always my turquoise two-piece, of course, but I was saving that for the wedding.'

'The iron is in the cupboard by the sink. Just help yourself,' Hildi offered. 'I'll just show you something else before I go to bed, then I'll leave you to your chores.'

She took Prue by the arm and led her up to the landing. There she opened up a huge old mahogany linen press. A row of six or seven dresses was revealed, all sealed up in transparent polythene covers.

'These are mine but most of them are too tight for me these days.' Hildi chuckled as she referred to her ample figure. 'They have been laundered recently, so if there's one you'd like to borrow, you can run the iron over it when you do the rest of your clothes.'

The dresses were attractive in a full-skirted sort of way and Prue flicked through them, considering, until Hildi plucked one off the rail.

'What about this one? It's really special and would suit you.'

'Yes, I had that one spotted already,' said Prue. 'It

looks about my size.'

The dress was made of fine white softly-starched cotton, snowy, the sleeveless bodice embroidered with white daisies. The skirt was short, flounced and lace-edged. At Hildi's insistence Prue tried it on. It wasn't exactly tailor-made to fit but after the waist had been taken in with a couple of safety pins, the effect was much improved and caused Hildi to clap her hands in delight.

'It's just right for midsummer,' she said. 'I'll lend you my Pink-on-Pink nail polish. Then you'll look really cool.'

'It's lovely,' said Prue, because it was. 'I almost feel like a Swedish girl in it! Thank you so much, Hildi, I'm so lucky. I'll iron it before I go to bed.'

Twirling before the long wardrobe mirror, she saw how it flattered her trim figure to perfection, and the knee-length skirt seemed to add inches to her shapely slender legs. She was so delighted she turned to Hildi.

'Big hugs!'

Smiling, Hildi obliged.

In the morning, awakened by noise and chatter coming from outside, and even a few notes of music, Prue dressed in her lilac jeans and a white sleeveless broderie anglaise top that she had borrowed from Hildi's clothes rail. It was quite a good fit and matched her new sunny mood.

The ironing she'd done the night before was hanging on the wardrobe door including Hildi's 'special' dress. Prue wondered, not for the first time, what had happened to her lapis lazuli beads. Not that she could wear them in the state they were in! Fortunately she had a few bits of other jewellery in her suitcase. A thin gold necklet and a matching bracelet assured that she looked a little 'dressed up.' She would wait until later to change into Hildi's white dress so it was fresh when the celebrations were ready to start. As she planned to help where she could, she didn't want to risk getting it dirty if she wore it too soon.

While she was dressing she glanced through the window now and again. The grounds were a hive of industry. Several people had arrived and the lawn was strewn with birch branches.

Anna-Karin, crisp and pretty in green, sat with Rolf, who was showing off his impressive, hairy-chested torso today. Both were busy attaching leafy twigs all over the prone maypole, with Hildi supervising. Prue noticed that her friend was wearing Swedish national costume as were some of the other ladies in the garden. White lace caps, white blouses, full royal blue skirts and waistcoats combined with a yellow apron - they were all such a pretty sight. Gunnar was at the picnic table drinking coffee plus now and again drawing a snatch of tune from his concertina. Garden and grounds were flooded with sunlight.

Outside the bedroom door, on the floor in a little box, was a bottle of nail polish. The Pink-on-Pink that Hildi had promised to lend! There was no time like the present, Prue decided to use it.

A little while later, pleased with her newly painted nails, she hurried downstairs to find that the kitchen, too, was full of activity. Friends and relatives were helping themselves from a basket of cloth-covered hot breakfast rolls and a marble platter of cheeses. Fru Dahlgren sat on the back steps hulling strawberries, and beside her was Aunt Agnetha with an open sewing basket. She was stitching a button on an aubergine coloured shirt which, presumably, belonged to the shirtless Rolf. Like Hildi, both ladies were resplendent in national costume of white lace cap, white blouse, waistcoat and full royal-blue skirt with yellow apron.

Thoroughly captivated, Prue went to exclaim over the ladies and their appearance. She even persuaded the sisters to stand and do a twirl so she could admire their lovely outfits before offering her assistance in preparing the food. Sadly, the one person she'd banked on seeing, was missing. If he'd been anywhere about, she would have felt his presence, she was sure of it.

'Prue, there you are! I've got a little job for you!' Hildi waved at her from a little distance. She was a much healthier colour today, and the sling had been discarded altogether. 'Would you find some flowers? They must be wild flowers; seven different kinds.'

Munching on a cheese roll, Prue strolled over to join her friend, acknowledging the 'God morgons' as she went.

'Seven,' Hildi emphasized darkly.

Prue raised her eyebrows at the precise

instruction. 'Strange request, but first I want to say how beautiful you look. Second, I left my phone upstairs in the bedroom, but I hope someone is taking lots of photos. I must have some souvenirs to remember this day.'

Then she obediently went off through the orchard into the meadow beyond. There she gathered buttercups, white dog daisies, blue flax, shepherd's purse, wild sweet peas, large purple ones, and pink ragged robin.

She wandered back with the scented posy and when she came up through the orchard, she smiled to see Anna-Karin skipping towards her, arms outstretched for a hug.

'Hello, darling.'

Prue gave the child a cuddle in greeting. They then sat together on the edge of the lawn. With a serious expression, the little girl went through the flower collection.

'...tre... fyra... fem... sex,' she counted before shaking her pale-blonde curls and wagging her finger at Prue. There were only six different sorts.

'Ah!' Immediately the child had a solution and she raced across to the picnic table where she'd been decorating a headband. She returned with a deep blue cornflower, but they had a witness.

'Anna-Karin! Nej. Nej!' Hildi called sharply. 'You must pick the flowers yourself, Prue!'

'Okay, sorry! Message received and understood.' With an apologetic wink at Anna-Karin, Prue handed the cornflower back.

Prue chuckled to herself because she realised what was going on. She was being gently manipulated into following an old Swedish tradition. At a guess, the maidens, the single girls, had the task of picking seven varieties of wild flower at midsummer. To put a love spell on some young man, maybe? She could only hazard a guess but if it was supposed to make her dreams come true, she would go along with it, all the way! After all, where getting together with The Maestro was concerned, she needed all the help she could get! So, smiling to herself, she did as she'd been ordered and chose a few from a shy clump of tiny red blooms like bee orchids.

Taking care to use all seven different sorts, Anna-Karin showed Prue how to fashion a decoration, a sort of chaplet, on a thin circular wire frame. The chaplet was to be worn on her head, while the left-over flowers would be woven into the maypole.

By this time the men were setting up a long table composed of separate trestles in the garden and Hildi, pointing to her wrist watch, indicated to Prue it was time to get ready and change. Before complying, Prue quickly ran to fetch sketch book and pencil. She simply had to get down on paper at least the flavour of a whole Swedish family preparing for midsummer. It would be the work of a few minutes only; she was very practised with her pencil and sketching pencil.

A short time later she went inside to change into Hildi's white dress. Clearly the result of hours of patient needlework, the dress was truly romantic. It was crisp and smelled of starch, and when she looked at her reflection in the mirrored wardrobe she noticed something amazing. Overnight the bodice had become tight fitting and shapely, simply because on examination she saw that it now sported four cunning hand-sewn darts. This, she guessed, had been dear Aunt Agnetha's first job this morning. The neckline was low cut and the new shapeliness showed off her bosom to perfection. She was still wearing the delicate gold chain and the bracelet, simple finishing touches that enhanced the whole outfit. Her white sandals were in the porch. They were dainty and smart yet comfortable enough for dancing. Prue was sure there would be dancing. She hoped there would.

One last check in the mirror. Yes, the neckline was rather daringly low cut, yet becoming.

'If you entered a beauty competition dressed in that, you'd walk off with the Booby Prize,' she told her reflection out loud, smiling ruefully at her own unintended pun. Yet it was a bit late to worry about the neckline and she had to admit the material brought out the bloom of her skin, making it look as if it had been brushed with gold dust. Her dark hair was glossy with a silky sheen and her green-gold eyes were highlighted by a hint of green eye shadow. She had used extra lipstick today, too. This in addition to Hildi's pink nail polish on fingers and toes was all the colour the dress needed to set it off.

She took a last critical look at herself and passed an inward comment on the whole effect - not too bad, quite lovely actually, and typically Swedish.

Any remaining doubts she had about her

appearance were dispelled as she descended the winding stairs. She was greeted by a long, low whistle - the inimitable Rolf was vocalising his appreciation. At the same moment, Hildi entered the hallway carrying Prue's coronet of fresh flowers with its new decoration of green satin ribbon.

'Bra! Bra!' she cried approvingly when she saw Prue and soon set about fixing the flowered crown in Prue's hair.

Hildi herself was like an advert for tourism in her white and blue traditional dress and today, two plaits. Rolf, impatient in the background, bounced forward the minute it was possible to take Prue's hand in his, just as the pleasantly noisy bell-trimmed porch door flew open. Not one of them had heard the Volvo arrive.

There he stood, Torsten Norberg Dahlgren, commanding the scene, motionless for a second, still as a statue and weighing up the situation. He, too, was dressed like a member of the cast in a costume drama. Certainly he would be the romantic lead in his sparkling white full-sleeved shirt, mandarin neck buttoned to the top, Prussian blue jerkin, and fawn knee breeches. His stance was vaguely menacing, his hands were hooked into his silver-buckled belt. Certainly, in Prue's eyes, he was a true prince.

Today, no sun glasses hid the penetrating concentration of the blue-violet gaze directed at her. She was almost mesmerised by it and tremors began to travel along her inner thighs, shoulder blades, the backs of her arms, and into the spaces around her heart. In her ears was a whispering, rushing sound and she found herself sucking in a slow, shuddery breath. Rolf still held Prue's hand in his own and she hoped he hadn't noticed anything untoward.

'Torsten...?' Hildi broke the spell of silence by asking her brother a question in Swedish.

'Torsten has been in Lunneby all morning because he's going to lead the Grand Procession,' she translated the exchange for Prue. 'He's done it for years now; he took the job over when our grandfather got too old and frail. Our father couldn't do it because he can't play the violin. I've just asked Torsten why he has bothered to come back here.'

In answer to Hildi's query, Torsten stepped forward and claimed Prue's hand, snatching it, without ceremony, out of Rolf's huge paw.

'I have come for Prudence,' he announced, his tone instantly silencing any opposition. 'Kom, Prudence, you will ride with me to Lunneby.'

## CHAPTER SIX

Rolf wasn't going to be put off so readily. His face turned an angry red and he directed a brief explosive sentence at Torsten in Swedish. Torsten simply took no notice of him and led Prue to the front door where she slipped her feet into her sandals. Perhaps inevitably Rolf followed; he wasn't about to give up. Again he shouted at Torsten, and in this parting shot the name 'Ulrica' cropped up twice.

Ulrica, the blonde girl who had seemed on more than friendly terms with Torsten outside the church. Ulrica, who'd asked to speak to Rolf on the phone. Ulrica, *Scandinavia's* road manager. Against her will, Prue felt a pang of jealousy. Torsten, however, again ignored Rolf's peevish outburst and, politeness personified, conducted Prue to the waiting car, its engine still ticking over. Although she sensed that he was impatient to drive off, he first removed a violin case and a dark blue broad-brimmed hat trimmed with a white band from the passenger side to the rear seat. He handled both objects with reverential care before gallantly holding the door open for her.

As she clicked the safety belt into place, Prue felt confused, yet she couldn't repress the feeling of elation which produced a frisson of anticipation along her spine. She hadn't seen or spoken to Torsten since their clash in the music room and she wondered what could have happened since then to cause this change of attitude towards her – if change there was. She never could tell; his mind was so unreadable. Before she could draw breath, he was in the driving seat, his carved jawline set purposefully, a muscle visibly moving at the side of his cheekbone.

Seconds later they'd set off at break-neck speed down the track to the Lunneby road. Prue could feel the flowers in the circlet shaking. Seeking a clue as to his mood, she stole a glance at his profile just as he did the same in her direction. Mint green eyes met Swedish blue causing a quiver of amusement to tug at the edges of his mouth. Embarrassed, Prue immediately switched her attention to the road ahead.

She tried to compose herself, folding and refolding her hands in her lap. His own were within the range of her vision, slender but strong. Magic fingers, supple wrists - extensions of an ingenious, creative mind, they were a fascination in themselves.

Prue released her breath in a low, protracted sigh. In the game of boy-meets-girl she was still very much a beginner and nobody had told her what agony it was, being in love. Yes, at last, she was acknowledging the truth to herself. She was in love. Many questions hammered at her brain at this moment, but she said nothing, deeming it his place to speak first, to enlighten her as to the reasons for, and the meanings of, his present actions.

He kept his foot down along the road to Lunneby, perhaps translating the energy of his thoughts into almost reckless speed, and Prue gave thanks that the traffic was light. In spite of this, she was about to make some restraining comment when, abruptly, he swung the car off the road to park in a wooded layby. After the bruising, rushing ride, the subsequent stillness was unnerving. Only their combined breathing disturbed the air. All around them the trees in the saturated green of the forest seemed to wait expectantly.

'So you thought I was about to marry my own sister!' The sentence ricocheted off the windscreen like a bullet, straight into Prue's heart. 'I know we've got a racy reputation in Europe, but even we Swedes think twice before stooping to that sort of thing!'

'Oh, but I didn't... I mean... I...' Prue turned to face him as, horrified and rising to the thrown bait, she stammered her defence. 'I thought no such thing. At the time, in the church. I naturally assumed you were the groom. It was all a mistake... a horrible... '

'Steady, steady, it's all right,' he interrupted her soothingly.

It was only then that she came down to earth and felt foolish, realising that, of course, his accusations hadn't been serious. He'd been playing with her, winding her up, catching her off guard. A dimple appeared, deep and attractive, and his smile betrayed his teasing. Unfastening his seat belt, he manoeuvred his taut upper body around until it was almost square with hers, and covered her twisting hands with his own. Startled, she glanced into his face.

His eyes were so mesmerising she had to look away; his touch had triggered her pulses into racing. The sensual warmth of him flowed in waves towards her, opening the hidden place inside her, the place where her very soul lived. He was so unbearably close.

'Prue...'

Her name throbbed in the quietness and, unwittingly, she looked up again. Their glances locked only for a second before she quailed and glanced away again. This wouldn't do at all, she told herself; she was acting like a star-struck teenager. With strengthened resolve she forced her eyes to seek his once more.

'I've got...' he began, indicating the clock on the dashboard, 'just about eight minutes to make my apology to you, for the sake of cordial Anglo-Swedish relations, you understand?'

Once more she was confounded. What was he getting at? She frowned, her gaze sliding back down to her hands still imprisoned in his.

'I want to get something off my chest, as you Brits like to say. I wouldn't want you to think of me as vicious, a swine for the sake of being a swine.' He paused then commanded her, gruffly but gently, 'Please, look at me.'

Prue obliged reluctantly - how could anyone return his gaze at such close quarters, the steadfast, unblinking indigo of those eyes? With a mild sense of shock she saw herself mirrored in them, as if she belonged there, inside him. His breath stirred the invisible down on her cheek. A lock of his sun-touched hair fell forwards over his brow and he shook it back with the impatient gesture she had come to know. He seemed to be waiting for some input from her, something encouraging, but she had no intention of making his confession easy - she had her pride. If he was anxious to say sorry for his former boorishness, he was being a long time about it.

Even now his bearing betrayed not a shred of humility so, being deliberately provocative, she said, 'I could have got a lift to Lunneby, you know. I can't imagine why you thought you had to fetch me.'

'I came because I wanted to clear the air between us. It's not nice to have bad feelings around at midsummer. Everyone is supposed to be happy; beautiful, too, as you are with flowers in your hair and ribbons as green as your eyes.'

She felt the compliment bring a rush of hot colour to her cheeks, but it subsided as he changed the subject.

'I heard you were going home. Not staying for the wedding.'

This was a bit of a shock. Prue had forgotten for the time being that she'd been prepared to leave. 'That was yesterday, I changed my mind; it's what we women do. Who told you anyway?' Her response was automatic, defensive but superfluous. It could only have been one person.

'Rolf, who else? Never trust him with a secret, he likes to cause mischief. Seriously, though, please don't leave before the wedding. Hildi would be most upset and it would be my fault. Hers, too. My sister is a naughty girl - I suspect she's been trying to put a little scheme of her own into practice. She means well, though, and we should forgive her. After all, it's midsummer, so I suppose I'll have to overlook her interference in my life, just this once.'

So he, too, had twigged that Hildi had been trying to match-make the pair of them. This knowledge, in itself, was a relief.

'I did consider going home early. It was because I thought you were Hildi's boyfriend... er... bridegroom.' Again she felt the heat of the flush creeping back into her cheeks at what she was about to say next. 'You have to admit you made a pass at me, so I thought it best to make myself scarce. It seemed the only sensible thing to do at the time.'

To Prue's astonishment he was nodding. 'I can well see how you got mixed up and got the wrong end of the stick. With Hildi's accident and everything, nobody thought to explain anything to you.'

Prue was disconcerted by his calm understanding of the situation. 'All along you've been convinced that I'm a... a... conniving so-and-so,' she said. 'Yet, all of a sudden, you're finding me not guilty. But there's more...' Her words tumbled out, falling on top of one another in their haste. 'You are the famous Sten Norberg.'

He took a deep breath. 'That I am.'

'But I had no idea,' Prue continued. 'Even when I found out you were Hildi's brother, Torsten Dahlgren is a name that didn't exactly ring any bells with me. I only realised the truth after Gunnar arrived on the scene.'

Sten Norberg - Prue still had difficulty in taking it in, the fact that he was Mr Sex-On-Legs with the talent and singing voice of a husky angel. He was the unattainable dream of millions of females and yet, here he was, sitting beside her, in a car, in the whispering green gloom of a forest layby. The windows were open, the breeze soft on her face, birds were singing in the trees. Magic was in the air.

'Make no mistake - I understand all your dilemmas. I've taken the trouble to work it all out; the hows, the whys and the wherefores of everything,' he said. 'As a matter of interest, family members and close friends call me Torsten, business people, the press, and acquaintances use Sten.'

'What should I call you?'

'Torsten,' he almost whispered.

Torsten. Her heartbeat accelerated. So she was more than a mere acquaintance.

He gave a cough then took up his explanation again. 'Using my middle name was the idea of Ulrica, my agent. She thought "Sten Norberg" had more of a commercial ring to it than "Torsten Dahlgren". I guess she was right. She usually is in matters of that sort.'

So, at last, the tangled ball of suspicion was starting to unravel.

'I can't believe you're saying all this,' she breathed. 'It seems too good to be true after everything that's happened.'

At Prue's words he had the grace to look repentant. 'Sorry about that, but I've been taken in before by beautiful women with easy, friendly ways, who've turned out to be serpents. I've learned to trust no one. I never used to be secretive, but now I lock up everything - fans find me everywhere and take away my possessions for souvenirs. Clothes, bits of precious equipment, anything they can lay their hands on. I love my fans and depend on them but some can be unthinking, even vicious.'

'You still haven't explained what made you realise.' Prue quizzed him impatiently, bringing him back to the original subject.

'I'm coming to that.' He squeezed her hands to silence her. 'I accept that you've been speaking the truth all along. Hildi likes you a lot, but my dear sister is very naive and you might just be an excellent actress. I've been through it all before, you see. Some women are very clever; I've learned to trust no one. The occasion that told me that you were entirely innocent of any guile was when I overheard you talking to Rolf yesterday morning, just after Gunnar arrived. I was in the room overlooking the log pile.'

Prue pressed her fingers to her lips, thinking back - yes, she recalled the conversation with Rolf, the open window above her, the blind rattling in the wind.

Uneasy, all the same, and not daring to believe all his doubts about her had actually evaporated, she filled her lungs with the pine-scented air of the nearby trees, ready to play her own Devil's Advocate.

'How do you know I wasn't putting on an act for your benefit? You know, pretending I'd only just found out I was sharing a house with, perhaps, the most famous musicians in, yes, the whole world?'

His face took on a puzzled expression. 'You didn't know I was listening, you couldn't possibly.'

'It was reasonable to assume you were still in bed,' she pressed on, her brain working overtime. 'A seasoned schemer would've had all that sussed out, the location of your bedroom and so on.'

'I take your point, though I can't think why you want to make it.' His eyes crinkled at the corners, his mouth twitched with humour. 'Especially as in this case your argument doesn't hold water.'

'Why not?' Prue was enjoying herself.

He pressed her hand, teasingly. 'Because the room in question isn't my bedroom. It's my grandfather's study, kept exactly as it was when he was alive, and never used since. I'd only gone in there for a minute to fetch what he used to call his "midsummer hat", plus his old violin. I always use both at midsummer to lead the Lunneby Grand Procession, just as he did.'

So, the nightmare was over. Finished. Done. Relief flooded through her. Yet he'd come to fetch her then, not out of any concerned affection but simply motivated by guilt and an anxiety to cleanse the atmosphere at the approaching wedding of any bad vibes.

Happily, only a moment later, her sour conclusion looked to be premature, erroneous even.

'You'll forgive me? Yes, I know you will.' His voice was low in his throat, a gentle rumble in her ear, and there was a little click as he pressed the release button of her seat belt.

What his intentions were, however, Prue never found out for at that precise moment a large silver car drove past the end of the lay-by.

'There goes Gunnar,' she commented, rather unthinking, but at this, Torsten paused and turned to look at the dashboard clock.

'Herregud!' he exclaimed. 'We must go! We're late!'

He took his sun glasses from a side pocket in the car door, looked at them but then put them back.

'No disguise today then?' Prue teased him as he started the engine.

He laughed. 'No point. Not when I'm performing, they all know it's me. I'll drop you just before we get there if you don't mind. Otherwise you might be harassed for a "statement" by journalists from what I call the scandal-rags.'

'Oh no, I wouldn't like that.'

True to his word, he stopped at a bend in the road where he suggested she alight. 'You'll see the crowds just round this corner. Everyone you know will be there. You won't be on your own.' With that he blew her a kiss and drove off.

Almost immediately round the bend she watched him pull up outside the brown-shingle-clad village hall. A procession had already formed and was waiting for its leader. The family were all present; Aunt Agnetha, Anna-Karin, Herr and Fru Dahlgren, Hildi and Didrik. As Torsten climbed out of the car a cheer went up.

The ground being bumpy, Gunnar wasn't propelling his wheel-chair himself but being pushed along by a tall woman in a white trouser suit. It was the exceedingly elegant and serenely beautiful Ulrica. With her hair the colour of harvested hay and a smile for everyone, she was turning not a few heads.

She was also wearing an expression that said, 'I'm in charge!'

Yes, as road manager, she would have to be. If Gunnar was here, then Rolf would also be somewhere around, and that was the whole group, complete. Rolf had already mentioned that they had assembled at the summer house to make music for midsummer. Wherever they went, Ulrica wouldn't be far behind, arranging things; supervising the transportation of stage equipment; doing the paperwork.

Recalling that Ulrica seemed also very close to Torsten, Prue pondered this for a moment. Were they just good friends, or was there more to their relationship? Whatever the answer was, it made her feel uncomfortable. Torsten may not be cheating on his bride, as she'd initially believed, but was he guilty of trying to cheat on Ulrica?

While Prue was taking all this in, Torsten removed violin and bow from their case and tossed the hat onto the back of his head at a rakish angle. Then with pride in every inch of his bearing, he took up his position, like a character from a Hollywood costume epic, at the head of the colourful band of villagers and friends.

Drawing a single note from his instrument, he nodded at the nearby group of expectant violinists, established a beat with his foot, and the music started up in a joyful burst of sound. People moved around and about, catching the scene on phone cameras, some even shouldering television cameras, and as she went to join Hildi, it struck Prue for the first time that the media were out in force.

The long curling line of the Grand Procession started off down the main street, participants skipping to the simple lively tune while escorting the village maypole across to the green. A crowd of onlookers, which included Hildi and her parents and friends, Rolf, Gunnar and Ulrica, Aunt Agnetha and Anna-Karin and Prue, brought up the rear.

'After procession, the boys and Torsten will play music for the dancing,' Hildi said with a smile. 'I'm glad you wear my dress, it suits you.'

'Someone has been working very hard on it since yesterday.' Prue's hand moved over the darts that had miraculously appeared during her sleep. 'It fits me perfectly now!'

Hildi giggled and then took her arm to guide her over to the stunning blonde. 'Here's someone you should meet. Ulrica, this is Prue, my English friend.'

'How do you do?' said Prue as Ulrica greeted her with a firm handshake.

'Hello Prue, nice to meet you. I have two jobs, agent and roadie. So, you see, I'm a vital cog in the *Scandinavia* wheel, indispensable.'

Ulrica accompanied her statement with a small laugh while her light blue eyes seemed to be studying Prue very intently. This made Prue wonder if the Swedish girl saw them both as rivals for Torsten's love? It was a thought based on pure instinct.

Ulrica seemed very attached and protective towards Gunnar, however, and privately Prue applauded this sympathy for the musician. The wheelchair made slow progress on the hummocky ground of the village, but finally they joined the swelling crowd just as the giant maypole was raised into place to the beat of the fiddlers' tune. Its rainbow ribbons fluttered bravely in the breeze. 'Huzzas' went up from scores of throats and Prue was charmed anew by the splendid theatricality of it all. Dancers started linking hands and Hildi gave Prue an encouraging push towards them.

'I shan't be doing much dancing myself today,' she said ruefully indicating her bandaged leg. 'But you must join in because...'

'Don't say it - because it will bring me good luck?' Prue interrupted. She jokingly touched the circlet of wild flowers on her head.

'Dance!' Hildi instructed her with a broad smile. 'And less of your cheek!'

Not knowing even the tunes, Prue was unable to sing along with the villagers as she danced in one of the several circles within circles. Despite that, she felt exhilarated and so privileged to be taking part in this ancient tradition.

The well-trodden grass was lush and green, with

that sweet overpowering new-mown-hay smell she really loved. The white skirt of her dress flounced up and about, swishing with her movements, and Prue felt like a little girl making her first party dress swing out. She hoped Torsten was looking, then saw that he was otherwise engaged, earnestly teasing and coaxing music from his grandfather's old fiddle. Someone else had her eyes on him, too, Prue noticed - Ulrica. She maintained close attendance on Gunnar, but her gaze wandered continually to the leader of the strings.

After about an hour or so, the crowd broke up into groups with much shouting and laughter. Totally belying the legend of 'solemn Swedes', they went off to their own various private functions, as did the Dahlgrens and their friends. Prue returned to Norrtorpet in the Volvo with Torsten and Ulrica. The blonde had headed straight for the front passenger seat as if her rightful place was beside Torsten, so Prue now sat in the back.

The conversation was mostly conducted by Ulrica. Torsten was fully occupied in negotiating, calling to, and often hooting the cheerfully abusive merrymakers thronging the road on foot and on bikes.

In her smooth English Ulrica chattered about London which she seemed to know better than Prue herself. Perhaps previously primed by Hildi, she made a point of drawing Prue out on the subject of her work with The Great Kate Trust.

'Your job must be really fascinating.'

'Yes, it is, but it's nice to have a break from it. Coming to Sweden is the opportunity of a lifetime for me.' Prue spoke with sincerity. 'It's great here, and it's so exciting to be invited to a Swedish wedding and to make so many new friends.'

'I'm just very glad that Hildi is recovering so well from her fall,' said Ulrica. 'What a pity she'll miss my name day for the first time since I've known her. I believe she'll be in Crete for her honeymoon then.'

'What is a name day? We don't have them in England.'

'Oh, no, you don't. Let me explain. In Sweden, apart from a birthday, everyone has a name day to celebrate. We have a special cake and everything. "Ulrica" is always on the fourth of July. Your name day is in February, isn't it, Torsten?'

'On the twenty-third,' he confirmed.

A few minutes later Torsten brought the car round into the entrance to Norrtorpet, and Ulrica turned in her seat, fixing Prue with her pale gaze.

'Men don't usually bother much about their own name days, but we girls like the excuse to hold a little party. I've invited a few friends round to my flat in Gustavskrona. I hope Torsten will bring you along.'

'That would've been lovely, but I shall be flying home as soon as I can after the wedding,' replied Prue. 'My boss has been very good in letting me stay on for an extra fortnight.'

In truth she had her own ideas about that. Maybe James had reasoned that it would give him time to get to know her mother without too many distractions. Of course, she couldn't say that aloud.

'In all fairness I must get back to work,' she concluded.

'What a pity.'

Ulrika didn't look too disappointed, however, but faced the front again and gave Torsten's fingers a squeeze as they lay on the steering wheel.

Seeing this, Prue's heart felt heavy. The two were evidently very close, and it seemed that Ulrica wished Prue to be aware of that. It was ironic. Today she'd allowed herself to hope that her feelings for Torsten might be reciprocated. In the light of the show of affection for him from Ulrica, though, her dreams were evaporating into nothingness. It could be that she'd been reading too much into his earlier words of apology, his actions. Yes, she was an idiot, stupidly fanciful. The sooner she was on that plane back to England, the better.

At Norrtorpet the family's home-made maypole had already been erected and tied to a wooden post near the flagpole. Tables had been set with blue-and-white checked tablecloths under the shade of the maple trees, and today the famous smörgåsbord came into its own. It consisted of sill, shrimps, Norwegian salmon, caviar, gravad lax and salads. White wine was chilling in buckets together with aquavit and cloudberry liqueur. There were hot dishes, too, all kept warm over silver table heaters. The smells combined to tantalise the taste buds and fill the garden with appetizing aromas.

Torsten and Ulrica sat together. At Hildi's suggestion Prue sat opposite them, reflecting despondently on a certain a fact of life - as one problem was solved, another one presented itself. In her case, that problem was Ulrica. She had to accept that her holiday encounter with the man of her dreams would soon become just a bitter-sweet memory.

Sitting at table next to Fru Dahlgren and Anna-Karin, Prue filled her plate with home-pickled herring and salad, but the food turned to cardboard in her mouth as she had a good view of Torsten and Ulrica, chatting together and smiling. Now and then, Torsten flashed his marvellous grin in Prue's direction which she answered with a nod, but most of the time she talked about all the delicacies on display with Aunt Agnetha – the mashed turnips; waxy potatoes; whole buttered onions; chicken portions in a creamy sauce. Aunt Agnetha was only too delighted to pass on the recipes for them all. Prue also did not forget to voice her gratitude for the alterations Hildi's aunt had done on the dress.

Later, in the warm, light evening, when every last bowl and dish had been cleared away by an army of helpers, Prue went with the crowd to Lunneby once more, to the open-air disco. A van arrived and the set of drums was loaded up. They left in convoy, Prue getting a lift this time with Hildi and Didrik.

There now stood a piano on a small platform by the maypole in Lunneby. The drums were soon set up and, in next to no time *Scandinavia* were playing the music that had made them famous; music that had no difficulty in imposing its uplifting beat on Prue's heart. The cascading notes of Torsten's piano-playing were nothing short of miraculous and his full-throated singing voice was heart-rending.

Prue didn't lack partners, many men being eager to sweetheart the English girl with her dark-haired beauty, to admire her wild green eyes with their darting lights. However, she declined several invitations to share a midsummer watch, totally not persuaded by promises of romantic love-making. She looked for romance from one source alone, never mind that that source now seemed effectively barred to her. Yet strangely, none of this mattered. She was in love with him. she acknowledged it to herself. It was a fact, and she was stuck with it!

As usual she found herself glancing round for Ulrica. Finally she spotted the Swedish woman sitting in a chair near to the music platform. She was listening intently to a piano-and-voice solo just begun by Torsten, who was accompanied by Gunnar on the concertina. Curious, Prue also found a chair and moved it close up to the stage and beside Ulrica where she had a clear view of Torsten - and, incidentally, he of her.

The song had begun softly, Torsten's voice almost a whisper. It gradually became louder, until the melody gained pace, building to a climax as Torsten repeated the words caressingly, in his smoky baritone.

*Where did you come from... beautiful girl?*
*Whenever I'm near you... my head's in a whirl...*

*I'll love you forever... if you'll only stay
and kiss me, my darling... on Midsummer's Day.'*

His eyes seemed only to be for Prue, apart from when his gaze flicked back to the music manuscript propped up on the piano before him. Prue caught her breath. She couldn't believe it, her heart raced; there were butterflies in her tummy. She watched, overcome with emotion, while Ulrica sat statue-still, no doubt also fascinated by the new tune. As the song ended, Prue took a quick peep at Ulrica's face. The look of pleasure, the smile she saw there seemed to indicate that Ulrica was also relieved that Torsten had been inspired to compose more music at last - and a love song into the bargain. At second glance, Ulrica's expression almost seemed to indicate that she assumed... Prue suddenly felt cold. Could the love song have been written for Ulrica? Prue was sitting close to the agent-cum-road manager, so was she mistaken in thinking that Torsten's eyes were only for herself? Was it sheer wishful thinking? He could so easily have been focusing on Ulrica and probably had been! After all, the two had been an item since the early death of his wife according to the information she had found online.

Realising her mistake, Prue felt utterly dejected.

The sweet music ended, Gunnar took up his drums again and the mood switched with a rousing rock-and-roll number.

The time passed quickly and at ten o'clock Hildi declared herself to be exhausted. So, after lingering on to hear a repeat of the haunting new tune, Prue accompanied Didrik and Hildi back to Norrtorpet. The song was already working its way into Prue's brain patterns and she was surprised to find herself humming it in the car on the journey back. Didrik hummed along with her.

'The new love song, it's great,' he commented.

'Ja,' said Hildi with obvious satisfaction. 'Torsten's working well, at last. I like the words, I think you say "lyric", and the music's lovely, don't you think?'

Prue couldn't agree more. 'I do. It's wonderful.'

She recognised the tune from that fraught night she'd been together with Torsten in the music studio. Afterwards the same divine melody had echoed through her day-dreams. That was when he must have started to compose it, but there was still one burning question on her mind.

Who was the song written for? For Jill, his poor deceased young wife? For Ulrica? Maybe, against all hope, even for herself, although this now seemed highly unlikely? Torsten could only compose if he was in love, she had been told. So he must be in love with somebody, but whom?

Back at the summer house, a couple of hedgehogs scurried across the grassy garden. Nightingales were singing on cue for Midsummer's Eve, and Prue, her mind and heart full of the new song, was amused to find Anna-Karin fast asleep in her bed with all the dolls tucked in beside her. Aunt Agnetha, mellow with aquavit, was herself almost asleep in the music room. Hildi had gone to bed too, as she'd been tired.

Judging by the strip of light under the door to Didrik's bedroom, he, too, had retired.

Prue would have no alternative but to bed down on one of the red Ikea couches in the sitting room. There were cushions there and a blanket. Perhaps she would keep the dress on as this was rather a public spot. Although the night was still light, she was suddenly feeling tired. She removed the midsummer coronet, the flowers now sadly wilted, and snuggled up under the blanket. A few minutes later, she was asleep.

How long she had slept, she didn't really know, when she was awoken by a sound. There it was again, a cry in the night, someone singing, in the nearby lanes. Young Swedish people most likely, making the most of this midsummer night. There were more noises. Prue sat up, suddenly wide awake. The first thing she saw was a large photograph of Torsten propped up beside her couch. Someone had placed it there as she slept. Someone? It would have been Hildi, no doubt complying with the old superstition. The first person a young girl sees when she wakes at midsummer will be her husband or sweetheart or whatever. Dear Hildi, she hadn't given up trying! Prue pulled a rueful face and looked out of the window. The night was light, but the sun had gone. It must be some time after two o'clock in the morning, at a guess.

She went into the kitchen. The revellers' bursts of laughter could be heard even more clearly here. Perhaps tonight was the night she should go exploring.

Quickly she went to the little cupboard on the wall and opened it. Among the keys hanging inside on hooks, there was one, larger than all the rest. She took it and read the label, tied to the key with string. It bore the legend, 'Wasakappellet.' Silently Prue thanked Rolf again for informing her of this.

She borrowed a knitted multi-coloured shawl that was hanging from the row of pegs in the hallway, just in case it turned chilly, and at the front door she slipped her feet into her flat sandals then stepped outside into the sweet-smelling garden. Didrik's red car was parked nearby, the black rubber torch in full view in the back window. Luckily, the car wasn't locked. In no time, the torch was in her hands. A quick press on its button produced an effective beam. Yes! Result! She turned it off; she didn't need it yet. The night was warm and quite light. She set off for the lake.

Reaching the chapel took Prue longer than she'd anticipated. She'd worked out that if she kept to the lake-edge, she would automatically come to the little building, but this was easier said than done. Here and there the tiny secluded beaches were occupied by couples, paddling and splashing about in the water, sitting at the lakeside, drinking wine, whispering, kissing and cuddling. Romance was in the air.

One of the girls gave a screech when Prue appeared. In the white dress, she probably resembled a ghost. A wistful, envious wraith though, she mused, wishing that she, too, might have a lover of her own to sit with, to share this magical night.

After that first intrusion she was more careful where she walked, partly out of consideration for the young people, partly because she suddenly had a dread that Torsten might be sharing the midsummer night with Ulrica at this very lakeside. That was a scene she didn't even want to imagine, let alone actually stumble across. Yet she couldn't avoid the lake altogether, or she would surely get lost.

It was rather gloomy under the tree canopy so she switched on the torch to light up the path. She could smell, almost taste the astringent forest perfumes. She could still hear the occasional shouts and laughter from the young people at the margin of the lake but they were few and far between now, fading into the night. The frequent forest clearings were grassy, studded with glow worms and awash with midsummer light but, in general, the thick carpet of pine needles irritated her feet. However she never lost sight of the lake and frequently returned to it to check her bearings. She could still see Nortorrpet across the water, the sharp outlines of its gables black against the sky, and even a lighted dormer window. Finally she calculated that she was almost at her destination. She turned back through the trees once more and a few minutes later the small building she was searching for stood before her, knee deep in infant pine and wild blueberry bushes, silent, waiting. Wasakappellet. The Wasa Chapel.

Its wooden exterior was stark, forbidding, and a shudder took hold of Prue. All at once she felt truly alone, yet this was no time for faint-heartedness.

Giving herself a mental shake, she walked boldly up to the entrance. The door opened easily and silently with the key which she left in the lock. Before she'd even stepped inside, she was assailed by an odour, insidious, smoky, almost tangible and so strong she felt constrained to turn her head to gulp in a lung-full of fresh air before lifting her foot over the threshold. The smell was stale, indefinable. Incense, perhaps, lavender, certainly; essence of roses, old candles, lamp oil, mildew and rot.

It was dark inside the chapel. The stained glass windows were high up, admitting little illumination, so she flashed the torch around. In that same moment something small and fast scuttled across the floor and out of the door. Prue let out a small scream. Positively unnerved now, she was on the brink of turning tail and running.

A second later all misgivings were swept aside when the torchlight hit the wall and caught a flash of colours; blue, deep reds and yellow ochres - wall paintings. Her interest quickened and she aimed the torch more directly. She picked out Gothic lettering; dates; people in rich medieval costumes; a king wearing a crown - and then the wondrous gilded ship built of a thousand oaks: sails billowing and with more than sixty guns, the ill-fated vessel that, in the end, had proved too top heavy to float. Its name was written on its side. Wasa.

With growing excitement, Prue moved in closer, the better to examine these glorious pictures;

surroundings forgotten in the moment of discovery. It was dark now,juk but she vowed to return later, with a good camera even if she had to borrow one.

She let the torchlight glide along the wooden wall, where she discovered holders containing half-used candles and shelves of little pierced pots similar to nightlights. As her eyes slowly became accustomed to the dark, she identified soft brocade wall hangings which she fingered gently. Not centuries old, she estimated, more like several decades. The originals had no doubt rotted away and these would be replicas. Yet they in their turn were wearing away she realised, wrinkling her nose at the ensuing faint stench of mildew. Such a shame because they were beautifully done, depicting ships of the Swedish navy in the seventeenth century; sailors in their uniforms; a marching band; the king on his gold throne in royal regalia, scarlet, blue and ermine, with a crown on his head.

She couldn't say how much time had passed, so completely was she lost in this intriguing world of olden days when she heard a subdued noise in the silence - a slight, soft tread, hardly discernible. Prue gasped, her heart started thudding. Was there someone there? She couldn't be a hundred per cent sure yet with the unthinking reaction of self-preservation, she turned around and pointed the only weapon she had at the open door - the narrow beam of the torch.

Yes, a figure stood there; erect of stature, broad, a riot of heavy hair, silhouetted against the dusky light at the now gaping doorway. A marauder, a drunken reveller, a stranger intent on mischief? Her heart went into overdrive as she raised the beam of the torch to the intruder's face. Blinded, he jerked his head away, but in the depths of her being, she recognised him. How could she ever mistake this prince among men for anyone else! It was Torsten, of course. Sten Norberg.

# CHAPTER SEVEN

'Will you never stop meddling in affairs that don't concern you?' His voice cut through the darkness. 'This building ... it's the one place I never visit. I avoid it at all costs!'

'Why are you here, then? Nobody asked you to come!' Prue sliced back. Her voice shook slightly, but her confidence hadn't completely deserted her. So much for his earlier words of sweet reason. It certainly hadn't taken him long to get back into his old ways of attacking her without good cause.

'I distinctly remember telling you that you'd need a guide.' He was speaking through clenched teeth, his tone building up, stoking the furnace of his charges against her. 'You might have been tempted to light the candles. In case you hadn't noticed, this structure is built entirely of wood; the place is a tinder box that could easily turn into a death trap.'

'I'm not a smoker; I don't carry matches or a lighter.'

'You wouldn't see much then. Candles are the only illumination here. That's why you need an experienced guide.'

'People are all having such a good time tonight, making lots of noise, and I couldn't sleep. I was just so curious, I couldn't wait any longer. I'm sorry.' She had to acknowledge that she was the intruder here, not him. 'I couldn't ask Hildi to bring me because of her ankle. I didn't know where you were and I knew you wouldn't be keen to come with me anyway,'

'Pity,' he said. 'Hildi would have loved to show you around – and she'd have suggested coming across in the dinghy as I've just done. A rowing boat's not difficult to manage even if you're not used to it. The lake is very smooth.'

So this accounted for the fact that his white shirt was unbuttoned to the waist and why his knee-breeches were looking a little grubby – he'd been rowing across the lake.

'Well, apologies again,' she said, trying a more softly-softly approach. 'I'm truly sorry to have upset you. The Wasa is bound up with the Great Kate, so surely you understand why I've been dying to explore this place.'

As she pleaded her cause, she reminded herself she was a guest and rather a rude one at that. After all, earlier he'd mentioned that he'd taken on all the expenses of Norrtorpet, so it was only right that she should have consulted him before taking matters into her own hands. She really had no right to be here. Still, here she was and not prepared to leave without a struggle. 'Anyway, you might tell me why being in this wonderful chapel upsets you so.'

'That's my business! Now let's go!'

There was no answer to that. She picked up the shawl from where she'd left it on a small chair.

'I didn't mean to pry.' She tried to sound really contrite as he turned for the door. 'I know I'm being a nuisance but, all the same, I wish you'd let me explore a little now I'm here. I promise not to touch the candles.'

He whirled around. 'And how much do you expect to see with that silly little torch?'

'I'll be able to see enough!' Her heart lifted for in spite of the acidity of his retort, it seemed to indicate he might be caving in! 'How did you know I was here? I didn't tell a soul.'

He was suddenly beside her in the semi-dark and the sheer closeness of him made her head swim.

'I got back to Norrtorpet late after the concert, where incidentally I was still doing encores well after midnight. The fans didn't want to go home. Then I got tied up with friends and dismantling our equipment and making sure we left the field in a reasonably tidy condition,' he replied. 'The first thing I noticed was the key cupboard in the kitchen. The door was ajar. Then I guessed you were here, the key to the chapel wasn't on its usual hook.'

'You don't miss much,' she commented.

'In any case, you didn't seem to be in the house.'

'How could you know that?'

'I have to admit I'd been looking for you.'

He sounded quite matter of fact, but her stomach quivered at the notion.

'Whatever did you want me for?'

'Anna-Karin was asleep in your room so I tried the sitting room - the pine couch in there is often used as a spare bed.' His tone was still super-cool. 'I drew a blank yet I could tell you'd been sleeping there - the midsummer coronet was hanging over the chair back. I knew it was yours, I noticed the green ribbons.'

But, please, not his photograph on the chair!

'Someone had put a photo of me there, too,' he continued. 'Knowing my sister as I do, I guess that was her doing.'

'It certainly wasn't mine,' Prue confirmed quickly.

'So that's why I'm here. For one thing, somebody had to warn you about the candles.' A slight worry line appeared between his eyebrows. 'Incidentally Rolf was down at the lake with Ulrica and a few others. They had seen you going towards the chapel a bit earlier.'

Rolf and Ulrica together at the lake! So presumably Torsten had had no intention of spending Midsummer Eve with Ulrica, as Prue had assumed. A wave of relief and yes, joy swept over her as he continued speaking.

'I was worried and wanted to take the quickest route, so I opted for the canoe.'

'But wait a minute, you still haven't told me why you were looking for me.'

She tensed up and awaited his reply, her breath caught painfully somewhere between her ribs. He in his turn seemed relaxed and she noted that he'd found a piece of furniture, a cupboard, maybe, to lean back on.

'In Sweden many young couples make a big thing out of waiting to see the sun rise at midsummer. I thought that you and I could watch it together.'

A midsummer watch with the man of her dreams!

She hadn't even allowed herself to hope for such a romantic invitation.

'We can still do that,' she said with a breaking sigh. Her head was spinning with the implications of his suggestion, but her renewed expectations were cruelly shattered by his next words.

'We'll see. At least, it would be an experience for you, a memory of one of our Nordic traditions. Keeping a midsummer watch with a pagan Swede. Think how the tale would amuse your friends, intrigue your grandchildren. '

'I suppose so.' Acute disappointment drained her vitality. 'What time will that be?'

'Around three-thirty.'

Romance seemed to be the last thing on his mind after all, so reluctantly she put it out of hers. It would be sensible to change the subject.

'Do we have to go back just yet? Now you're actually here in the chapel, you could sort of supervise me if you're afraid I'll do some harm.'

'I've got my own reasons for disliking it here,' he said, his voice hard. 'This place does something to me, I loathe it!'

In the face of so much feeling, Prue's determination wavered. She mustn't forget her manners. In her enthusiasm, her selfish thirst for new knowledge, she had barged into something very private, and yet... if she capitulated now, he would lock the chapel forever and throw away the key.

'Whether you let me see it or not, I'll never get over the wonder of it, the uniqueness,' she murmured. 'A shrine to the Wasa, here, when she went down so far away, in Stockholm. The history behind it must be absolutely enthralling.'

'Women!' Torsten exploded, throwing up his hands in exasperation. 'Do you never give up? All right, since you've got me inside, and I swore never to set foot in here again, ever, let me give you the grand tour. You've badgered me into it!'

'Great!' Prue wasn't altogether surprised by his U-turn; it was what she'd been counting on.

'Lights!' he announced. 'We need lights, and lots of them!'

'But you've already told me that there are only candles here, and they are dangerous!' she pointed out.

'I am used to candles; I am a Swede after all – and I know where the fire extinguishers are stored. You'd never have found them in time if you were in a panic and surrounded by flames in a burning building you're not familiar with.'

With a sure tread he crossed the room in the darkness and began to move things about, opening drawers and boxes, searching. Prue shone the torch so he was better able to see what he was doing. A minute or two later he struck a match and from it lit a long taper.

'To be absolutely safe, the trick is never to leave a room empty with lighted candles in it,' he said. 'If there is nobody left in the room, put the candles out. Better safe than sorry.'

In the soft glow she could make out a small table,

candlesticks, and a carved wooden crucifix - the altar.

'Excellent!'

The taper gained in strength, and above it his face was taut, unsmiling, all sharp shadows - a Norse god in a Christian temple. It was a face suffused with strong, perhaps conflicting, thoughts.

The tense atmosphere increased her nervousness. Oddly enough, now she'd got her way she felt a little afraid and had no idea why.

'I didn't intend to harm anything,' she said. 'I'm quite used to treating antiquities with care and respect. After all, I work with them all day and every day. I didn't want to cause any trouble, only to have a quick look, and we don't have to stay long.' It was strange but the atmosphere of the chapel was starting to get to her, making her uneasy, nervous.

'Too late to back off,' he replied. 'I've made up my mind you shall see it all. You asked for it - you've got it! So, let's get on with it!'

So she stood aside, aware that a low, pulsating anger was now fuelling his movements. She'd been misguided ever to come here, pig-headed, and at this instant she suddenly wished she could leave and never look back; forget everything to do with the place. She sensed she'd stirred up a nest of hornets...

She put the shawl on the chair again. Switching off the torch she placed it by the door - the battery was giving out. Then she waited and watched, a hand nervously fingering her cheek. Her eyes followed his figure darting around, lighting candles and pottery oil lamps.

The small flames started to glow, endlessly flickering, growing and brightening, casting a soft aura over the chapel. Simultaneously, Prue wrinkled her nose at a subtle yet all-pervading new aroma.

'Can you smell the aromatic oils?' he asked. 'Jill, my late wife, had a passion for them. She believed strongly in the mystical power of exotic perfumes.'

His laugh was mirthless. He was plainly still very much affected by the loss of his beloved partner, Prue realised with an empathy that began to colour her recently jaundiced judgement of him. The next second every thought was knocked out of her head as the wall pictures began to come into focus, springing silently to life - ruby-reds; aquamarines; courtiers in blazingly beautiful costumes; gold leaf ornamentation. Prue gasped. Slowly she moved to the centre of the room, taking everything in, and her artistic spirit went out to the master painter who had created it all, maybe centuries ago.

She waved a hand to encompass the richness around her. 'All this must have been a great influence on Hildi when she was growing up.'

'It was,' he replied. 'From when she was a child she never wanted to do anything else but work with the Wasa. She steeped herself in its history, and it was certainly this that got her the job at the museum. Working in public relations suits her well. She's very gregarious.'

'It's so amazing,' Prue whispered, over-awed, as he put lights to yet more sconces. 'But why is it here?'

'Patience! I'm just going to show you.'

He walked over to her and placed his free hand in the small of her back to propel her forward to the opposite end of the room. There he swept aside an ornate tapestry to reveal a narrow archway, and through it a cosy alcove. In the alcove was a luxuriously-cushioned divan bed, upholstered in smooth deerskin. Again the light was meagre and he was already at the task of lighting more pottery vapourisers. They punctuated the alcove - on brackets and small gilt tables. A number of them stood on the floor and Prue was cautioned to watch where she was walking as she went round to examine a shelf that had caught her eye.

The fitment was crowded with bottles labelled with exotic names - ylang-ylang, armoise, camphor, jasmine absolute, melissa, petitgrain, sweet almond and many, many more. Then, as if pleading for recognition, on a panel above the divan, a painting came into view, almost into relief, with the increasing brightness. It was the likeness of a young man, life-size, six feet tall, maybe more. He wore a blue hat with a brim, blue shirt and navy blue breeches. If it was a uniform, it wasn't smart, perhaps just the garb of a lowly sailor. Below were a name and two dates.

'Anders Norberg, 1606 - 1628. ' Prue read the inscription out loud, suddenly aware of a lump in her throat. 'Only twenty-two when he died. So young, what a waste!'

'Anders Norberg was in the Swedish Navy, just an ordinary sailor as you can see by his plain clothing.

He was on board the Wasa when it went down. Many men drowned that day. Obviously the lad was a member of our family and they built this chapel to his memory. He happened to be betrothed to an accomplished artist. She spent the rest of her life doing this, decorating these walls. She never married.'

'How tragic, and how incredibly moving.'

'Yes, love of that quality is very rare.'

He seemed calmer now. The way he'd said it, his voice giving the words an extra dimension, a meaningful tenderness, made Prue look up at him. Had Torsten, too, experienced such a love, such a lifetime of commitment, reaching across the boundaries of death itself? It was an outdated notion but a romantic one, and it could be the reason why he hated coming here. He could be anxious to avoid any vivid reminders of the love he had lost, of his beloved Jill.

The atmosphere was emotionally charged. The heavy scents of the aromatic oils seemed to be seeping into Prue's very veins, affecting her mind even.

'I can't wait to tell my mum and my work colleagues about all this.' She spoke almost to herself. 'It's absolutely unbelievable.'

Having finished lighting the candles Torsten sat himself on the divan bed. He leaned back on his elbows while seeming to consider his next question carefully. His marvellous physique was in almost full view, his honed six-pack, the glistening hairs on his chest, all were revealed owing to his shirt buttons still being unfastened. Prue couldn't take her eyes away. Her insides had turned to jelly. She swallowed hard and took a deep breath, to try and control her emotions as he spoke again.

'When Hildi first mentioned you I got the impression you worked at the Mary Rose Museum in Portsmouth, but I understand I was wrong. So tell me about it.'

This was a new departure, a civilised discourse, at last. How temperamental he was, erratic.

'Oh, it's very similar to the story of the Wasa. The wreck is called 'Catherine Queen of the Waves' and I'm employed as chief illustrator. I make drawings of the artefacts the divers find on board the old ship. Oddly enough, drawings can show the details better than photographs. But that's enough about me, let's talk about you and your band, about *Scandinavia*.'

'You probably know it all, already. We have an excellent publicity machine, thanks to Ulrica.' He gave a little laugh.

'My mother will be thrilled to know I've actually met the great Sten Norberg. She loves your music, we both do.' Prue hesitated. 'The tune of the new song is very catchy. Er...did you write it for Ulrica?'

'Ulrica? No. She's an excellent road manager and we pretend to be in a relationship simply for the sake of my sanity.'

'Oh? How does that work?'

'There are so many females who want to attach themselves to a famous, wealthy, and I repeat, wealthy man. It's to send out the message to the fans that I am "spoken for". We ham it up for the media but in reality, Ulrica and I are just good friends.'

Just good friends. Wasn't that what they all said? Men could be as devious as women and Prue didn't quite know what to think, but she decided to trust his word. The world of show business was a mystery to her. 'At least she looked really pleased that you'd written something new.'

'I know. It is a while since we were in the music charts.' He got up from the divan. 'By the way, there's something else you might like to see.' Giving his wayward locks an impatient finger-flick he drew back a net curtain opposite the divan.

Another life-size painting was revealed. A blonde angel with braids round her head, strangely compelling. The face was beautiful with large blue eyes, and notwithstanding her gentle smile, Prue received the impression of inestimable sadness.

'That's the artist herself,' Torsten explained. 'People say she's the image of my wife, although Jill's hair was darker. Would you agree with that?'

Sensing a pressure in his words, she was a little confused. 'I'm sorry. I do recall reading about the dreadful accident she had. In Spain, wasn't it? But I'm sure I've never seen a photograph of your wife.' She fell silent, hoping she hadn't exposed a nerve in him.

'Of course, I'd forgotten her photograph was suppressed. I have Ulrica to thank for that. She took control of everything at the time. No photographs of Jill were released to the press, out of respect for the privacy of my wife's family, and mine. Ulrica even tried to suppress the story altogether, but that wasn't possible.'

'Hurrah for Ulrica,' said Prue, rather lamely. 'But what do you think? Does the angel remind you of your wife?'

'There's a likeness,' he replied. 'Although Jill looked different, of course…'

So that was probably the reason why the painting was now hidden behind the curtain. It would have been common talk among family and friends, the likeness of the angel to his beautiful wife. Someone – maybe Ulrica – must have realised that, as such, the sight of the painting was not welcome to him, and organised the net fabric to cover it up.

Prue relaxed a little. 'She must've been stunning then, your Jill. I can see now why this chapel is such a painful reminder for you.'

'Yes, that's one thing I can say for my wife. She was beautiful, more than beautiful. Magnetic, with an insatiable appetite for… life.'

He returned to the divan. Looking down on it, he gave a little gasp and picked up a small object that had been lying there unnoticed, till now. It was tiny, and as he held it up close to the light, he sucked air in between his teeth while he examined it. He then pushed it into the pocket of his breeches before sitting down, his expression grim.

Prue rested her back against the wall. 'You shouldn't go on letting your tragic loss upset you. Try to be grateful you knew great happiness once. It's a precious gift not given to many. I'm sure Jill wouldn't want you go through the rest of your life suffering, prolonging your bitterness.'

He was up in a bound, drawing himself up to his full height, dwarfing everything around him.

'Don't be so damn patronising!' he thundered. 'What do you know about us, about Jill and me? Nothing!" His instant frenzy was terrifying in that small space. The candle flames wavered unsteadily, and even the very walls seemed to shudder. 'Please keep your opinions to yourself!'

Thoroughly alarmed, Prue recoiled from this verbal attack. The blistering, uncalled-for words pierced her mind like sword thrusts. Her heart hammered. What on earth had happened to wind him up like this? Was the scented, insidiously intoxicating atmosphere affecting him? She'd heard about these hot oils, heard they were powerful mood enhancers. Now she came to think about it, she felt more than a little drunk herself, yet kind of overwrought, dizzy, all at the same time.

Indeed, the alcove had become overlaid with a glowing apricot-orange light, plus the pungency of many blended aromas, and a definite mist hung in the air. At the centre of it all, Torsten loomed, magnificent, features full of anguish, tormented by some immense inner grief.

Her blood racing, Prue's eyes quickly scanned her surroundings for an escape route in the face of such towering anger. Unfortunately, Torsten was standing in front of the narrow arched entrance to the alcove, cutting off her one point of retreat. She had to go through the archway, only then she would be able to leave the chapel. She knew he wouldn't follow her because, by his own account, he had every last candle to douse before he dare leave the building.

'See what you've let yourself in for by getting me over here?' his voice rasped.

'I never wanted to get you involved, you know I didn't.' She took a fortifying breath, the better to lance him with her own temper. 'You'll find I'm not so easily intimidated, not even by a spoilt media star like you. Now, if you'll just stand aside, I'd like to leave.'

'Oh, yes, you want to run away now you've made your mischief, do you? Typical!'

'What are you talking about? Let me pass, please!'

He stood, rock solid, as she tried to squeeze by him.

'Not so fast, miss. You wanted this experience. You shall have it. There's more to see, much more.' He reached out and took her shoulder. 'I insist you...'

'I've seen all I want to, thank you,' she interrupted him, dodging out of his grasp and trying once more to escape through the opening.

She managed to step into the archway, and then she heard tearing. When she looked behind, there were further ripping sounds. Dear heaven, another catastrophe! How much more could she take?

'Now look what you've made me do! The dress - it's not mine, and it's caught on something!' The culprit was a nail in the wood lining the archway. She levered the material off as carefully as she could in the circumstances, but the damage was done. 'Whatever will Hildi say?'

'Trouble all round, aren't you, Miss Claybourne? Accident-prone as well as pushy; a walking disaster area! Goodness only knows why I can't stop wanting to kiss you.'

'Don't you dare!' she spat at him.

Yet it was strange, a curious thing, but he posed no physical threat. She felt it in her bones. Somehow she knew he'd made up his mind not to touch her. There would be no kisses, mocking or otherwise. It was something to do with this place. The whole time they'd been here, he'd been careful to maintain a distance between them, he never even came close. Despite this, she didn't deserve such a tongue-lashing. Into the bargain he'd caused her to spoil Hildi's lovely frock by being awkward when she wished to leave.

'You're a little spitfire!' he snapped at her, but he stood aside and made no more attempts to stop her as she walked through into the main chapel and out through the door.

Her head was singing, her veins and arteries flooded with fumes from the perfumed oils in the atmosphere. Indeed she was so light-headed that she stumbled a little on the path when she was outside. Aware of the lake nearby, she slowly headed in its direction. She would be able to find her way better if she walked back to Norrtorpet along the shore line.

Away from the aromatic perfumes of the chapel, thankfully, her head was beginning to clear.

As she approached the lake shore, she tripped in the undergrowth several times, but she was soon there and turned in the direction of the summer house. There were merry-makers about still, singing occasionally, shouting. She would have to keep a sharp lookout as she didn't want to meet up with any of them. The lake stretched away into the distance, calm and black under a night sky that wasn't quite dark. The sun had set around half past ten, she knew. It would rise again about three thirty in the morning, Torsten had said.

Slowly, in the freshening breeze, the last of the strange toxic perfumes that had invaded her bloodstream, cleared away. Prue stopped to examine Hildi's dress more thoroughly in the half-light. There was quite a large tear in the skirt at the back, she could feel it, and a couple of inches at the waist had come unstitched. In addition, her stumbling through the undergrowth had stained the pristine white. It looked to be beyond repair, symbolising her dreams, her wishful thoughts, now all in ruins. Covering her face with her hands she sank to the ground, unsuccessfully trying to hold back the tears.

She heard his footsteps even before he spoke.

'You left the torch behind.' His tones were surprisingly moderate as he approached her. 'And I brought this with me. I thought you might need it.' He was carrying the shawl.

Goodness, yes, she'd forgotten the borrowed

torch and shawl, and the wind was quite chilly now. Prue squeezed her eyelids together - she wouldn't let him see her crying.

'So I'm a beast, am I?' He came up to stand over her. 'You're so right. Please accept my profound apologies. I'm not myself in the chapel. It's a house of God but also a place of evil - sacred and profane.'

Astounded by his complete change of attitude, Prue wiped her eyes and made no reply. Although his referral to the chapel being a place of evil made her agog to know more, to ask him to explain, she had determined never to speak to him again. He was contemptible, monstrous, all the horrible names she could think of; a self-centred, volatile man. And yet, to be fair, he had just apologised really nicely and she couldn't deny that she was relieved to see him. She hadn't realised how lonely she'd felt in a strange place, in the middle of the night. She gave a little shudder.

'Oh, here, you're cold.' He draped the shawl round her shoulders, letting his fingers linger.

This brought on another bout of crying. Recognising the tears for what they were, self-pity, she tried to stem them on the skirt of the damaged dress.

'Is something wrong?' His voice was tinged with concern.

'Wrong? You could say that! What do you expect?' she blurted out between sobs, forgetting both her vow not to give way to tears, and her vow not to speak to him. 'I've never been treated like that before. Never! Blaming your atrocious behaviour on the atmosphere in the chapel is oh, so easy. Cowardly!'

He sighed gustily. 'There are things you don't know about, things I can never, ever bring myself to talk about. Certain... events have left their mark on the building; sights which have affected me deeply. I lost control in there just now. It was unforgivable, I know.' He made a half-turn towards the nearby beach. 'Time to go. The dinghy's over there.'

'I got here by myself,' said Prue. 'I'll find my own way back, thank you.'

He'd started to walk off through the trees, but now he returned.

'Don't be difficult, Prue.' He bent to take her hand, gently but firmly, and pulled her to her feet. 'Be sensible. I can't leave you here alone. The woods are alive with guys who've taken more *brannvin* than is good for them. Listen!'

His statement was confirmed by distant raucous laughing and frequent shouts ringing through the air.

Finding her hand was still in his, Prue snatched it away. 'A bodyguard is the last thing I need, thank you.'

He gave an exasperated sigh. 'What about our midsummer watch? It's time. Look, the sun!'

Majestic, he stood in the dawn light gazing over to where a blaze of brilliance was edging up from behind the forest screen. His face was stilled like a sculpture, his head held high, the cheekbones hazed by a flush of excitement.

She stood beside him and followed his gaze, catching her breath at the glorious spectacle of the rising sun. Vivid bands of apricot, gold, amethyst and apple green stretched across the midsummer sky. Her artist's eye saw it all as a wide canvas of sheer heart-stopping magic.

'We did it,' he murmured finally. 'Together we watched the sunrise.'

Birds were beginning to twitter, insects flitted clumsily past. The scent of pine was strong and heady while he stood, motionless as if in a trance, long back erect, worshipping. His profile was unmoving, his hair stirred in the dawn wind. Down the centuries this tradition had been kept alive by lovers, maybe even by Anders Norberg and his beautiful angel. Prue had an instant mental image of the two of them, perhaps at this very spot. Standing here, at Torsten's side, sharing the wonder of the dawn and being part of it, suddenly she felt that she belonged. It was a good feeling.

'Do you know what lovers are doing all over Sweden tonight, Prudence?' His voice was little more than a husky whisper. 'Can't you feel it in the air? They're making love.'

There was a catch in his throat as he faced her, his hair backlit against the sky. His mouth was only a breath away.

Prue trembled, profoundly affected by his words. 'I should've guessed Sweden was a romantic place, *Scandinavia*'s songs are all about love. I imagine Rolf never thinks about anything else!'

Betrayed by a primal sweetness in her loins, she waited eagerly, but the kiss she had anticipated did not come. In a flash his expression changed. It was as if her feeble attempt at humour had triggered off a thought and the spell was broken. Frowning, he reached into the pocket of his breeches and brought out a small object, no doubt the one he'd picked up earlier from the divan inside the chapel. He studied the tiny thing with displeasure in his face, loathing even. Then, abruptly, he turned on his heel and marched off towards the canoe which was beached further along the lake shore.

'Kom, Prudence, time for bed!'

He threw the instruction over his shoulder and with a sigh, she hurried after him.

# CHAPTER EIGHT

One thing was certain; Torsten was too temperamental by half. Prue felt sorry for any female who got entangled with him. How could any sane person keep up with his changes of mood?

When she arrived at the canoe he helped her to climb aboard and settle into the seat. Then he pushed the boat off the beach, jumped into his own seat and began rowing towards Norrtorpet. The journey passed in silence. When they landed, he beached the boat and tied it to a tree while Prue went up to the house and made straight for the sitting room. There, she collapsed onto the couch and wrapped herself in the blanket. She hoped for sleep to claim her immediately.

In the morning she aroused slowly and the first thing that came into focus was the torch beside her pillow. Her midsummer coronet had gone but her blue lapis lazuli beads were hanging over the back of the chair. They had been re-strung. Prue gave a little cry, sat up and picked them up. Every last bead was there and, shining in the morning light, they looked beautiful. What a kind thought! It must have taken Torsten an age to locate the lost beads in the music room. Next to the necklace was a message on a slip of paper:

*Hope these are O.K. I am looking forward to seeing you wear them again. Aunt Agnetha has re-strung them for you.*

*Please forgive me for everything. I am not a perfect human being. T.N.D.'*

How could she resist such an endearing apology? Memories of the previous night were crowding in, the midsummer watch, the abrupt and disappointing ending. He was a flawed character, spoiled in many ways, but most of the time he meant well. She was getting rather used to it.

Seeing her beads again had cheered Prue up immensely. She would find Torsten and thank him and she mustn't forget to thank the stalwart Aunt Agnetha, too. She was a lovely lady and every family should have such an auntie!

'Midsommardag' was one of Sweden's flag days and, glancing through the window Prue saw that somebody had raised the yellow-and-blue national flag on the pole next to the apple tree in the garden. It hung there proudly, ruffled by the breeze. Yes, today was a day to be happy, and Prue decided she would be!

She'd slept soundly until she was woken up by a disturbance. Angry male voices engaged in a full-blown row somewhere in the house, but it didn't last long and it was almost time to get up anyway.

As she tidied up the make-shift bed, she reminded herself that she should find the time to make some notes on her laptop today to record her impressions of the Wasa Chapel and the story of Anders Norberg - but at this moment her first task was to fetch something decent to wear from her luggage upstairs. She found a summery green top which she teamed with one of Hildi's short skirts, a dark green one which fitted her surprisingly well. She also took great delight in wearing her newly strung beads. Then, anxious to look her best, she brushed her hair and put on a little eye make-up and coral lipstick. Her second task was to summon up the courage to confess the shame of the ruined dress to Hildi.

To get the ordeal over, she brought it up over breakfast, which was a help-yourself affair in the garden. She joined her friend who was standing by the table, in the shade of a tree.

'Everyone seemed to be in the woods so I thought I would see what was happening. Unfortunately I fell over, more than once,' she lied. 'I can't apologise enough, Hildi. Of course, I'll pay for another dress - if it can be replaced.'

She hadn't mentioned the Wasa Chapel because she didn't think Torsten would want her to talk about it. It was a feeling she had. Just a guess.

Surprisingly enough, Hildi just laughed, obviously not at all upset about the damage. 'Silly girl, it is midsummer, everyone's clothes get spoiled.' She winked at Aunt Agnetha who had just come out of the house. 'That dress has been mended a few times before, I can tell you.'

Prue was much relieved to hear her words.

'Now, please take a dish and fill it up, then eat!' Hildi went on. 'Did you, by any chance, go on a midsummer watch?'

Prue nodded.

'With Torsten?'

She nodded again.

Hildi's face broke into smiles. 'Then you are completely forgiven.'

Prue gave her friend a warm hug and then went over to the buffet table to help herself to a mug of coffee. She still felt guilty about the dress, but it was time to say 'thank you' for the re-stringing of the lapis lazulis.

She turned to Aunt Agnetha, who was piling up her plate with cold meats, cheese, bread, and fruit chutney. 'I'm so grateful and you are such a clever lady. Is there anything you can't do?'

Agnetha, in a white-and-peach trouser suit this morning, smiled in her sweet-natured way. 'I like to do hand crafts. I am glad you wear beads today.'

Prue smiled back at her and took a little of the cold, sliced pork, a hard-boiled egg and a sweet bread roll onto her plate. Everything looked delicious.

Aunt Agnetha found a seat at the table, while Prue joined Hildi. They sat down nearby.

'We are a bit backwards... I mean, behind with the wedding thanks to my little mishap, but Torsten will entertain you, I'm sure.' Hildi sent Prue a meaningful glance.

Her friend must have jumped to all the wrong conclusions about the night's events, thought Prue. She herself hardly knew where she stood with Torsten and in the full light of day she would have to give the matter some consideration. One fact came over loud and clear, and that was that Torsten was still besotted with his poor deceased wife. From her own wishful thinking, Hildi had clearly come to the conclusion that Torsten and Prue were now an item.

If only... She tightened her lips, resignedly. We shall see what we shall see, she mused. Anything could happen, and usually did. Life never really went according to plan.

Family and friends were still in noisy evidence at the leisurely meal that was really 'brunch', and they meandered in and out of the garden and house, or sat about, eating, talking, and laughing in the sunshine. Prue was only half listening to the chat, though. She was alert for one person and one person only. He must be around, somewhere, because his car was still on the drive.

'I wanted to show you Wasakappellet, but I'm too afraid I shall fall over.' Hildi pointed to her bandaged foot and shrugged. 'I very much wanted to take you myself, but I'm going to ask Torsten to give you a tour instead. I just know you'll love our hidden treasure in the woods.'

Prue didn't know what to say to that. She took a bite of her breakfast roll then ventured. 'I saw the chapel yesterday, and Torsten showed me round. I was so overwhelmed that I am absolutely lost for words. I'm going to record everything I saw on my computer before I forget. My colleagues at The Trust will want every detail. My mother will too, not to mention my friend, Claire.'

'Oh, great! Torsten never goes to the chapel these days, I don't know why, so I'm glad he went with you.' Hildi's eyes scanned the group of people in the garden. 'I haven't seen him this morning? Have you?'

Even as Hildi spoke, the strains of music that were just starting to pour forth from the studio told their own story.

Prue changed the subject. 'I've borrowed one of your skirts.'

'And you look nice and summery. I'm so pleased you're able to use some of my things. Wear whatever you like.'

'I'd like to do some painting later.' Prue glanced up into the sky. 'The light here is so special, so clear - a painter's light.'

'That's good. I don't wish you to be bored.'

Not much danger of that, thought Prue. Torsten must have had breakfast very early this morning. She ached to see her 'not perfect human being' as he'd described himself so touchingly in his note. At least, she knew where he was. She could still hear the music from what was plainly a rehearsal going on in the studio. It was odd, really, because she'd seen Rolf wander down the garden, not five minutes ago, and wondered why he wasn't rehearsing with the other two. It was then that she recalled the heated exchange that had woken her earlier. Men's voices. Had Rolf been involved in that, with another band member? Torsten, maybe?

When Hildi had finished her breakfast, she began to stack some of the used crockery on a tray.

Prue got up to assist. 'Leave this to me, Hildi, you should be resting.'

Hildi laughed. 'I am quite well, truly, but you can carry the tray if you like, I might drop it.'

So they cleared up together, walking back and forth to the scullery and round the sunlit garden, chatting and joking, as Prue was introduced to new arrivals. She also said 'Hello' to Ulrica and stopped to talk to Herr and Fru Dahlgren and Anna-Karin.

There were plenty of willing helpers in the scullery, washing the dishes, or drying them. Yet all the while, as she socialised and engaged with the extended Dahlgren family and friends, Prue was listening intently. The moment the music stopped she started to scan the doors anxiously, her heart beating its own tattoo. When the music started again she felt so disappointed. She was just longing for the sight and sound, the feel, of this outrageous, brilliant, lovable person who, in spite of their ups-and-downs, had irrevocably taken possession of her heart.

More 'help yourself' food was prepared for later by Fru Dahlgren; herring, salmon, salads and cold vegetable dishes, just in case anyone felt peckish in the afternoon. Then suddenly Hildi, in the process of putting wine to chill on the tiled larder floor, looked at her watch and said something in Swedish.

'Mamma and I have to visit with the dressmaker and she is a very busy lady,' she explained to Prue. 'It's time we went. We mustn't be late as it is very good of her to see us today. I think I mentioned it to you earlier. We had to cancel the appointment with her last week because I was in hospital.'

'I imagine all businesses are closed at Midsummer,

all the shops,' observed Prue.

'Most of them are, but some shops will open for a short time. Many restaurants and cafes don't close at all, of course. I must go and find Didrik. He will drive us there. We're leaving Aunt Agnetha in charge while we're away. If there's anything you want, you can ask her.'

Prue walked Hildi, her mother and Didrik to the Saab, at the same time returning the borrowed torch that now held a new battery. Ulrica came running up at the last minute, shouting out in Swedish about Gustavskrona. Prue knew Ulrica's car was having a repair at the garage and guessed she was asking for a lift. She gave her a smile. Ulrica smiled back and Prue was struck again by the classic beauty of the road manager. How glad she was that Ulrica's relationship with Torsten was merely a pretend romance for public consumption only.

Eventually the lack of sleep was catching up on Prue. She trudged back to the house and up the steps to the scullery, massaging the back of her neck, in desperate need of an aspirin and a bit of shut-eye. There were a few people in the kitchen including Rolf, who was drinking coffee at the table.

'Good morning, Rolf. You're not rehearsing with the others, then?'

All the reply she got was a scowl. Rolf's head shook slightly as if he were drunk or angry, or maybe both. The movement caused his earrings to glint as they caught the light. Two of them, for a change - so he'd matched up his single stud with its twin.

Without even looking at her, he polished off his drink and banged his mug on the table as if it disgusted him. 'You go Wasakapellet? No?'

'Yes,' she answered. 'Divine place. Unique, a real gem.'

'Maestro, he hate it. Did he tell you about secret thing there? No? Still he not talk about it. Ha ha!'

Rolf stamped off into the hall and up the stairs.

Totally taken aback, Prue watched him through the door he had left ajar. Obviously the man wasn't having a good day. She opened a kitchen cupboard. Now where was the aspirin?

Rolf's words stayed with her however. What could be the secret that Torsten wouldn't talk about? With her own eyes she'd seen that being in the chapel had profoundly upset him, angered him even. He'd made that clear. It brought back too many memories of his beloved wife and Prue could understand and appreciate such depth of feeling. He'd made one strange remark though - he'd referred to the chapel as both sacred and profane. That, Prue could not fathom, it didn't seem to make any sense whatsoever. But one thing she did know: Torsten was a 'one woman man.'

Yes, it seemed that he fancied a summer romance with Prue; he was male after all. Yet it would be a passing flirt, a brief affair that would bloom and die within a short space of time. That was the last thing Prue was looking for. She longed for love that would last a lifetime. She craved Torsten's love and a permanent commitment, not a holiday fling. With these matters lying heavily on her mind, she went upstairs to try and catch up on her sleep.

After a short but restorative nap in the bedroom with the dolls' house, her headache had largely gone. If only she could empty her mind of unpleasant thoughts as easily. She'd also managed to have a strip-wash, being now quite practised at heating up water and coping with the old fashioned jug-and-basin set in the bedroom. The shampooing of her hair could wait, she decided, as she combed it into a becoming frame for her face. The Swedish summer air seemed to suit it.

She took up a 'painting position' at the far end of the garden, making herself comfortable on one of the picnic rugs left out for guests to use. She'd worked out that, from this spot, she would be visible from many windows in the house and that Torsten would see her easily. Suspicious as she was about his motives, that his interest in her would be just a passing thing, she was still obsessed with him. She couldn't help it. What was that common expression, 'the spirit is willing but the flesh is weak?' That saying fitted her current situation very well. She felt cross with herself, yet she couldn't resist him. The music had ceased and she wondered where he was at this moment. A few friends and family sat about the garden, two groups playing board games. They waved to her and she waved back.

For a while she busied herself measuring up the house, drawing it, sketching in a few trees and shrubs. She had mixed up some burnt umber and started to fill in the outlines when a taxi drove up and hooted. She paused and watched, curious. Was it a new guest or Ulrica returning? Was it here to pick somebody up?

The mystery was soon solved. Rolf, loaded down with suitcase and guitar, came out of the house, bad-temperedly kicking aside the ramp provided for Gunnar's wheelchair. Without so much as a 'Goodbye' to anyone, he climbed into the taxi and was whisked away.

Prue frowned, curious about Rolf's departure, yet she saw that she had problems enough of her own right now. For a start, several small insects had crawled onto her wet painting. She was an idiot; she shouldn't be sitting so close to the bushes. In addition, the impressionistic study of the house didn't please her anyway. It simply wasn't good enough. She tore the picture up and went to retrieve her laundry which she'd earlier put into the washing machine.

When Hildi and Didrik returned a couple of hours later, Torsten and Gunnar appeared for the first time that day. Prue had dealt with her washing, hanging it on the clothes line in the drying area outside. Now she was involved in preparing chicken for Flying Jacob - the dish Hildi was going to cook for their evening meal. Hildi had described the process and Prue had been delighted to hear about a new and interesting recipe. So she'd been working hard, removing the skin and bones from the cooked chicken and slicing it up into small pieces and putting it in a bowl. She placed the chicken in the fridge beside the chili sauce and cream that would also be part of the dish. Some of the other ingredients, bananas and peanuts were ready in the pantry. After washing her hands she set about frying the bacon, her ears straining, heart fluttering. She was conscious of Torsten as he went about the house, could hear his voice, talking to the others in Swedish about Rolf. This seemed to indicate that Torsten knew of Rolf's departure.

The kitchen door opened and she knew straight away it was him. At long last he was here. Prue deliberately didn't look round but continued to cook the small squares of bacon so they were crisp but not burnt, collecting them in a pile on a plate lined with kitchen paper. She was aware Torsten was watching her.

'So busy.' He said at last and coming up behind her, moved her hair to plant a lingering kiss on the back of her neck. 'And you're wearing your beads.'

Startled, thrilled, melting inside, she took the pan from the heat and had to remind herself sternly that it was merely the great and spoilt Sten Norberg, who was conferring his favours on her, knowing that no female in her right mind could resist. But he'd mentioned the beads, and yes, she mustn't forget her manners. She turned to him.

'Thank you so much for getting my beads repaired.' Lightly, she touched them with her fingertips. 'I thanked Aunt Agnetha this morning - so kind of you both.'

'My pleasure.' He put his arms round her in a big hug. 'Now I have work of my own to do. We, Gunnar and I, have lost our guitar player. I have to make some phone calls to find a new one.'

'Rolf,' she said, to confirm that she already knew something was going on.

'He's gone and good riddance. I know some excellent session musicians so finding a new guitarist shouldn't be a problem - but it's more than urgent.'

He released Prue but held her face in his hands for a moment or two. How could she stand this? He was wearing a fawn, shadow-checked shirt with slim, matching trousers, all recently ironed, and smelled so fresh. Drowning with love and longing, she told herself she must stay strong.

'How are you feeling?' he went on. 'I was so weary after last night I fell asleep in the studio. Gunnar did, too.'

'Gunnar was tired?'

'Yes, he was up in the early hours.' Torsten turned his blue-dark gaze on Prue, eyes glinting with mischief. 'And in case you're asking, he hasn't got a girlfriend right now, but he stayed up late, playing cards with our neighbours. They live across the road.'

As Hildi came into the room, he helped himself to a piece of bread and creamy Swedish cheese from one of the dishes in the fridge then left.

Hildi's face wore a beaming smile as she took the rest of the buffet food out of the fridge and put it on a tray to take outside. 'Prudence, you have prepared dinner! All I have to do now is find a big casserole dish.' She wagged a finger. 'Naughty girl, you are not here to work, you are a guest!'

'And you are injured and are doing too much.'

Prue held her hand up meaningfully and the friends gave each other a high five after which they both collapsed into laughter.

'Torsten was just telling me about Gunnar. He likes to play cards with your neighbours,' Prue said as they recovered from their mirth.

'He does. When they can't find him, he's always with Stina and Stig.' Hildi handed her the tray. 'If you could take these outside just in case anyone is hungry, please. I will bring the elderflower cordial.'

In the garden Gunnar's sister was with the family, playing Trivial Pursuit. Prue was invited to join the game which she was happy to do. She assumed Torsten was busy trying to locate a guitar player. The group wanted to make a recording of the new song soon, so time was of the essence.

Later they had dinner, and the Flying Jacob was judged a great success. Unsurprisingly, Hildi had placed Prue next to Torsten at table. So near and yet so far, because they hardly had the opportunity to speak a word to each other – everyone wanted to know how the rehearsals were coming along. To Prue's great pleasure Torsten announced to the assembled company that he had the choice of two very good guitarists to replace Rolf, and they were to meet up and rehearse together very shortly. The guests looked puzzled, not being aware that Rolf had left *Scandinavia*. Indeed there was a clamour to find out what had been going on. Torsten however was giving nothing away, nor was Gunnar. A few minutes later the two men excused themselves from the dining table and went off to do more rehearsing.

Prue followed them with her eyes. What had Rolf done that had been so drastic, just when they were set to make a new recording? It was a mystery.

A little later, in the long light evening and trying to throw off feelings of dejection, Prue wandered out into the garden to the clothes line to check her laundry. As half expected, it wasn't yet dry. So, on impulse, she sat down on the nearby swing under an apple tree where she could hear the honeyed, throaty sound of Torsten's singing voice. The recently-composed love song now seemed to be honed to perfection. She closed her eyes and swung easily back and forth to its pulsating rhythm, head thrumming with its insistent refrain. Over the last two days the music had worked itself into her brain patterns. Drowsily she began to hum along.

'You approve of the new song, then?' Torsten came up and sat on a nearby bench.

Her eyes flicked open and she stopped humming, while the melody continued in the studio on Gunnar's concertina.

'It's... um... lovely. The tune is beautiful, and so are the words.' If only she knew who they were meant for! 'It'll be a Top Ten hit, I'm sure of it.'

When he smiled, she realised how worn out he was. His face was drained with the effort of creativity and lack of sleep, his eyes bruised with shadows, and his skin waxy with fatigue.

'You're very generous,' he said and sniffed the air. 'It's nice and cool out here; it gets so stuffy in the studio.'

He snapped off a grassy stalk, chewed on it thoughtfully, companionably, and she wondered what it was about him that even in this tree-shaded spot he seemed to glow, to be surrounded by his own aura, a sort of splendour. Just looking at him brought on a feeling she could not name. This was history repeating itself, although right now they were good friends. She was not only hopelessly in love with him, she also liked him. So this was that elusive feeling. It wasn't just lust but Love with a capital 'L.'

No doubt, to him she was still just a passing English tourist, a light interlude in his exciting life. Nonetheless, she told herself to enjoy this moment of peace, calm and companionship.

'You must excuse me,' she said. 'I think it's about my bedtime.'

She made to rise from the swing but in a split second he'd moved towards her, steadying the rope with one hand. With the other he caught her at the back of her head, holding her firmly.

The stalk of grass fell to the ground as he whispered, 'Not just yet. Stay awhile, let's...'

His face was close, his lips slightly parted, seductively so. This time, however, she was ready for him. It was not 'Playtime with Prudence' again. If he'd wanted her, there'd been a time when he could have taken her in the proper manner. Only last night in the forest, she'd been in a fever of joy for him. Yet, what had he done? He'd remembered something in his pocket; something not shared with her, and then stalked off with no explanation. The same sort of thing could easily happen tonight if she yielded. In any case, she didn't want to be just another notch on his bedpost. Enough was enough, she had her pride.

'No!' She jerked her head back, shaking free of his clutch.

'Prudence, please…'

'I'm grateful for my beads and I was thrilled to see the inside of the chapel.' Her words were measured, dignified. 'But this is as far as I go. Friendship. Not just another conquest for the great Sten Norberg. I'm sorry. It's never been my intention to lead you on. This has been a fantastic experience for me, unique. I love your sister, in fact, I love all your family and I'll never forget these last few days.'

Having delivered her heart-felt speech, Prue dodged out of the way of his reaching arms, ran across the lawn and up to her room with its comforting little dolls, and flung herself on the bed. Despite her brave words, she felt her world had ended. When her breathlessness had finally begun to subside, a series of sharp rhythmic sounds could be heard from the garden below. Curiosity drew her to the window.

Torsten was arched over the silver birch logs; arms raised high in the act of swinging an axe up, then down, splitting the wood, fiercely, but with the accuracy and ease of long practice. Frustration was spelled out in the set of his jaw, the clamped line of his mouth. This all seemed to indicate that he was not used to being thwarted, turned down. Oh well, there was a first time for everything, she supposed, and his temporary irritation was nothing compared with her own anguish, her shattered dreams.

Even so, half mesmerised, she watched him, fascinated, as he attacked the logs with total disregard for any damage that might be caused to his precious hands. At this moment, he was a Swede through and through, a natural lumberjack, a creature of the forests. A stain of fresh sweat was spreading into the front of his fawn shirt and across the swell of his shoulders as he kept up the murderous pace, passion unleashed. For the umpteenth time she pondered on the dark secret connected with the chapel and hinted at by Rolf before he left. Would she ever discover what it was?

The next morning, Torsten and Gunnar left the house early. While she was brushing her teeth, Prue caught sight of them driving off in their separate cars. It was Monday, a small yellow van drove up to return the drum set that had been used at the festival in Lunneby, and Hildi went off to keep an appointment with her doctor. Aunt Agnetha and Anna-Karin had gone home the previous evening so Prue sat, undisturbed, in the peaceful garden. From here she could see a new pile of split logs stacked, shoulder high, the full length of the back wall.

She worked there and afterwards at the lakeside,

until she'd produced a set of water colours of the house and its surroundings which satisfied her. They had to be just perfect before she would present them to the bride and groom, to Hildi and Didrik. It took her all of the morning and most of the afternoon, but when the couple turned up later, the pictures were complete, mounted and framed. She had no proper wrapping paper, but she did have some pristine tissue paper in her luggage.

Hildi and Didrik both enthused over Prue's gift.

'They're lovely,' said Hildi. 'All your own work, too, and you've signed them.'

'We shall treasure them,' Didrik put in, a smile on his chubby face. 'What a day we're having, a wonderful wedding present, and the doctor is very pleased with Hildi's progress. So we're going to sacrifice one of the bottles of wine we've been saving for the wedding.'

'Yes.' Hildi grinned. 'We are in the mood to celebrate.'

The three of them spent a happy evening together, chattering and laughing. Prue grilled some Baltic halibut while Hildi dressed the salad. A bottle of Chablis was opened and they toasted one another, but Prue couldn't help wishing that Torsten was here as well.

'I expect your brother and Gunnar are busy today,' she said, casually.

Hildi nodded. 'They went to Ulrica's flat to interview the guitar-players. I know they won't be back for dinner tonight. Ulrica has invited them all to stay for a meal.'

Prue could see that was thoughtful of Ulrica. She obviously didn't want to burden Hildi with any more entertaining, especially so near the wedding day. It was Ulrica's gain, too. She never seemed to like being far from Torsten. However, Prue reminded herself firmly, the relationship between Torsten and Ulrica was definitely not any of her business from now on. Hadn't she made her position abundantly clear? She was definitely not the kind of girl who went in for one-night stands, not even with Sweden's great hero composer, thank you very much!

She held up her glass for a refill. 'Does anybody know what happened to Rolf?'

'He had to go home because his father was taken ill,' said Didrik. 'That's what Torsten told us. Rolf's parents live in Karlstad, a long way from here.'

Prue wondered about that. If it was true, she was sad for him. Somehow she doubted it though. His behaviour before his departure indicated anger, not sorrow.

After the meal was cleared away, Hildi suggested a game of Monopoly. Prue smiled. Swedish Monopoly - that would make an interesting change. The Swedes liked their board games and they liked to eat 'al fresco', that much she had learned about her new Scandinavian friends.

Preparations for the wedding were now well under way and during the following days early guests started to arrive at the summer house, from Visby and from

Gothenburg. Prue found herself the centre of much interest among the new arrivals, which didn't displease her. Yet, underneath, she felt dismal and there was a tight knot in her stomach that wouldn't go away.

Torsten was absent and this should have been an excellent thing for now she dreaded seeing him. It should be a case of out of sight, out of mind yet to be honest absence was making the heart grow fonder. She missed him like crazy. Yes, the passionate longing was there too, underneath, barely below the surface.

She took off one morning, alone, with her field set; painting boards and sandwiches of smoked salmon with cream cheese. The day was fine; indeed, the weather in Sweden had come as a pleasant surprise to her. She'd heard that the summers were generally short but she'd found that the days were often settled with hours of sunshine and endless birdsong. As it turned out, she did next to no work. The woodland paths were secluded, conducive to quiet introspection. She made herself comfortable in a small grove, thinking to draw some of the jewel-coloured flowers - yellow coltsfoot and wild mignonette, so rare in the English countryside today, destroyed by herbicides. So first she found her mobile phone and took some photographs to use later as a memory aid. But in the end, she did little actual sketching. Concentrating was impossible because of the thoughts which came crowding in.

Torsten was a man, who could take his pick of

women, so surely his desire for her was a compliment, not an insult? Why shouldn't she take the flirtation lightly, enjoy it and depart with no hard feelings? She immediately rejected the idea.

'True love is worth waiting for.' She almost uttered the expression out loud. It had been one of her granny's favourites. There would be no going back on her resolve. For whatever she was, she had her standards. So that was that, settled, done. No further argument on the subject, not even with herself. Tired but hopeful that she had, at last, expelled Torsten from her system for good, she made her way back to the summer house. He was the love of her life, but he didn't love her back. She would have to live with that.

As soon as she arrived, one of the early guests from Gothenburg - a narrow-faced young man with white-blonde hair, took it upon himself to flirt with Prue in halting English. 'My name is Magnus. And your name?'

'Prudence.'

She didn't reply unkindly, but she didn't want to lead him on. He wasn't discouraged, however when he discovered she was unattached. From thereon in, he shadowed her everywhere like an adoring puppy.

What the heck, she thought, he was probably still at school, but he was rather cute. No, more than that, he was mega eye candy, and at least he was pleasant company and very attentive. There weren't many people of the lad's own age at Norrtorpet and in any case, Prue realised he was keen to practise his

English.

She was introduced to his parents who were also pleased to talk to her in English, his father asking her about football, the Premier League, which Prue knew very little about.

The rest of the week passed swiftly and included a barbecue one evening. Torsten turned up for this bringing with him pork chops and sausages, which he helped to cook, clad in a big green apron.

He was already coaxing the barbecue into life when Prue spotted him from her bedroom window. She stiffened. She'd been working on her laptop, catching up on her notes. Before she'd even given herself time to think straight, she was changing into her pretty yellow shift dress, the one she'd ironed earlier that day. Her discarded clothes were thrown untidily onto the bed, black leggings and one of Hildi's loose tops. The man had put her in a state of agitation once again. Her hands were shaking as she closed down her computer. She immediately made herself stand up very straight and draw a few deep breaths to calm down. Then she freshened her make-up, put on her stiletto-heeled shoes and went outside, giving her best to look carefree, to join Magnus who was in the garden with his parents.

'Hello,' she said to Torsten very civilly, just to let him know there were no hard feelings.

He responded by giving her a salute with the barbecue tongs and a penetrating, questioning look, rather a sad one. She turned away but was aware he was watching her as she moved a chair to sit with her new friend and his parents at a picnic table on the edge of the grassy area. Doing so, she couldn't help overhearing the conversation of three ladies sitting nearby, talking to one another in Swedish. A name sprang out from their conversation more than once: Jill.

Prue smiled at Magnus. 'This sounds like an interesting conversation. These ladies next to us, can you translate what they are saying?'

Magnus fell into the trap, naturally assuming she was merely testing his linguistic skills. 'They are say... er... about Torsten's wife, Jill, and he is... was... loved her very much... and it...'

He stumbled on and Prue gathered that the discourse was all about how awful it was that Torsten's wife had died so tragically. How sad Torsten was that she was not here, still, to attend Hildi's wedding. How he had written another song, the first for ages. A love song to his wife, in honour of Hildi's midsummer nuptials.

A man came to sit with the ladies and more was said on the subject, according to Magnus' slow interpretation. Prue had heard enough though.

'That's excellent, Magnus,' she interrupted gently. 'You are improving so much.'

Magnus was chuffed. 'One day I come England and I speak very good.'

'Er... yes...' Prue returned, doubtfully. She hoped he wasn't getting the wrong idea. To string the boy along was the last thing she wanted to do.

'Come and get it!' Torsten called out, in English, and he was soon busy dishing out the results of his labour. Magnus and his father fetched platefuls of food for the four of them. Torsten was still on Prue's mind and she could hardly bear to look at him. She was glad he was so fully occupied, and tried her best to concentrate on the conversation with Magnus and his parents.

After a while, Magnus went off to find ice cream. Meanwhile, his parents decided to go for a walk down to the lake.

'You come?' Magnus' mother suggested.

'Well, I haven't quite finished eating and,' Prue stretched out a leg to indicate her high heeled shoes. 'I couldn't walk through the wood in these. Sorry!'

They laughed and nodded at that before excusing themselves, while Prue picked up a pork chop and delicately bit into it. She was just finishing off the salad on her plate when Magnus returned complete with ice cream for them both.

'Ah, little alone-person. Where are Mamma and Papa?'

Prue explained, while Magnus put her ice cream bowl on the picnic table.

'Tomorrow, my parents and I, we go to Orrefors,' he said, tucking into his own portion. 'Famous glassworks. You will come with us?'

Wiping her hands on a paper napkin, Prue was busy trying to work out a way of declining politely when another voice broke in, snatching the conversation.

'It's a long drive to the glassworks from here and the weather's going to be very hot.'

Torsten, still in his multi-stained, barbecue apron, sat beside her, uninvited. 'And why are you avoiding me?'

'I'm sure you know the answer to that one.' With false enthusiasm, Prue turned to the young Swede. 'I'd love to go to Orrefors.'

That would show him. It would be a long while before Torsten Dahlgren bothered her again; she had intentionally burned all her boats this time. She regretted her rude behaviour, but at least he would surely get the message now that it was best if he kept his distance from her. How else could she learn to cope when her heart was breaking with the thought that they would never be together; that nothing would ever match his love for his late wife? She was trying to teach herself to hide her feelings, and his presence just made it so much more difficult. He had spoken rather sharply and she wondered if Torsten was jealous of Magnus, perhaps just a little.

Prue stood. 'Great food, you're a man of many talents.'

She picked up her plate and swept off with a well pleased Magnus. Unfortunately, the anticipated sense of triumph was missing. The only reaction she felt was a yawning emptiness in the region of her heart.

The next day she tried to put her feelings of despondency behind her on the outing to the glassworks. She made a big effort to be a pleasant companion. It had been very good of Magnus and his parents to include her in their visit. Torsten, however, had been right. It was a long journey to their destination and it was exhaustingly hot in the car. The fractured conversation was tiring too; Magnus and his parents had little English. On their tour of the famous glassworks they stopped to watch the glass-blowing which was totally fascinating, but the heat from the furnaces was uncomfortable. In the factory shop Prue purchased a wine decanter for her mother, and Magnus insisted on buying her a small swan ornament.

'I am decide. Say nothing,' he silenced her when she tried to stop him spending his money on her.

She could have wept, he was being so sweet. Later she bought them all lunch at the restaurant in the visitor centre. It was the least she could do after all their kindness. A trip to this same interesting place with Torsten was an image constantly on her mind. Oh, why had she been so aloof and cold with him yesterday? If she thought about it, apart from a few misunderstandings, he had only ever been nice to her. She had looked for fault where there had been none. Now he would never speak to her again and she was not sure she could stand that!

On Friday, a mother-of-the-bride reception was held at the Dahlgrens' residence in Gustavskrona. Strangely neither Torsten, nor Gunnar appeared at this eve-of-wedding party which was an essential part of the nuptial celebrations. Prue felt she'd been let off the proverbial hook as she'd dreaded bumping into Torsten again. At least she could relax a little, enjoy laughing and talking with the relatives, many of whom wanted a 'selfie' taken with her. These were members of Hildi's family that she hadn't met before, who lived locally. She even took a few minutes out to ring her mother.

'I can get a signal on my phone here, Mum, so I thought I'd bring you up to date. I'm at a 'mother-of-the-bride' party. It's a tradition in Sweden.'

'Darling, lovely to hear from you. I'm sure you're having a wonderful time!'

The two went on to chat happily for a few minutes. After the phone call, Prue reflected on her mother's words. She was having a truly wonderful time, maybe. Yet she frequently found herself watching the door, dreaming of the man who should be walking in and sweeping her into his arms. Where was he tonight, for goodness' sake? Of course, there would be a good reason for his absence. Gunnar wasn't around either. Logic told her that they were bonding with the new guitarist, in readiness for the recording session, but where? Maybe they'd gone to Stockholm. Torsten had a residence there, in the Old Town, or so Hildi had once mentioned - and the recording studios were in Stockholm. Prue tightened her lips for wherever he was, Ulrica would be nearby and other females, too. The world was full of pretty girls who wouldn't say 'no' to Sten Norberg.

And then he arrived. Clad in a leather biker's jacket, he came in with Gunnar and Ulrica and the new guitarist.

'Ah, Torsten,' said Magnus. 'He is here, from Stockholm.'

She hadn't been far wrong then. Busy with his music business, working with his new musician, signing contracts; whatever it took for before a new recording could hit the air waves. People crowded round the four of them, his mother brought them food and drinks, and there was much kissing, meeting and greeting going on. Prue waved to them across the room. It was the least she could do but her heart was heavy. Perhaps luckily Torsten was in constant demand, he was never alone, his family and friends obviously were eager for all his latest news.

This was what Prue had longed for yet it didn't make her happy. Torsten was so near and yet so far. He was out of her league if she faced the truth. Hiding her heartache, she spent the rest of the evening pretending to enjoy the party. In point of fact, she drank rather too much schnapps and danced the night away with Magnus to music from a CD player in the Dahlgren's town garden.

The next day was the big day, the wedding day and Prue had reason to regret having spent so much time with Magnus. He was such a pleasant boy, so anxious to please, and she'd plainly given him the wrong signals. This came to light when he came to sit beside her in the church, instead of with his family.

'You are beautiful. I love you,' he whispered, gazing at her adoringly.

Prue chuckled. 'Oh, Magnus, you are funny. What you mean is, "You look nice, and I like you." ' She had developed the habit of correcting his use of English at his own request.

'No,' he replied, his face earnest as he covered her small hand with his large one. 'You are beautiful and I love you.'

Prue felt her cheeks go hot. She knew she was looking her best – her hair was glossy and she was wearing her best turquoise satin-sheened outfit with its pretty mini skirt and pearl-lustred tights. Admiration was not unwelcome but not from Magnus. Too late she realised that the young man had fallen for her. She'd never meant for this to happen.

Conscience-stricken, she removed her hand from his as the ethereal sound of the Trumpet Voluntary filled the birch-bough bedecked church. As if by an invisible thread, her gaze was drawn to a certain spot, the nape of a certain neck. Visible only occasionally in the crowded church, the neatly barbered hair was not yet tangled by one of his unthinking raking movements.

Wagner's Bridal March struck up and the congregation rose as one and turned to face back down the main aisle. The bridal group made a tableau before taking the long approach to the altar together, led by Anna-Karin and the other bridesmaid, both delightful in frilly pink dresses.

Hildi, overflowing with happiness, beamed round at all her guests. She wore ivory wild silk, a gold-and-crystal bride crown on her head, and carried a bouquet of lilies and dark mauve cornflowers. Her injured hand was hidden by a lace mitten. Didrik was a handsome foil for his bride in his sharply pressed navy suit. Moved by the sheer glory of the moment, Prue swallowed the lump in her throat. Truly, the bride was radiant. In her mind's eye she could picture herself in this same church, with this same music, standing before the altar with Torsten by her side. It was an impossible dream and, like all such dreams, was destined to dissolve into thin air.

The service continued, with interesting and unrehearsed distractions. During the vows, for instance, Anna-Karin slipped her, possibly uncomfortable, feet out of her white pumps and did a little jig to ease them on the large platform in front of the altar, in full view of the guests. Aunt Agnetha, in exceedingly high heels today, stumbled but recovered gracefully on the altar steps after her Bible reading.

Everywhere Prue looked, the scene was a feast for the eyes. She loved especially the soaring pillars, this morning adorned with garlands of ivy. On every pew and window sill, on every table and patch of floor were jugs and bowls of freshly gathered wild flowers: bell-flowers and cornflowers as well as moon daisies, the combined scents of their nectars subtly pervading the whole glittering church. For Prudence nothing could spoil this marvellous, memorable event. And nothing did, or did it?

After the service, the sun-bathed courtyard and

steps outside were teeming with paparazzi and movie cameras; all were represented there - popular magazines, newspapers, television. This was indeed a note-worthy occasion, because for the first time since the untimely death of his wife, Sten Norberg, at this moment putting on his inevitable sunglasses, was once again in the public eye.

Journalists followed the wedding party walking down from the church to the nearby quayside and onto a hired pleasure boat, ready for a trip round the skerries before the hotel reception. There was much shouting and popping of champagne corks on board as they left the harbour.

With a pang she couldn't suppress, Prue noted Torsten in a group which included Ulrica - a figure impossible to miss in ruched shocking pink. Was that Magnus standing right beside the handsome pair, casting around as if looking for her? Quick as a flash Prue grabbed her handbag and hurried down the steps.

On the lower deck, she paused to exchange a few words with Gunnar who was surrounded by admirers. Moving on, she lifted a second flute of champagne from the tray of a passing waiter then looked for a seat. She found one, in an empty, glassed-in section of the prow and sank onto the white slatted bench. Lost in thought, she watched the droplets of sea spray on the windows. This was it, almost the end of her visit. The happy couple would be on their honeymoon this time tomorrow.

She took a sip of her lively champagne. Soon all

the lovely people she'd met in Sweden would be just a happy memory. The thought made her so sad that tears welled up in her eyes, although she'd keep in touch with Hildi, of course.

'Not crying on this auspicious day!'

The silver-grey perfectly tailored suit and white shirt became Torsten very well. Tousled by the sea wind, locks of hair strayed over his brow.

'Of course I'm not. I was just thinking that I've never, ever been to such a beautiful wedding before. It's the champagne making my eyes run,' she lied and dabbed them with a silk hanky. Her words covered the leaping up of her heart. She mustered up her resolve and delivered a broadside. 'Long time, no see... er... Maestro.'

'Watch it!' he said laughing and wagging his finger at her.

'Well, you must have better things to do than to hang out with the likes of me.'

Why had she said that? Would she never learn to bite her tongue? She had him here, all to herself, yet she couldn't stop herself making stupid, hostile remarks.

'For the last few days, I did have other things to do, important things. Now I've done some of them, at least. Our new band member is a great success. We have more work to do together, and then we shall be releasing the new song. The publicity machine is already at work, radio stations have announced that *Scandinavia* are soon to issue a new recording.'

'I'm pleased for you, I hope it does well.' She toasted him with her bubbly then took a sip. Her blood was heating in slow, heavy tides already, betraying her once more. They were true then, all those clichés she'd heard about sexual chemistry - she could feel it right here, in this tiny cabin, discernible, electric. 'At least one of us is happy then.'

She'd done it again! Put a damper on the conversation! It must be the champagne, she'd completely lost control!

'Yes, life is good. Our fans haven't deserted us, but what about you? You seem, how shall I put it, prickly?' He held onto the cabin door frame while the boat came round into the wind. 'You're not still mad with me because of what happened at Wasakapellet, are you?'

Waves were breaking over the window and Prue clutched the edge of the seat. 'No, I'm sorry if that's what you think. It's all forgotten.'

Was this really happening? Was fate giving her a second chance? The boat shuddered a little, or was it her heart? She scarcely knew.

'I did apologise at the time,' he went on. 'It was an aberration. It won't happen again. From now on I'll make it my mission in life to convince you I'm not all bad. By the way, you can't fool me, you are crying.'

'Nonsense, I'm neither crying, nor upset.' Prue jutted her chin out defiantly. 'It's the champagne, it's affecting my eyes - I'm not used to it. Are you trying to make me feel stupid or something?'

Her outburst prompted by his accurate

assessment of her situation was uncalled for. He was holding out an olive branch and she was rejecting it. She definitely wasn't used to alcohol.

'What an ogre you make me out to be. May I?'

Without waiting for her assent, he moved into the small prow section and seated himself opposite. Their knees were touching.

'Do you have ogres in England? In Sweden, ogres, giants and trolls are mythical monsters that live in remote forests.'

'I know.' She hardly trusted herself to say more. Everything kept coming out wrong.

Prue watched him bite his lower lip but whether from amusement or irritation she wasn't sure because she couldn't see his eyes.

'For goodness' sake, take off those sunglasses!' she said, her manner mock severe. 'Will you never stop hiding behind them? You don't need to disguise yourself here; we all know who you are!'

His reaction to her jibe was to laugh out loud, an engaging rumble of hilarity in his throat. His dimple deepened in his cheek. 'Oh dear, fireworks already and we've not been together more than five minutes. For your information, today I'm wearing the shades simply to protect my eyes from the sun, as you do.'

He removed the glasses and slipped them into his top pocket. 'Anything to oblige, though, as you English like to say.'

The gaze he turned on her was celestial blue as if all the colour of the sky was there. Prue blinked and looked out of the window. A rocky grey, foam-wreathed Baltic island was just disappearing from sight. Beneath her feet the engines throbbed insistently, or again, was that her heart beating, pounding, vibrating through and through her body? Oh, why did this man have such an effect on her?

'Now I've taken off the Ray-Bans, you won't even look at me.' His complaint bore a trace of humour. 'You're not being very nice to me, you know - today is my sister's wedding day. Everyone should be happy.' He paused. 'By the way, I'm not an idiot - you were having a little weep. Was it at the thought of leaving me? I understand you're going home to England tomorrow.'

She faced him again. In a way she was back to square one. Was he teasing her, or was he being serious?

'Your family have been kindness itself and I shall be sorry to leave them. As for you, you're a world-famous man. You could have any woman, yet you'd like to add me to your list of conquests. That's just being greedy.' She shook her head. 'So nothing doing, matey, as we Brits say.'

There, she'd said it and she was heart-broken, worn out with the see-sawing of her emotions - hope one minute, despair the next - but she could see now that he just liked to play with her feelings. He was Sten Norberg and he could get away with it.

The next moment stretched ahead, the silence heavy, his face was bleak. At last, he spoke.

'That's a "no", then, is it? Believe me, Prue, I know all about rejection - I could write a book about it, but you haven't rejected me. Not in your heart, you haven't.' His expression was definitely serious now, grave even. 'You see this as pay-back time because I lost my head in the chapel. Retaliation, retribution, call it what you will - you've got this inbuilt need to fight me, when I want us to be friends.'

Friendship? So that was all he was offering, anyway? Not even a little romantic affair, a fling. Friendship sounded dishearteningly lukewarm. Time was pressing, she felt it suddenly. He was right, deep down inside she had a place for him, always would have. Tomorrow she would be homeward-bound. She sighed. She was weary of the game, of being unpleasant, and had, at last, discharged all the bad feelings from her system. It wasn't in her nature to be so vindictive.

Making a great effort she summoned up a smile.

'That's better,' he said, rewarding her with a joyful grin, just as the boat was brought round to head back to town. He leaned forward. 'I've got some business in London in connection with the new single. We are working like crazy. You will have noticed that we've also invited the press today.'

Prue nodded, not sure what to think about this fact.

He placed a hand on her arm guessing, correctly, that she was about to object to cashing in on his sister's big day. 'Before you say anything, I got Hildi's approval first. She was all for it, she knows the publicity will be worth a fortune to us. She's really glad that we're making music again - commercially, I mean.'

'I'm pleased for you, too - honestly.'

'Did you meet our new guitarist yesterday? His name is Rutger Sunstedt. We were lucky there - I had a job to persuade him to join us.'

'What happened to..?'

'Rolf? Don't talk to me about him, he drinks too much. Now listen!' Torsten leaned forward. 'I have to go to London. I've been asked to appear on a chat show there. It will be good publicity for the new song.'

'Will... er... Ulrica be going with you?'

He looked grim. 'Ulrica will soon be making other plans.'

'Wh..?'

There was a sudden flash of pink and the two were gate-crashed by Anna-Karin. The girl climbed up next to Prue and nuzzled against her in a way that needed no common language.

'Pru-dence, I... like,' she said, nodding her blonde curly head and looking pleased with her attempt at English.

Guessing she'd been primed to say this by Aunt Agnetha, Prue hugged the little girl.

'I like you too, very much. In fact, I love you.'

She went on to tell the child how clever she was, how pretty she looked in her satin, and how well she'd done her part at the ceremony.

She smiled at Torsten. 'Did you see this little madam, skipping up and down on the altar without her shoes?'

Not waiting for his reply, she turned back to the child.

'You're so cute.' Sad to think they would soon be parting, she gave Anna-Karin a tender kiss, before the little girl scampered off.

'Well, what do you think?' Torsten's voice sounded urgent.

'About what?'

'Oh, forlat - I'm sorry. Perhaps I didn't make myself clear. I'm offering you a lift in my car back to England.'

Prue sat up. Accepting his offer would mean to be alone with him for two, maybe three whole days. She made an effort to compose herself, trying not to give her feelings away.

'We'll drive to Malmo, get onto the ring road and cross into Denmark by the Oresund Bridge - you'll like the bridge, it goes over the Baltic. Then there'll be a couple of overnight stops, one in Holland and one in France somewhere. We'll eventually be taking the Cherbourg Portsmouth route to England.' He was studying her face carefully. 'That's quite convenient for you, isn't it? You live near Portsmouth, don't you?'

Prue nodded and licked her lips that suddenly felt very dry. Of course, going home with Torsten would mean she wouldn't be able to start work until, what, Wednesday? At one time, because of her work ethic, her total dedication to The Great Kate Trust, she would have declined the lift. In fact, to extend her trip to Sweden was distinctly taking advantage of her boss' generosity. Today, though, to turn Torsten's offer down was unthinkable to her. How she'd changed since first coming to Sweden! Nothing was more important to her now than time spent with the man of her dreams although she was nervous about it, too. Things could go wrong, would go wrong. She was miserable without him and certainly not comfortable when she was with him.

'I've got a plane ticket, a "standby" because the flight I wanted tomorrow was full. I have to turn up at the airport and hope for the best.' She laughed. 'No, just joking. I think you get a seat on the plane if there's an empty one, a non-arrival, it's called.'

'You won't need that then. Also if you come with me, it'll save someone in the family the trouble of driving you up to Stockholm airport.' There was a wry twist to his mouth. 'Young Magnus lives in the opposite direction, in Gothenburg, and has to take his parents home anyway.'

So he hadn't missed her meaningless flirtation with Magnus.

The next second the boat started dipping and plunging quite alarmingly; obviously it had hit choppy waters. Holding onto her seat, Prue glanced out of the window. She felt she, too, had hit choppy waters. How should she handle the present conversation? She didn't want to go with Torsten, yet she desperately wanted to go with him - what a dilemma! Also, she didn't want to seem too eager.

She turned back to him. 'You must have trains or

buses in Sweden. I can make my own way to Stockholm. Or, you could take me to the airport.'

Why had she said that? Nothing could be better than being alone with him on a car journey for three whole days. She could kick herself because she wasn't thinking straight!

Happily he ignored her comment, going on to explain that all expenses would be paid for by him. 'I'm not a poor man, and the cost of such a trip will be trivial. In any case, Gunnar was coming with me, but he's changed his mind and decided to fly in on Wednesday, for the chat show. In point of fact, the rooms are already booked in advance, so you can have Gunnar's room. Simple!'

'Not so fast! How do I know you'll have the strength to resist me on such a long drive?' She spoke light-heartedly, putting all the humour she could into her question, and watched his arresting face alter, the contours soften.

'Maybe I won't be strong enough - I'm only flesh and blood, you know.' The tenor of his voice changed, becoming tender and intimate, rough with emotion. 'Do you dislike my kisses so very much?'

He moved across the cabin and put an arm around her, pulling her close. At that precise moment there was a flash, and another. Prue looked up, startled. Then there was a third one.

'It's just the press,' said Torsten. 'Ignore them. Ulrica gave them permission to be here, it's free publicity. Now could you answer my question?' Sounding quite anxious, he released her.

Did she dislike his kisses? She hesitated but couldn't resist speaking from the heart. 'You can kiss me anytime you like.'

'Aha, that's all I need to know,' he triumphed. 'Excellent. It's on, then. Today it feels like I'm starting again; new guitar-player, new song, and a new sweetheart. Be packed and ready by six in the morning. We've got quite a trek across Europe ahead of us.'

So it was settled. If there was any joy in the world at that moment, it seemed to be concentrated on that Baltic pleasure boat, in that tiny glassed-in cabin in the prow. He'd probably always be in love with his late wife, but who said life was perfect? Nobody. She was glad she'd determined to grab the opportunity with both hands, instead of spoiling it by saying something cutting as she usually did. This would be her last chance. She was overwhelmed with happiness.

The boat docked and landed its passengers outside the hotel for the wedding reception, and the rest of the festivities passed in a whirl. The majestic yellow-and-gold reception room was candle-lit even though it was broad daylight, and the happy couple received each well-wisher in turn beneath a romantic arch of flowers and greenery.

'Congratulations,' said Prue. 'You both look so beautiful.'

The traditional almond wedding cake on its plinth beside them was a wondrous vision of fragile fretwork. Prue took photographs on her mobile phone of everyone and everything.

The table was set out in the shape of a large 'U' so that everyone was connected. Prue found a seat with Aunt Agnetha, Magnus and his parents. Didrik gave his bridegroom speech in a mixture of Swedish and English, which was considerate of him. Then it was Herr Dahlgren's turn to address the guests. During the speeches and the singing of the old Swedish community songs, Prue's mind kept returning to the proposed journey home with Torsten. The very thought of it made her feel quite lightheaded. She had accepted that she would see little of Torsten at the reception because he had an official role to play. He was acting as toastmaster and leader of the traditional games.

Later, when the tables were cleared away he became DJ for the dancing. Not surprisingly, at one point in the evening he rounded up Gunnar and Rutger to help him perform the new song for the guests. He announced that the song had been written specially for his sister's wedding. Hildi glowed.

As the applause for the song died away, Torsten strolled over to Prue.

'Would you like to dance?'

Would she! She nodded and was sure she was the envy of most of the females in the room as they moved round the floor to a slow, smoochy number. An expert dancer, he held her so close, she was in heaven. Afterwards he danced with his mother and Ulrica, while Prue danced with Magnus.

Later in the evening she made a point of going up

to Hildi and giving her a sisterly hug.

'I can't begin to tell you how happy I've been in Sweden. Thank you so much for inviting me to share your marvellous Swedish traditions. Be very happy, Hildi! Didrik is such a nice man.'

'Thank you, dear,' said the beaming bride. 'I'm so glad you were able to share our wedding with us. Have a safe journey home.'

'I wish you a wonderful honeymoon, Crete's a lovely place.' Prue smiled. 'I might not see you before you go in the morning, but make no mistake, I shall keep in touch with you, come what may. Keep checking your emails!'

When Prue went to the Ladies' Room to powder her nose, it was already the early hours of the morning. In the cloakroom there were two girls at the communal mirror who soon left together, chatting animatedly. Just when Prue was about to leave, the door flew open and in walked Ulrica. It was soon plain she had been watching Prue's movements and was now quite smug to have cornered her in here. Wasting no time on preliminaries, she sat on a small sofa and waved her iPod at Prue.

'Look at this! It's an article about the wedding – it's already online.'

Curious, Prue sat down beside her and took the iPod. When she looked at the screen, she couldn't believe her eyes!

# CHAPTER NINE

The wedding was front page news – 'Sten Norbergs Syster Gifter Sig', which, Prue guessed, translated as – 'Sten Norberg's Sister Weds'. However, strangely enough, there was no actual wedding photograph. Instead there was a blown-up head-and-shoulders picture of Torsten and herself! Prue gasped, scarcely about to get her head round it. It had clearly been taken in the cabin on the boat, when Torsten had his arm about her shoulders. The text below was in Swedish. Ulrica scrolled down the page so Prue could see the two photographs below it. One was of herself, taken from the group photograph of all the wedding guests probably. The one beside it was of Jill. The accompanying text was again in Swedish, no translation, however, was necessary. For, staring straight at Prue from the iPod was the evidence from which she could draw only one conclusion. Torsten's late wife and herself looked almost identical. Jill's hair was dark like Prue's, the lips maybe slightly narrower, but in fact the two girls could have been twins, or at least sisters.

Prue didn't need Ulrica's smug expression to tell her that the newspaper was pointing out the similarity, even speculating on Prue's relationship with Torsten.

"Has Sten Norberg found a new Jill?" would be the gist of the news item.

'You have Jill's face; her smile; her hair; her small stature,' Ulrica gloated. 'Surely you know you are her doppelganger?'

'No! Of course I didn't know!' Prue was aghast at the implications that were starting to dawn on her.

Ulrica looked amazed. 'Strange no one mentioned it to you,' she said with an ugly twist to her mouth.

'Well, no one did!' Prue shook her head. 'Now I come to think, people did react to me in an odd way. Aunt Agnetha, Rolf... but it didn't seem too significant at the time. I have no Swedish at all, you see.'

Hurt and anguish probed keenly at the base of Prue's spine. Previously unexplained incidents slid into focus - Torsten's own first double-take of her at the wedding rehearsal, for instance. No wonder he suspected Prue of engineering their meeting. If she'd been that kind of girl, she could have gambled on making capital out of her likeness to his adored Jill.

The others, Rolf, for example, must have, on first acquaintance, assumed the same thing - that Torsten had found a substitute for his dead wife, an almost identical replacement. Hildi, too, from the best of motives - the welfare of her beloved brother - had brought Prue and Torsten together because of the likeness.

'Oh, Hildi, Hildi, what have you done?' she moaned to herself.

'Excuse me?' Ulrica didn't even try to hide the triumphant gleam in her eye.

'This is awful, horrifying.' Prue was talking half to

herself. 'I am me, I am not Jill. I'm not a pale imitation of another person.'

'You are to Torsten – you're just a re-make of his wife. You amuse him because you are her "twin", but he will never love anyone else the way he loved her. He adored Jill.'

Images from the past came rushing in, jostling for attention. She recalled the conversation in the Wasa Chapel about the angel, the self-portrait of the woman who'd devoted her life to the memory of her dead lover, Anders Norberg.

'It's said the angel looks like Jill, my late wife. Would you agree?' Torsten had asked, almost casually.

In the light of the recent revelations, it was plain he'd been testing her. She couldn't bring her reply to mind exactly, but it had been non-committal, and it must have clinched everything. Her answer at that time had revealed to Torsten that Prue had no clue at all as to Jill's appearance – that she'd been exquisitely tiny and dark, and nothing like the six foot blonde angel-artist with her bold facial features. If there had been any lingering fears in Torsten's mind - for example, that Prue might be playing an exceedingly clever game - it must have been at that point he'd dismissed them.

Not that Torsten's attitude had instantly softened towards her – after all she was female and every girl he came across was suspect, a potential gold digger. Perhaps, though, that moment in the chapel had been the one when seeds of trust were first planted.

Prue sighed deeply. At least things were clearer now, thanks to Ulrica - or rather, no thanks. She would've enjoyed keeping her illusions a bit longer, relishing the drive across Europe with the man who'd captured her heart. Now, it was unthinkable.

'You know, even if you had had a romantic get-together with Torsten, it wouldn't have lasted long,' said Ulrica. 'When he realised that you might look like Jill, but you are definitely not her, he would have come to his senses. You would be discarded without further ado!'

It sounded like a perfectly feasible scenario. To Torsten she would simply be a flash in the pan, nothing more. We don't choose the person we fall in love with - it just happens, she reminded herself, dolefully. Love just is. Yet, in spite of everything - his hostility, his moodiness, his arrogant assumption that she found him irresistible - despite all that, she was irrevocably in love with him.

Ulrica's ultra-precise English broke up Prue's train of thought. 'My car was out of action over midsummer. It was at the garage, being repaired, but I got it back today. I'm going up to Stockholm tonight, within the hour. I could take you to Norrtorpet for your baggage, and then drive you to Arlanda airport...'

Prue nodded, subdued. She was defeated, totally beaten.

'It will probably mean you'll have to spend the night at the airport. Are you all right with that?' said Ulrica.

'Yes, I'll be fine,' replied Prue in flat tones. 'I'll sort out my ticket when I get there.' There was no point in worrying about a flight home, there would be one eventually. All she wanted to do at this minute was to get away. She was past caring about the details.

'Hello. Mary Claybourne speaking.'

Her mother's voice at the other end of the line gave Prue the sense of comfort she badly needed at this moment.

'Mum - it's me. Sorry to be such an early caller, but I'm at Stockholm airport, and this is a payphone.' Prue rushed her explanation along. 'I just wanted to let you know that I should be home before very long.'

'Oh, Prue, darling! I can't wait to hear how it all went. By the way, Claire phoned. She's looking forward to seeing you when you get back.'

'I'll get in touch with her as soon as I can. Give her my love if you see her.'

'I will - and I've got some news for you.'

'Come on then, spill,' said Prue, rather wearily after a night without sleep.

'There's so much to tell you. The lifting frame is in place over the Great Kate, well ahead of schedule, and the weather forecast is excellent. James is so over the moon about it. Oh, and talking of James, congratulate me, darling. We're going to be...'

Unfortunately, the warning pips were already punctuating the pay-phone line and her mother's animated flow was cut off. Prue guessed her mother's news anyway.

'Oh, Mum, I'm so happy for you!' she shouted and hoped against hope her enthusiastic good wishes could still be heard.

Quite fazed by this new development, she replaced the receiver and took a long, steadying breath. Her mum had sounded so excited, so happy, and the more Prue thought about it, the more pleased she was - James was such a nice man; hard working, dependable and excellent company. Mulling the stupendous news over in her mind, she stepped away from the phone booth.

Thankfully the question of the plane ticket had been sorted out by Ulrica. There'd been some finger-wagging from the airline official, but Prue was to be allowed to join an earlier flight to Heathrow, space permitting.

Automatically she glanced across to the uncomfortable bench where she and Ulrica had just endeavoured to snatch a couple of hours' sleep and where Ulrica was, at present, sitting with the luggage. Prue looked again and quickly dodged back behind the phone hood, for there was someone with Ulrica. Torsten! How had he materialised?

Prue's heart started thumping; it felt, in an instant, too big for her small chest. She commanded herself to calm down - the Torsten Dahlgren/Sten Norberg episode of her life was at an end. Over. Finished. Definitely and forever.

She hovered, out of sight, every nerve quivering

and her eyes intent on the two of them - Ulrica and Torsten. Both seemed to be having plenty to say, they were arguing – more than that. They were fighting, verbally, at least.

Ulrica jumped up off the bench, her eyes glinting and her cheeks red with anger. Prue shrank back and waited, bewildered. She needed time to think. She wasn't keen to get dragged into their dispute, they were shouting at one another in Swedish anyway. She didn't even want to take sides. Ulrica had been good to her. Pointing out Prue's resemblance to Jill had done her a favour and had prevented her from making a grave mistake. Ulrica had stayed with her at the airport, too, and arranged a flight for her. The best thing was to hang on here, out of sight, until the two of them had sorted things out between them.

And yet, here was the man who could have been her whole world. He'd driven alone through the night, perhaps to demand an explanation - and he deserved one. After all, she'd left in a great rush and had said 'goodbye' only to Hildi's parents. Prue felt suddenly ashamed.

Finally, the shouting stopped. Prue peeped out from her hiding place to see that a small crowd had gathered round the arguing pair. Some were even taking photos. At that moment Ulrica slung her bag over her shoulder and stomped away towards the exit. Prue, who hadn't even merited a parting glance, was left with a great churning inside her.

What now? Torsten was still there, next to her luggage, and he looked likely to stay. Biting her lower lip, she watched him comfortably settling on the bench, his long legs across her bags, and calmly opening a newspaper. She was due to check in now, so she needed to pluck up the courage to go up to him and claim her luggage. At length, there was nothing else for it; she was forced to reveal herself.

'That took you long enough,' was his nonchalant greeting, tossing the newspaper aside as she approached him tentatively and hoped she looked reasonable after several hours drive through the moonlit Swedish countryside. Before the journey she'd changed into white jeans and a pretty lemon long-sleeved top so at least she was presentable.

'Don't imagine for one second I didn't know you were over there.' He folded the paper and got nimbly to his feet. 'Just follow me. The car's outside.'

'What?'

He was all orders as usual. Dumbstruck, she watched while he picked up her luggage and made for the exit. No wonder he was anxious to get out. The crowd of onlookers had thinned out considerably, but he was still the centre of attention.

'My plane's due to leave soon. I've got to check in,' she remonstrated, running after his retreating back as he negotiated first gates, then swing doors until he reached the street. Agitated, she tried plucking her case and bag away from him.

Just as if she were an irritating insect, he shook her off. 'You're coming with me and I'm not letting you out of my sight again. You've got into a terrible habit of disappearing, Miss Claybourne, and we need to talk.'

'Well, I can't think what about!' Prue flashed back, with returning spirit. Her body was flooded with adrenalin, her head buzzing from trying to sort out the complexities of the situation. Sweet heaven, what was going on?

'You left Gustavskrona in a tremendous hurry,' he said, making for the Volvo on the airport car park. 'It was very rude of you, unpardonable. I think you owe me an explanation.'

'Ye-es, I... I'm sorry about that.' Prue had had a whole night to regret the manner of her departure. 'I did say goodbye to your parents, but Ulrica thought we should leave without fuss. It seemed like a good idea at the time.'

'Ulrica would, wouldn't she?' he asserted sourly. 'Luckily Mamma mentioned you'd left. Mentioned, did I say? She made a point of finding me to tell me, and that's why I'm here. I've managed to prise the whole sick story out of Ulrica.' He clicked open his car, stashed Prue's luggage inside the boot and closed the lid smartly.

'She was looking after my interests,' Prue interposed.

'I don't think so and as you might guess, I'm now on the look-out for a new manager. Ulrica won't be easy to replace. She was an efficient worker, dedicated to her job.'

Prue was confounded. 'Ulrica resigned?'

'Not exactly. I fired her. She's a mischief-maker. I showed great restraint and decided not to give her the bad news until after the wedding, but we had a row at the reception, about you as a matter of fact, so I told her then. I couldn't bring myself to wait any longer. My friend, my former friend, Rolf, wasn't backward in spilling all the beans on that lady.'

So that was what he had meant when he'd said that Ulrica 'had other plans.' She would be looking for a new job, and perhaps that wouldn't be difficult for a person with her experience.

Torsten opened the passenger door and indicated Prue should get in.

'Here we go again.' Prue glared at him rebelliously and folded her arms across her chest. 'In case you didn't know it, kidnapping is against international law, or perhaps you're above such petty considerations.'

'This is not a kidnap. You're free to go when and wherever you please if that's what you really want. Bear in mind, though, you've no luggage. It's safely locked in the boot of my car.'

'But, that's called... er... coercion, I think.'

He laughed aloud, a rich sound, and executed a mocking little bow. 'Whatever it is, my darling, you're in my power.'

She was, she couldn't deny that, and for the time being she had to accept it. With a sigh of resignation, she got into the car.

'Isn't this where we came in?' she said, making a feeble joke as he joined her and started up the engine. 'Why do you always end up getting your own way?'

Small talk, however, seemed inappropriate under

the circumstances. Prue stared stolidly out of the side window and kept any further thoughts to herself, while they left the airport and edged out into the Stockholm morning traffic. Meanwhile, her companion whistled quietly under his breath as he motored expertly through the city and finally into the cobbled ways of the picturesque Old Town.

'I know you like this part of Stockholm - Hildi told me,' he commented. 'I love it, too and I have a house here, however the place is full of workmen at the moment. They're doing a few repairs to the walls and the roof so I'm keeping out of their way. Until the work's finished I'm renting a suite of rooms in a local hotel.'

Prue made no reply. She wanted answers and they weren't forthcoming. What was the mystery concerning Ulrica? More important, what was she, Prue, doing here with him? If only he could see inside her, see how in the last twenty-four hours her heart and feelings had cruelly see-sawed from hope to near-despair.

There was a limit to what she could tolerate, though, and that limit had been reached. She was emotionally drained. This time there was no light on her horizon.

Outside, the streets of ancient timber buildings, yellow and blue and red ochre, were like a pantomime backdrop. Around every corner one expected to see scenes from the Old Norse folktales. Prue was vitally aware of Torsten's every movement - there was something about the way he performed even the mundane actions of driving that she found disturbingly sensual. His hold on her was primitive, not-to-be-denied. Oh, how would it all finish up? In tears, without a doubt.

The Volvo came to a standstill in the private courtyard of an impressive black-and-white timbered building. Clearly this was the hotel. Torsten levered himself out of the car.

'Come with me,' he said tersely. He opened the door for her to alight and she followed him into the hotel.

He spoke a few words in Swedish to the receptionist then turned to Prue. Taking her hand, he led her upstairs. 'I've ordered breakfast for us. I hope that's all right.'

She shrugged but made no reply.

'Please, Prue. Give me a chance,' he said. 'We've got to call a truce. Ulrica's been feeding you poison - something she's quite good at. Surely you're fair-minded enough to hear my side of things?'

The unexpected plea shattered Prue's resistance. 'It can't be worse than what I've already imagined,' she said. 'So why not?'

Fifteen minutes later, her hands around a mug of steaming coffee, she was standing on the balcony of his suite. The balcony was square with a wooden bench on each side, both adorned with comfy, blue cushions. The hot drink and the thought of the food waiting on the breakfast trolley - rolls, butter, jam and soft Swedish cheese - soothed her and made her feel less edgy. With a refreshing sea breeze caressing her face, she began to feel cleansed and invigorated.

The wondrous panorama of the city was spread before her. She loved the majestic pale buildings with their jade-green roofs. Steeples and spires soared into the sky; a hundred pretty stone bridges spanned a hundred arms of the silver Baltic; yachts rocked gently at their moorings – Sweden's capital city seemed to be sailing on the sea, as befitted a true seafaring nation. Prue felt overwhelmed with gratitude that such awe-inspiring beauty could exist - already the scene was working its eternal magic.

Below, the waters of Stockholm harbour shimmered in the sunshine. On a similar bright morning near this very spot, the flagship Wasa, sails billowing, had foundered more than three centuries ago. Prue could almost hear the excitement of that day; the music; the crowds; the pageantry of the king and his retinue - and soon after the horror and despair sweeping over the scene as the fully manned ship had turned over and gone down without trace. She shuddered, sensing sorrowful ghosts abroad.

'It's quite a view, isn't it?' His voice brought her back to the present. 'Do you know it takes thirty years or more for the copper roofs to turn that colour?'

She nodded. 'I knew it took a long time. It's the most marvellous shade of green, but I was thinking about Anders Norberg. He drowned somewhere near here.'

Sad at the thought she turned away and her gaze fell through the open balcony door on the room behind her. Panelled in polished wood and furnished luxuriously in cream and blue, it was faintly reminiscent of the ancient church where Hildi had been married - was it only yesterday?

'I love it here,' she said. 'Very plush. Extravagantly expensive, too, I'm sure.'

'But worth every krona.'

Torsten parried her banter with a grin as he pulled off his tie and stuffed it into the pocket of the grey wedding suit which he was still wearing. He returned into the room, shed the jacket and slipped it over the back of a dining chair.

How pleasant the room was with its sunny balcony, a baby grand piano in the opposite corner and the aroma of coffee filling the air!

The waiter had left the breakfast trolley between the blue-tiled wood-burning stove and the dining table. The next moment they were both helping themselves to more coffee, sitting at the table and enjoying their meal. After a while, Torsten gravitated towards the piano. Rolling up the sleeves of his white silk shirt, he sat down and ran through a few melodious chords. Immediately his features took on a dreamy, far-away look. The smudges beneath his eyes reminded Prue that he had driven hard and fast through the small hours and was, like herself, without sleep.

'We need to talk. So let's get it all straight. Ulrica got you to steal away like a thief in the night. That wasn't very nice, was it?' His supple fingers rippled over the keys. 'Did you forget you'd just promised me three whole days of your company? I assumed we had a deal, you and I. What's more, because you've been a silly girl again, we have an even longer journey to look forward to.'

This was it – confrontation time! Prue put her empty coffee mug down on the table. She took a deep breath. 'The reason I left was that Ulrica pointed something out to me. In fact, it was splashed all over the news: I'm your wife's double! I look like Jill.'

He raised his fine eyebrows at her but didn't stop playing. 'That's where you're wrong. Oh, you have the same colouring as my dear wife and you are English as she was, it's true. It is also true that when I first met you I assumed you were trying to cash in on the very slight similarity - but a lookalike? Never!' He executed a few tuneful flourishes on the keys.

'But I am like Jill!' Prue insisted. 'Ulrica showed me the photo of her, of us both, on her iPod. We could be identical twins!'

'The press needs to attract readers. The photographs were air-brushed. Doctored to make you and Jill look alike. Don't forget I bought a newspaper at the airport, so I've seen the photographs. I was reading it while I waited for you. It makes a good story and it fitted into Ulrica's plan so well. She just wanted to get you away. It was sheer spite. She's... she likes...'

'She's in love with you! Is that what you're trying to say? I know that, it must be obvious to everyone. She's mad about you.'

Torsten nodded. 'I don't have feelings for her and I have been straight with her about it, but she doesn't listen.'

'She lives in hope, I know the feeling. But to get back to your Jill and my supposed likeness to her…' Prue's head was ringing with this new revelation. 'Everything clicked. My likeness to Jill was the reason why Hildi invited me to the wedding on such short acquaintance. She deliberately didn't warn me that you were the great Sten Norberg and took a chance that I wouldn't recognise you without your beard. She didn't want me to be frightened off before I'd met you."

'Hildi certainly saw something in you that reminded her of my wife. Maybe it was merely that you're English. She meant well. '

'She just wanted to throw us together, you and me, to see what would happen. She did it with your happiness in mind, knowing how devastated you'd been when you lost your wife. How sad you still were. Hildi wanted to... to replace Jill for you.'

'But not because you're a lookalike for Jill. Simply because you're a nice girl and she likes you - and she knows I admire dark hair.'

'Well, that's why I left. Ulrica explained, showed me the photos and offered me a lift to the airport. She guessed correctly that I wouldn't want to be a substitute for Jill. Ulrica seemed to be doing everything out of kindness, looking after me and staying with me... and...'

'Only because she wanted to make sure you got

on that plane,' he interrupted. 'One day maybe I'll show you a true likeness of my wife, a photo that hasn't been doctored - although I must admit I destroyed all I could find a while ago.'

He spoke slowly and the music ceased as he looked round and engaged her eyes with his own, azure meeting luminous green for a moment.

'You must believe me, Prue. You've got a sweetness of expression all of your own, and sometimes a lost look which I love.'

'Such gallantry!' she countered as hope began to surge inside her once more, and love for him flooded her being. 'When I think about it all, I feel awful. About going to the Wasa Chapel, I mean.'

Looking away from his intense gaze she went over to the breakfast trolley. She took her time in choosing a hot roll and after a while he returned to his piano-playing.

'It must've been torture - you loved your wife and the chapel was too much for you to cope with. I suppose the memories all came flooding back in there, in her favourite place.' Prue paused as she buttered the roll and spread it with raspberry jam. 'Her presence is probably still very strong in the chapel. I felt something in there myself. I can't explain what. Perhaps we should remember that death is not evil, only tragic, and Jill wouldn't want you to be... '

The music stopped abruptly, her sentence was cut off. 'But you've gone and got it all wrong as usual, haven't you!'

Torsten's accusation resounded in the spacious room.

Completely caught off balance, Prue dropped the roll onto her plate, appetite gone, yet she schooled herself into keeping a cool head. 'No. I'm right; otherwise you wouldn't be reacting so badly. We don't stop loving a person just because they've gone away.'

Torsten took a deep breath and started to play again, the heart-stealing notes of the new love song. It opened softly and gently, gaining strength and pace as it moved along, then quickly resolving itself in the most beautiful harmony. Then he began to sing, haltingly at first, as if overcome by emotion.

*'Where did you come from, beautiful girl?*
*Whenever I'm near you my head's in a whirl.*
*I'll love you forever if you'll only stay,*
*And kiss me, my darling, on Midsummer's Day.'*

The lyrics were romantic beyond measure and blended magically with the tune. His singing faded away altogether, but his fingers continued to perform.

'I wrote this for you,' he said quietly. 'But you realised that, I'm sure.'

Prue was stunned; jolted by the casual way he'd delivered his earth-shattering disclosure.

'No, I didn't!' she said, flustered.

Composing the song for her must mean that he loved her, that he was in love with her. She was moved to the core of her being. Indeed she felt so emotional she could hardly cope with it as she went out onto the balcony for some air, once more. The magical rooftops, the spires and green copper domes of Stockholm sparkled in the sunlight and added to the overwhelming sense she had that what was happening to her was beyond imagining. It was cool out there, though, and after a few moments she was brought down to earth. Reality re-emerged, the raw truth as she saw it. Leaning back against the balcony balustrade she pondered on it all.

She was feeling exactly the way he'd planned, but her head was clearer now. What better way to soften a woman up, to get her into bed, than write a love song for her? Or pretend it was written for her? She was not such a gullible fool. The protective wall she had earlier built round her heart was still strong. Impregnable! To go to all that trouble, he most definitely wanted her to consummate what he saw as a good relationship, but love with a capital L? That was a whole different ball game, especially to a man who could have his pick of the crop when it came to women.

She went back into the room. 'I'd like to go now. If I could have my things, please.' She delivered her request with a steadiness she was far from feeling. 'Reception will get me a taxi for the airport, I'm sure.'

There was no Ulrica to guide her through now but, hey, what the heck! She'd buy a new plane ticket if that's what it was going to take to get home. This time she'd had enough, she was mentally and physically drained.

Torsten was still sitting on the piano stool. He

slapped his forehead with his hand. 'You are something else! Cra - zee! Think what you're doing, for goodness' sake! I chase after you for miles through the night! I rescue you from Ulrica! I write a song for you! What more do I have to do to convince you that I want you?'

'But the "Beautiful Girl" in your song is not me. It's Jill. Ulrica told me you'd never love anyone else, and she should know. As a close friend and would-be girlfriend, one who had to pretend to be your partner even if it was only for the media, she must've fathomed you out a long time ago.'

'You know, perhaps I am somewhat to blame for Ulrica's attitude. I've never thought about it before. When everything went wrong in my life, I did rely on her for moral and emotional support. She helped me to keep going, to get over the shock, but I think she read more into the relationship that grew between us than I intended. I've said before that the public at large thought we were an item - and that was deliberate and for my own protection.'

'Yes, you told me about it.'

'I am a bit paranoid when it comes to predatory ladies,' he went on. 'I've had to put up with so much of it, you see. It's quite likely that Ulrica read more into our little arrangement than I wished. I probably gave her the wrong impression. It was selfish of me, I can see that now.'

'Yes, she's obviously been living in hopes. Even though she told me that you'd never love anyone else like you loved your wife - that was just a smokescreen to put me off. From the start she probably believed that you'd tire of Jill, perhaps because she was foreign to you, English and...'

'Oh, why do you keep harping on about my late wife? Jill! Jill! You're obsessed with her!' His hands crashed down on the keyboard and the sound of clashing chords echoed discordantly around the room. He glared at Prue, his eyes blazing. 'Perhaps we should get one or two things straight, things I've never discussed willingly with a single soul before. Perhaps I should acquaint you with the history of my dear departed spouse; then maybe you won't feel quite so jealous of a dead woman.'

*Jealous!* That did it. In the face of the anger she'd always found intimidating, a matching fury shook her own body - largely, perhaps, because he'd hit the nail fairly and squarely on the head. She was jealous of Jill, as jealous as hell! Yes, she craved Torsten's love, but she wanted him to love her for herself, not because she was small and dark-haired and English, bringing back memories of his first great romance. She could stand it no longer!

'I still should leave,' she said. 'My luggage is in the boot of your car.'

By way of reply Torsten jumped up, came over to her and, taking her hand firmly, led her into the bedroom. She struggled against him but in reality, she was done. The sleepless night was taking its toll. He gently pushed her down so that she was lying on the bed. He then gently moved her legs so that he had room to sit facing her. Prue gasped in protest but stayed put.

He brought his face close to hers and looked into her eyes. 'Prudence. Do you love me?'

She caught her breath. 'I might ask you the same question.'

'Answer me! I love you, I've been trying to show it for long enough. I'll ask you again. Be honest! Do you love me?'

She closed her eyes. 'Yes, I do. I love you with all my heart.'

There, it was out, and it was true. When she opened her eyes again, he was looking at her, gazing intently.

'Min karesta, then you are mine, all mine.' His fingers touched her lips, softly. 'So listen and don't interrupt.'

His brow was knotted with tension, a pulse quickened in his neck. The very air around him seemed to be charged. His thigh touched hers, burned into her. He seemed to be locked into some kind of angst, his features distorted as he appeared to search for words. Then he began. The story came out slowly at first, haltingly, but with increasing conviction.

'A long time ago, a very long time ago, Jill was...' He paused, choking a little then he coughed and continued. 'She meant everything to me; that is, until I found her out. One day I came home to the summer house - I hardly ever went there as our studio was here in Stockholm at the time. Ulrica had told me there was an urgent message and that I was to meet Jill at Norrtorpet.' He paused, clearly affected deeply by the process of dredging up the details of the memory.

'When I got there, I found a note in Jill's writing pinned to the door. It wasn't meant for my eyes. "Lars, come straight to the chapel," it said. I wasn't suspicious - I was a trusting soul in those days. I was curious, mind you - for one thing I knew no-one called Lars. So I went to the chapel, and what did I find?' Torsten's face twisted with internal pain and there was a long pause before he carried on.

'I'd known for some time that Jill was into aromatherapy, that sort of thing. I was pleased she'd found an interest - she got so bored hanging around the studios while I was rehearsing, or composing, or attending to business. So this day I went to the chapel and there she was, in the Anders Norberg shrine with... with at least three others. Men, all men, and all...naked!' His words came hesitantly as if they were strangling him.

Shaken to the core, Prue gasped. 'No! Never!'

'Believe me, it's the truth,' he returned. 'The candles were alight - the smell of them so sickly... evil. I didn't wait to think, to take it all in, the massaging, the...' His eyes closed for a long moment. 'I just lashed out at them all. I was beside myself, out of my mind with shock!' His hands were twisting together as the sordid story unfolded, beads of sweat gathered on his brow, betraying how much the horrendous scene had affected him.

'How could she!' Prue was equally astounded,

uncomprehending.

'I damaged myself as well as them,' he continued. 'My fingers were a mess and for a long time afterwards I was afraid I'd never be able to play the piano again.'

He spread his hands before him, regarding them, and then looked up at her again. Prue was spellbound, incredulous. She reached out to him, entwining his fingers with her own. 'Go on.'

'The family never found out about it. I told them I'd injured myself felling trees in the forest. As for Jill - she went off to Spain with a girlfriend, and you know the rest.' His body juddered visibly as he relived his nightmare. 'I'll never forget that scene, the smell of those hot perfumes - mind numbing. To this day certain scents make me want to retch.'

'Indescribable! Detestable!' Prue's response was a hoarse whisper, her throat constricted with compassion. 'Why would she even think of straying in any way, shape or form, when she had you?' It was completely beyond Prue's comprehension.

The confession explained so much - his ambivalent feelings towards her; his uncertainty at times; his arrogance at others.

'And yet you're still in love with her.'

'In love with her, after that? How could I be?' He combed his fingers through his hair.

'We can't switch off love just like that, it's impossible,' she replied. 'When you look at me, do you see Jill? I have to know.'

'I see you,' he answered her tenderly. 'Until

Midsummer Night, when I was in Wasakappellet with you, I'm prepared to admit that Jill was still a part of me. A bad part, it's true. But there, with you, I said goodbye to her evil spirit - forever.'

'You finally buried her memory.' She spoke softly, understanding.

'Something like that. Perhaps you kissed away the nightmare, broke the spell.' He leaned forward and gently took her hand in his. 'I was really vile to you in the chapel. Can you forget it?'

'It's forgotten already.'

Prue ached to fold her arms around him to help him put the trauma behind him forever, but he wasn't through with his story yet.

'Right from the start I wanted to keep you away from the chapel and its contaminated atmosphere. Don't ask me to explain why, I don't know. I used to ask myself why it mattered, particularly when I took you for a gold digger. Some women are so devious, you see, as I keep saying.'

'Men, too.'

He made a noise between a snort and a laugh and held up his hands in mock defence. 'Okay, I agree. Rolf, for one, but let's talk about Ulrica first. She was the one who'd pushed me into going to Norrtorpet that evening. There was, of course, no urgent message from Jill, but Ulrica knew all about Jill's carryings-on. She wanted me to catch my charming wife in action.'

'And Rolf?'

'My good and faithful friend, I don't think.'

Torsten's eyes clouded with yet more pain. 'That night, in the chapel with you, I found his earring. You couldn't mistake it - a gold stud with a ruby.'

'Yes, I remember that. You changed in an instant and you hardly spoke to me afterwards. It was plain that what you found had knocked you for six.'

Torsten nodded. 'Sorry about that, I was speechless at the time. Rolf sets great store by his earrings; they're of great sentimental value to him. They belonged to his late mother and he's always looked upon them as his lucky charms. He was very upset when he realised he'd lost one and after that he started swapping the other one round, sometimes in the left ear, sometimes in the right.'

'I never noticed,' said Prue. 'Maybe he thought doing that would keep the luck going.'

'I suppose so. When I was with you in the chapel I spotted the damn thing, the one he'd lost, in a crease in the couch. It was obvious he'd been there at some stage, enjoying my wife's favours. He didn't deny it when I tackled him over it. He couldn't.'

'When I first met Rolf I thought he was a joker, a good natured rogue. But in truth he's absolutely despicable.'

'Anyway, after that he was happy to dish the dirt on Ulrica, how she'd set it all up for Jill, the whole damned operation. She saw Jill had an appetite for flattery and admiration, in short: for men - the more the merrier.' He paused, and pain flickered in his face.

'It's hard to believe that you've kept all this to

yourself. No wonder you're so touchy.'

He laughed. 'Not any more. You will ease the pain for me.' He frowned. 'Actually, I've always wondered who tipped the papers off about the "orgy". I'm sure it wasn't Ulrica, though, because she had nothing to gain. It must've been one of those other rats. One of them did it - for thirty pieces of silver, I shouldn't wonder. It was assumed I was involved, too, you see. The whole thing made me sick. I didn't bother to dignify it with a denial, but I stopped talking to the press from that moment on.'

'Ulrica had a motive for her wickedness, though,' Prue put in thoughtfully. 'She wanted you for herself and she wanted to destroy the love you had for Jill. Also even bad publicity is good for business, any business.'

'Maybe...yes, I daresay you're right.' Torsten sucked in a deep breath and released it in a prolonged sigh. 'But Ulrica was never my type. She was just a good road manager.'

As he spoke he lifted his legs up onto the bed and stretched his long length beside Prue.

'Enough of other people.' He reached for her and wound his arms around her. 'God, Prue, my darling. You don't know how much I want you. I need you.'

His embrace was soothing and arousing all at the same time. She didn't resist when he moved over her and buried his face in the hollow of her neck. Lovingly, she pressed her lips to the gold-bright hair. She closed her eyes as his mouth moved to hers and kissed her with aching tenderness. Her longing for him was sweet agony as his arms tightened and he pulled her pliant body into his.

'I adore you, adore you,' he repeated, again and again.

She responded to his ardour by moistening his long eye-lashes with her tongue, kissing his eyelids, the tip of his nose.

'I love you so much,' she told him quietly. 'You are the sun, moon and stars to me. I shall love you like this always. Whatever happens, my feelings for you will never fade.'

'That's because we're made for each other, my darling.' He dropped baby kisses across her brow, on her cheeks, down the line of her throat. 'Nothing can split us up now. Nothing will spoil what we have found together.'

She melted inside at his words, felt a throbbing in her loins and wished for these moments to last forever. Overcome by the divine scents of his skin, expensive soap and after-shave, she kissed his cheeks, his brows, his lips. His mouth tasted of coffee. She felt breathless with love for this most beautiful, talented man.

'This is bliss,' she said. 'When I think of the time that I believed you were Didrik and about to marry Hildi, I was so confused I didn't know how to behave. I hope you've forgiven me.'

'That's all in the past,' he told her as he kissed her.

Returning the kiss she moved further beneath him, making him groan. He trapped her with his legs, one each side of her and pushed his hands under her lemon top to hold her delicate shoulders. His mouth found hers again in a dynamic yet gentle yearning kiss until she felt she would dissolve away. She was part of him, they were one, and she was in paradise. The rapture and delight she'd found in this lovely smiling land with its lakes and forests and wild fruits and flowers had found a permanent place in her heart. It was her heart.

Their love was not spent, far from it, but they both eventually fell asleep for an hour. The night for them both had been long and quite arduous.

A few hours later they were sitting on one of the wooden benches on the balcony, a tray with coffee, milk and sugar on a little side table next to them.

'Yesterday on the boat I told you that I've been invited to a chat show in London.' Torsten smiled at Prue. 'Would you like to come on it with me? The whole world's agog to meet my Beautiful Girl. Curious is not the word.'

The glow of divine happiness was doused immediately. 'I'd rather not. I don't feel comfortable standing in the spotlight – or are you angry with me now for not wanting to come along?'

Torsten shook his head. 'Of course publicity is important - to me, to the band, to all the people who depend on us for a living - but I won't try to persuade you into going on TV if you're against it. As for the press, you won't avoid them. You'll just have to get used to ignoring them when we're man and wife.'

'When we're man and wife? You're very sure of yourself!'

'If I'm sure of anything, it's that we belong together. We can't escape it.' He bent forward and took her face in his hands. 'Prue, I do believe in marriage. Would you like to marry me?'

'Marry you?' Prue's mind hazed over. He couldn't mean it, there had to be a catch. She'd never let herself believe in anything again.

He pulled her into his arms. 'I'm asking you to be my wife, Prue. I love you. More than that, I'm in love with you, dammit! How can I make you believe I love you?'

His love washed over her then, his tenderly spoken phrases seduced her, finding their way to the centre of her being. She was again at his command, helpless and willing. Time stood still as he eased her gently back into the bedroom. This was how it ought to be.

He stroked the mass of her luxuriant hair, winding it round his fingers, while she gazed at him, taking him all in - the white-gold of his own hair; the blue irises; the red-gold of his unshaven chin. Incredible bliss flowed through her once more.

'Come on,' he prompted her. 'You haven't answered my question. Will you marry me?'

'You know the answer,' she said. 'Yes! Yes! Yes!'

'Once is enough to make me the happiest man on earth, my darling!' he teased her, smiling.

She smiled back at him. 'By the way, my mum's getting married again, she told me today.'

'Good for her! Love is in the air, then - all very right and proper at midsummer. Isn't it rather sudden, though?'

'I suppose it is, but then so is this - you and me!'

'We're special; ordinary rules don't apply to us.' He gave her a kiss. 'We're a couple in a million, a billion, a trillion, a zillion...'

She gave a small delighted laugh and pressed a finger to his lips, stopping his flow of words. 'My mum's special, too. She suffered so much when Dad left, she went to a shadow. Her new romance with James means she's got over all that.'

'James? Is this the same James who happens to be your boss?'

'Yes, and a great boss he is, too. He gave me permission to stay on here at short notice. Now I know why. He must've had his eye on Mum right from the start. I think they first met at Christmas - she was my guest at The Trust dinner.' Prue gave him a little kiss on his adorable dimple. 'I'm so happy for her.'

His smile gave way to a marvellous grin. 'Well, if you don't mind, I'm more interested in my own love affair right this minute.'

Gazing into his eyes, she lovingly stroked his hair.

He studied her face, his gaze flickering over her eyes, her mouth, drinking her in. With one forefinger he tilted her chin; with the other he lovingly traced her brows, her nose and the line of her throat.

'You're far more beautiful than Jill,' was his verdict, at last. 'Some of the time you're quite a sparky young thing, and yet you can be quiet, resolute, like nobody but yourself. There's gentleness and warmth about you that Jill never had.'

He bent forward and closed his eyes as his mouth met hers in a kiss that was softly abrasive, piquant, yet all humid fire. All the way from the tip of her toes she felt it, invading every part of her being with delight. His mouth moved to her cheek, her forehead, planting little kisses. He held her tighter and tighter as if he would never let her go. When he finally paused to take a breath, she marked the meeting edge of his eyelids, bordered by lashes so long, bronze-tipped.

'Do you think we'll quarrel after we're married?' She moved away a little. 'For my part I'll try not to. You have your music and your fame, and I can imagine nothing more exciting than to share all that with you. Even so, marriage is a big step, we might not get on.'

'We'll make it our life's work to get on!' His eyes flew wide, all blue fire. 'Can't you see we're blessed by the gods, as we say in Sweden? We've got the proof - in spite of all the bad things that have happened, in spite of the influence of my late wife, we're together. No more argument, you're mine and I'm yours and that's all there is to it.'

He spoke with great intensity and punctuated his words with kisses on her lips as if he couldn't get enough of her.

Once again she was breathless with the joy of it. Ecstatic! She loved him so much she couldn't really believe her luck.

Prue closed her eyes and remembered the wild flowers, seven different kinds gathered at midsummer; the magic seven. Magic they had been indeed, bewitching them both. A sigh shuddered through her. She leaned back and savoured the coolness of his breath stirring her hair at the temples as he dropped a shower of tiny kisses on her throat and then her mouth. The touch of his lips on hers was like spring sunshine after the longest winter, and this was her last coherent thought before he gathered her again into the haven of his arms.

# CHAPTER TEN

It was June again. The scents of roses and lilies filled the church and filled up the senses. The midsummer sun shone through the stained glass windows onto the crystal chandeliers, the mouldings and the carved cherubs and angels in the interior of the Church of Queen Ulrica Pia. A low murmur from the wedding guests mingled with the recorded classical music of Brahms and Bach.

The bridal party, the minister, bride, groom and bridesmaids, had gathered together in a retiring room near the church entrance as was the usual practice at Swedish weddings.

Prue had lifted up her floor-length ivory lace wedding dress, the better to put a knee on a cushioned chair and peep through the small window of the annexe into the body of the church. The altar was bathed in light. In perhaps half an hour's time, she would no longer be Miss Claybourne but Mrs Torsten Norberg Dahlgren - wife of Sweden's great music master, Sten Norberg. After his love song, 'Beautiful Girl,' had gone soaring up the pop charts, the group *Scandinavia* had been in huge demand. Hero-composer Sten Norberg was writing hit songs again! Pop music fans all over the world had been ecstatic!

Prue gazed through at the congregation. All the people that mattered to her in the whole world were here, together, in this heart-stoppingly wonderful place – her family as well as her friends. There was Hildi, stately in a lacy mauve skirt and top, six months pregnant and radiant with it. Beside her sat her proud husband, Didrik, her parents and dear Aunt Agnetha in a pink striped outfit.

'I can see your mother. She looks gorgeous,' Prue whispered to bridesmaid Anna-Karin. 'Agnetha! Gorgeous!' She hoped Anna-Karin would understand.

The little girl laughed delightedly. 'Mamma! Gorgeous!'

'You are gorgeous too,' Prue said, and so the child was, a vision in gold satin. 'Thank you for the flowers in my coronet.'

She indicated her head where her bride crown rested on the glossy mane of hair which now hung down her back, long and luxuriant, partly covered by a short veil. The crown was decorated with deep blue cornflowers, shepherd's purse, buttercups, daisies, wild sweet peas, ragged robin and blue flax.

'Seven different sorts of wild flowers to bring me good luck. Thank you, Anna-Karin. What would I do without you?'

The little girl had known exactly where to find all seven types of flowers that Prue had wanted specially to wear on her wedding day.

She turned again to the window and soon spotted Gunnar sitting near one of the pillars in his wheelchair. Near him was Rutger, *Scandinavia's* successful replacement for Rolf.

'May I have a peep?' This was from Claire, Prue's best friend from schooldays, who was visiting Sweden for the first time. She was also in gold satin and obviously loving every minute of being a bridesmaid. 'Oh, I can see your dad, Prue. I'm so glad you're friends with him again.'

'Yes, we're fine these days. Do you know where he went this morning? He did what Swedish fathers-of-the-bride do and gathered birch branches in the forest.'

'Whatever for?'

'The birches are to decorate the church and the reception room. Have a look, aren't they beautiful? It's for good luck. Torsten's dad went with him.'

'What a lovely idea,' said Claire. 'And your dad's obviously on speaking terms with your mum, as well.'

'Yes, Mum is so happy these days and that's all that matters.'

Indeed Prue's mother, now Mrs Bickford, was sitting with James in a front pew. Her hat was a riot of colour; an explosion of ruffles and roses; an expression of pure joy.

What could be better? After Great Kate had been raised from the bottom of Plymouth Harbour the previous year and established in her own museum, Prue had given up working for The Trust to be with Torsten full time as he travelled across Europe, Australia even, from concert hall to concert hall. Now that her mother was married to James, keeping up to date and in touch with The Kate team was no trouble at all. Never would Prue forget that it was Great Kate that had brought herself and Torsten together in the first place. Her life was a dream come true. Smiling she went up to him. He was the love of her life, her bridegroom, who at this very moment was giving her a long hungry look.

He turned to the minister. 'Doesn't my bride look fantastic? Couldn't you just eat her?'

The minister nodded and smiled politely, but Prue didn't think he understood much English.

'Alskling, I'm dying to kiss you,' Torsten said to Prue. 'Sadly I can't because I don't want to spoil your make up. You look fabulous, a perfect picture. I love you.' He put the tips of his fingers to his lips and blew her a series of little kisses.

'You're fantastic, too,' she returned. 'Exceedingly handsome.'

In his fawn knee breeches, full sleeved white shirt with its mandarin collar and vibrant blue, sleeveless jerkin, Torsten looked amazing. He was wearing Swedish national costume to please her, and because he was in church his blue hat was in his hand and not on his head. He was her golden boy, her hero. No wonder half the known world was in love with him the female half.

'Everyone!' The minister pointed at his watch. 'We go!'

He opened the door of the annexe room onto the church. It was time for bride and bridesmaids to claim their wedding bouquets from the side table and form a procession. Prue's heart filled with joyous tremors. She collected her flowers, a combination of white roses and deep blue cornflowers; the latter to match her necklace of lapis lazuli beads that held so many memories.

'Wait! said Torsten dramatically. 'Listen!'

So they all stood, statue-still, while a spine-tingling melody came stealing into the church. Then Torsten's voice, singing, harshly mellifluous, vulnerable, unmistakeable.

'Darling,' he said to Prue. 'They're playing our song.'

*Where did you come from, beautiful girl?*
*Whenever I'm near you…'*

As the last notes died away, Torsten took Prue's arm and tucked it firmly into his own. 'Come, my very beautiful girl. Let's get married…'

### THE END

Made in the USA
Charleston, SC
15 November 2016